W9-BTG-220

Charade

DONNA HILL

Charade

ARABESQUE®

3 9082 10110 8424

CHARADE

An Arabesque novel published by Kimani Press/May 2008

First published by Kensington Publishing Corp. in 1998

ISBN-13: 978-0-373-83101-2
ISBN-10:   0-373-83101-3

Copyright © 1998 by Donna Hill

www.kimanipress.com

Printed in U.S.A.

Acknowledgment

I want to thank the countless readers who have been steadfast and supportive of my work during these past years. Without them, I could not be where I am today. To my family and friends, who keep me "real." To my longtime friend Antoinette Howell, CSW, who was instrumental in helping me with the clinical aspects of this story. To my sister—and her best friend, Lisa—who sat and read page after page, doing her share of editing and doing a great job. To Gwynne, without whose extensive knowledge about so many things I would be adrift. To Gregg, who sustains me. And most of all to God, who has given me this wonderful gift.

"All the world's a stage,
and the men and women merely players.
They have their exits and their entrances,
and one man in his time plays many parts."
—William Shakespeare,
As You Like It

Prologue

The hair was gray now, barely there. The pale skin nearly parchment white. Breathing was difficult. The frail hand shook trying to complete the mailing label and stick it on the heavy, brown box. All the answers were there.

Inside.

Done.

Now, leaving this earth would be so much easier....

"Come on, Tyler, sweetheart. The social worker is here. It's time ta go."

Hot, searing tears coursed down Tyler's honey-brown cheeks, straining her baby-soft skin with streaks of salty white an instant before they slipped over her trembling mouth.

"Please, Mama Wilcox, I'll be a good girl. Please don't let them take me again."

"Oh, Lord, chile, you a good girl. Don't you ever think no different." Elsie Wilcox gathered the rail-thin, eight-year-old against her bosom, fighting back her own wave of sorrow. "Hush now, Tyler. It's gonna be all right. They's gonna take you to a nice new foster home."

"W…hat did I do? Why I gotta go?" She hugged Elsie tighter.

Elsie kissed the top of Tyler's head, the springy black curls tickling her nose. "That's just how it is sometimes, Tyler. These folks know what's best for you. Don't want you to get too attached to no one family till they can find you a permanent home."

Tyler looked up into Elsie Wilcox's face, her large, doelike eyes shimmering pools of brown. "Why cain't I stay with you?" she pleaded, her chest heaving in and out.

Elsie took a breath and straightened, gently brushing Tyler's curls. "Go on now, Tyler," she whispered, her voice weak with heartache. She eased her toward Ms. Lydia, the white social worker with the flaming-red hair, the one who always came, who now stood her ground in the doorway of the pale-green, frame house poised to take her away.

"You said it would be for always this time. I wouldn't have to go to no more homes. This was my home. It's what you said," she wailed. "You lied!"

Tyler's little body shuddered as she lost the battle with her sobs, her gaze rushing over the house that she had been a part of for two years; to the boy, Matthew, and to the girl, Lisa, who had been like a real brother and sister to her, who now watched her exodus in stoic silence.

"Don'tcha love me enuff to keep me?" Her dark eyes pierced through each member of the household, branding them in accusation.

With that she spun away, pushed past the social worker and ran down the plank-wood steps and across the dirt path to the waiting car.

She never looked back.

When the door of the car closed, so did a part of her heart. Never again would she let anyone get close enough to hurt her. When they got close and won your affections, they just threw you away.

She knew that now.

Chapter 1

Dream a Little Dream

On this marginal date: Trauma continues to manifest itself in client's inability to display genuine emotion or relate to anyone beyond the surface. Although outwardly social, detachment is underlying behavior. Fear of closeness continues....

"Come on, girl. It's quitting time," Lauren announced, popping her hip up onto the edge of Tyler's desk.

Tyler snapped her head up from the story she was writing and a slow, dimpled smile spread across her face.

"You don't give the second hand on the clock half a chance to get around to the other side before you're out the door."

"You got that right. When those cheap SOBs said no more O.T., that was my cue. Ain't got to tell me nothing twice."

Tyler laughed, shaking her head of spiral curls in amusement. She and Lauren Hayes had met five years earlier when they both attended Technical Institute, for secretarial studies. Their night-and-day personalities seemed to click and they remained friends. As luck would have it, they both landed jobs as legal secretaries at the law firm of Dewey, Cheetam, and Howe within months of graduation.

They were both good at their jobs, but Tyler wanted more, or at least she thought she did. A part of her couldn't see spending the rest of her life trying to please someone with "the fine job you're doing." She'd spent too many years trying to please, to be accepted. She wanted to create a scenario where everyone danced to *her* drummer. And she would one day, she hoped. Then there was that other part of her that still held the childhood scars of rejection. That was the side she did battle with every day.

"What are you working on now?" Lauren quizzed, trying to steal a peek at the handwritten notes. She tucked a stray dreadlock behind her two-holed pierced ear.

"Just another story…about a young girl who finally finds her family."

"Hmm. What are you going to do with this one, when it's finished—tuck it away with all the others?"

Tyler twisted her lips. "What if I do?"

"Then I'll ask what I always ask—what's the point in writing all of these 'alleged' great stories if you never show them to anyone?"

Tyler chose to ignore the remark, though it was on target. Lauren may have been her closest friend, but she sure knew how to work on her nerves. How many times did she have to tell her that her stories just weren't ready yet? Maybe she didn't want to show them to anybody. Maybe she just wrote for herself. Maybe... *Stop lying to yourself, girl. You know you want somebody to read them and tell you how wonderful they are, or else you wouldn't have done what you did. You're just too scared that they won't.*

Tyler sucked her teeth, switched off her computer, and locked her desk. Snatching up her oversize, black leather bag from the back of her swivel chair, she stood. "Don't bug me today, Lauren. Okay? Not today."

"How 'bout tomorrow, then?" Lauren teased, draping her arm across Tyler's shoulder as they headed down the carpeted hallway toward the bank of elevators.

"Good night, ladies," intoned Carl Dewey, senior partner of the fifty-year-old firm, as he passed the striking duo in the hallway.

"Good night, Mr. Dewey," Tyler and Lauren chorused in their best "professional" voices, instinctively turning off their sisterhood vernacular. "Have a nice weekend," Tyler added for good measure.

They both rolled their eyes.

"If the police asked him to ID the two women he'd just passed in the hall he wouldn't have a clue," Lauren uttered in disgust.

"How 'bout that? We might as well be invisible, for all they care. So long as we do the work and act like we like it, that's all that matters."

The elevator bell pinged and the gleaming doors

whooshed open. Tyler and Lauren stepped in, wedging themselves between suits that cost more than they earned in two weeks and gulping down clouds of designer perfumes and colognes.

With a staff of more than three hundred, DCH was one of the largest multifaceted law firms in Savannah, Georgia. Out of the three hundred-plus, if there were a dozen black faces—that didn't include the cleaning crew—it was a lot. There were no black managers and only three attorneys of color. Most of the black employees were relegated to the secretarial pool. Affirmative Action wasn't alive and kicking at DCH.

The doors glided open and everyone pretended to be courteous as they brushed by each other in a dash for the parking lot. Even a mere two minute lead time could mean the difference between getting stuck in traffic and making that blessed light.

"Wanna grab something to eat?" Lauren asked as they casually strolled toward the lot.

"Naw. I think I'm going to head home. I'm beat." Actually she couldn't wait to get home. She'd been holding her breath for nearly three weeks waiting for *the* letter. She hadn't dared to tell Lauren what she'd done. Lauren would've hounded her relentlessly until they both knew the outcome. Besides, if she didn't make it she didn't want anyone to know.

Maybe today was the day.

"I hear ya. I guess I'll give Jason a call and see what he's in the mood for tonight," she said with a wicked giggle, sticking the key into the lock of her leased Lexus.

Tyler turned to her three-year-old used Honda Civic,

pushing back a smile. She and Lauren made the same amount of money, but their lifestyles were light-years apart. Lauren religiously believed that the more she paid for something the better it was, and so was she. That fact was dramatized daily in Lauren's eye-stopping attire, getaway weekend, strings of leased cars and *House Beautiful* apartment. However, she didn't have a dime in the bank, and regularly disguised her voice on the phone to avoid her creditors.

Tyler, on the other hand, knew from painful, personal experience what it was like to do without. As a result she lived modestly but well in a cozy one-bedroom apartment in a converted carriage house located in the historic district on Chippewa Square.

The house, built one hundred and fifty years earlier as a private residence, boasted twenty-three rooms. The building had been faithfully restored and then converted into ten individual apartment units, each having its own fireplace. The building's centerpiece was its courtyard, constructed of brick and wrought iron, with hanging baskets of garlands, and magnolia and Japanese loquat growing between the pavers. The crepe myrtle that abounded was older than the house itself. Adding to the serenity were three beautiful fountains whose lulling sounds could cradle one to sleep.

To this day she was still amazed at how she'd gotten so lucky. It was a far cry from the places in which she grew up. These kinds of apartments were in mint condition and generally went for elaborate sums of money, which precluded most blacks from even considering them. But on one of her bargain-hunting sprees she'd wandered onto the grounds and met Wesley, who was both caretaker and doorman. They talked and she told him how much she'd love living in a place like that. He told her to leave her number and if anything came up he'd give her a call. Sure enough, several weeks later he called. He said the only thing she had to remember if she spoke to management was that she was his niece. He rented the apartment to her for a steal. That was five years ago and she'd never had a day of regret.

Being the consummate shopper, she bought most of her furniture secondhand, and painstakingly restored it herself. She usually waited until an item she wanted was knocked down twice before she bought it. She purchased classic clothing that was designed to endure the ever-changing fads. She had a decent amount of money in the bank, which she never touched. She was building her nest egg, just as her Nana Tess told her to do. "Always be prepared for a rainy day," Tess often warned.

Nana. She hadn't seen her ailing grandmother in nearly two weeks. She'd make it a point to call her when she got home and make plans to visit her during the weekend.

Tess Ellington was all the family Tyler had. She'd seen her mother, Cissy Ellington, killed right in front of her when she was only four years old, and she had no idea who her father was. When the social workers came to take her away after her mother's murder, it was Tess, her maternal grandmother, who stepped in and took the emotionally scarred child to her bosom.

Tess coddled and nurtured Tyler during the two years she lived with her, giving her all the love and affection she'd missed from her nightclub-singing mother, and the previously neglected little girl began to bloom under Tess's care until Tess became too ill with diabetes to take care of her granddaughter. Being taken away from her grandmother was yet another trauma that the young Tyler had to endure. But the occasional visits to her Nana Tess and the letters they shared during her adolescence had made the parting bearable.

But Tyler never spoke of that night that changed her life, not to her grandmother, not to the police, the social workers—anyone. They all believed that she had been so traumatized she'd blocked it from her mind.

She hadn't. At least not all of it. But to talk about it would make it real. What happened to her and to her mother would be real. If she never spoke the words, maybe it could remain someone else's nightmare.

Yet, even now, at thirty years old, she still saw the shadowy visions in her dreams that sometimes spilled over into her life.

A light tap on her shoulder startled her, shutting down the images.

"You okay?" Lauren's saffron-toned face, distinguished by striking green eyes, crinkled with concern. Gently she rubbed Tyler's back.

Tyler took a short breath, turned toward Lauren and forced a smile. "Yeah, I'm fine. Just thinking about all the stuff I have to do when I get home."

Lauren arched her right eyebrow. "You sure? You look like you just took a short trip down a dark alley, girl. Must be some might serious 'stuff' you have to take care of."

The subtle tone of Lauren's disbelief brushed against Tyler's conscience. She'd always wished that there was someone in whom she could confide. Someone who would listen and not censure.

As friends went, Lauren Hayes was the best anyone could ask for. Still, Tyler could not seem to move from behind the wall she'd erected around her life and her heart. She'd spent too many years building the nearly impenetrable structure. Keeping people at a distance was second nature. To the outsider, Tyler Ellington presented a picture of contentment and stability. She wanted to keep it that way.

"Positive. As a matter of fact," she said, checking her watch, "I'd better get rolling. I want to call Nana before it gets too late."

Lauren grinned. "Tell that feisty ole' lady I said hey."

"Of course. You know as soon as I mention your name she's going to want an update on your love life."

In a pseudo whisper, Lauren quipped, "Just keep the juicy parts to yourself."

"Girl, I couldn't even fix my face to tell her about half of your escapades."

"Ain't that the truth." She gave Tyler a quick hug. "Have a good one. If you want to get together this weekend give me a call." She looked at her friend for a moment. "Or if you just want to talk."

Tyler felt her false smile begin to waver. "Will do." Quickly she turned away, opened the driver's-side door, and slid behind the wheel, tossing her bag over the seat to the back, where it landed with a dull thud on the floor.

Lauren waved goodbye as Tyler sped away.

Tyler pulled into her parking spot adjacent to the building. The private parking lot was relatively new, having been constructed only ten years earlier after continuous requests from the high-brow residents. For all its beauty, grandeur and historic significance, the place never gave her the same feeling of belonging as Nana's house, with its sprawling country kitchen, wide front porch with a real bench swing, oversize bedrooms, backyard and henhouse. Tyler did boast a built-in microwave, dishwasher and laundry room, however—all of which Nana insisted she'd never have in *her* house. She couldn't understand why anyone would want to cook food using some kind of radiation, and according to her there was nothing like a little elbow grease and effort to get the dishes and laundry done.

From all she'd seen in her five years in Midwood Manor, Tyler was the only single tenant. Apparently everyone was married with children or involved in live-in situations. Everyone around her did their "thing" in pairs or in groups, which was usually fine with her. At least she didn't have to worry about anyone knocking on her door for a cup of sugar.

Sometimes, though, she wished they would.

Stepping out of the car, she slowly strolled toward the entrance and greeted Wesley, who would remain on duty throughout the night. Though her community was relatively crime free, she guessed one could never be too careful.

"End of another week, eh, Ms. Ellington?"

"Finally." She sighed.

"Plans for the weekend?"

"No plans, Wes."

He chuckled, then slowly shook his head. "Pretty thang like you should have your date book full."

"I…keep busy."

"Hmm." He rubbed his shaved head as if he could conjure up an explanation. "You have a nice evening, Ms. Ellington."

"You too, Wes."

"Hear from 'the Duke' lately?" he cackled, his rheumy cough rumbling in his chest.

Tyler grinned. "One day you're going to get tired of that old joke." He'd been teasing her about her last name being Ellington after the legendary bandleader since the day they met.

"I will when it stops makin' you smile." He winked his good eye, the other being covered by a black patch. "Old war injury," he'd bragged on many occasions.

"'Night, Wes."

"Same to ya." He crossed his legs at the ankles, leaned back in his aluminum folding chair and began whistling, in offbeat heaven.

Tyler strolled down the short corridor to the row of mailboxes. Stopping in front of hers, she fumbled for her key among the half dozen on her chain, and opened the narrow, bronze door.

Her tummy suddenly tightened and her breathing escalated just a notch. Briefly she shut her eyes. "Please, Lord, let today be the day." She shoved her hand in the box and pulled out a stack of envelopes of various shapes and two magazines. Quickly she sorted through the pile, her eyes racing over the return addresses. Second by second her light at the end of the tunnel began to dim.

The last letter.

"Nothing." She blew out a defeated breath of disappointment. Slamming the little door shut she walked up the one flight to her apartment.

Flipping on the light switch she dropped her bag on the refinished hall table along with the pile of mail and continued down the abbreviated foyer toward the kitchen, which opened to the rectangular living room.

Tyler pulled open the refrigerator door, stooped down and scoped out the assorted boxes of takeout in varying sizes and states of edibility.

Sucking her teeth in disgust, she shut the door, snatching the menu for a Creole take-out restaurant from under the magnetic apple that held it in place.

Looking over the options, which she knew by heart, she reached for the white wall phone. Just as she was about to dial her doorbell ding-donged. She flinched at the sound, making a mental note to tell Wes to have the bell fixed. Again.

Returning the receiver to the base, she retraced her steps to the front door. She wasn't expecting anyone and was sure it wasn't a neighbor dropping in for a sit-down. She slid the circular cover away from the glass hole and peeped out, surprised to see Wes standing on the other side. She unlocked her one lock and pulled the door open.

"Wes? Something wrong?"

"I must apologize, Ms. E." He dug in his jacket pocket and pulled out a legal-size white envelope. "This come for ya earlier. Had to sign for it." He tapped his shiny head. "Slipped my mind. Eh, eh," he cackled. "Know what they say…"

"What's that?"

"Memory's the first thang ta go." He handed her the letter.

Tyler's heart went off on a mad gallop. The return address was The Black Women's Screenwriters Association, in New York. Her hand shook as she took the envelope.

"Thank you, Wes." She stared at the letter.

"Sho' thang." He cocked his head to the side, peeking at her with his good eye. "You all right, Ms. E?"

She blinked, her head snapped up and she focused on Wes. "Oh…yes. I'm fine. Thanks, Wes." She put her hand on the door, hoping it would be his cue to leave.

"Well…good night, then." He started to turn away, then stopped. "Must be somethin' mighty special in that letter."

Tyler looked at Wes's weatherbeaten face and smiled. "I hope so, Wes, I sure do."

"Me, too, Ms. E." He turned, his slight limp taking him down the hall.

Tyler closed the door and pressed the letter to her breasts. "Please, please, please," she chanted.

Almost in a daze she walked into her living room and plopped down on her faded, beige velour couch. Taking a breath she stuck her finger in the corner opening of the envelope and ran her finger across it, ripping it open.

With slightly trembling fingers she read the enclosed letter.

Dear Ms. Ellington,
The Selection Committee of The Black Women's Screenwriters Association is proud to inform you that you have been selected for a one-year scholarship, to attend New York University's Film School.

The Committee members strongly believe that your essay and accompanying story were the most inspiring we have seen in a long time, and feel confident that your screenwriting abilities will be enhanced at NYU.

Congratulations on your achievement. Please sign the enclosed educational agreement and return it to us. Upon receipt we will issue your scholarship check along with registration information.

If you have any questions, please contact us. Again, congratulations, and much success in your future endeavors.

Tyler's heart was beating so fast she was sure she was going to choke. She pressed the treasured letter to her lips and did a "full-out hit-with-the-spirit" jig from one end of the apartment to the other, complete with mental music of Sundays gone by, shouting out her thanks with every step.

Exhausted, she flopped down on the couch, legs outstretched, and read the letter again. *Just to be sure*. No sense in making a complete fool of herself calling her Nana, only to find out she'd read something wrong—like the letter being addressed to the wrong person or something.

She checked it one more time. Sure enough, it was official. Even though she'd been a devout backslider over the years, the Lord must have seen fit to do her this one big favor.

Taking a deep, cleansing breath she tucked the letter back in the envelope, pulled out the enclosed agreement, read the particulars and signed with a flourish. The letter was going in the mail first thing in the morning. She'd take it down to the box right that minute if it would get to the sender any faster. Since there wasn't an iota of a chance that would happen, it would keep until morning.

With that she jumped up from her basking-in-glory position and rushed toward the phone. Now she had an extra reason to call her Nana.

By rote she punched in the numbers and waited, listening to the phone ring and ring. A little flutter of nerves flapped in her stomach. It seemed to take Nana Tess longer and longer to get to the phone. Her stomach never settled down until she heard Nana Tess's distinctive Gullah accent—a mixture of clicking African intonations and Southern soul all rolled into one melody— vibrate across the lines. Her grandmother had lived on Gullah, one of the Sea Islands off the cost of Georgia, all her life. A bulldozer couldn't blast her off.

Finally the ringing ceased and the sounds of the phone being fumbled with filled Tyler's ear.

"Yesss?"

"Nana Tess, it's me, Tyler."

Tess chuckled. "Of course it's you, chile. Who else gon' call me Nana Tess?"

Tyler grinned. There was nothing like hearing her Nana's voice to put an extra spark in her day, or lift her spirit.

"How you be, baby?"

"I'm fine, Nana. Better than fine."

"Sounds like somethin' good. Gettin' married?"

"No. Something better than that."

"What could be better than settlin' down with a good man and makin' babies? That's the fun part." She laughed a deep, soul-stirring chuckle that started way down in her belly and built with intensity as it rose.

"Nana, you are aw-ful! What am I gonna do with you?"

"Find me a good man, fo' it's too late." Her bubbling laughter filled the air. "Matter 'o fact, there's a nice, young man just moved in up the road, into the old Taylor place. Handsome devil, too." She laughed. "Says he takes pictures fo' a livin' or somethin'. Perfect fo' you."

"I'll try to keep that in mind." Between her Nana and Lauren always trying to set her up, she didn't know who was worse. "Anyway, I'm coming to visit for the weekend. My room ready?"

"Yo' room's always ready. When you comin'?"

"I'll drive down in the morning. I should be there before lunch."

"I'll work us up a good, hefty meal. Then you can tell me this news of yours on a full stomach. And you can take care of all this mail and bills that's been pilin' up."

Tyler worried about that. She always feared that her grandmother would have her lights or gas turned off because, as she claimed, "I ain't got no head fo' all that mess. Whatchu think I got you fer?" The truth was, Nana Tess couldn't read and had no idea what was inside all the little white envelopes. At least the house was paid for, Tyler mused. Her grandmother's voice cut into her thoughts.

"Maybe I'll even make that sweet potato pie you love so much."

Just thinking about it made her mouth water. Her Nana's sweet potato pies were "to die for." "Nana Tess, for one slice I'd clean your whole house."

"Well, you jes go right ahead."

Tyler giggled. "See you tomorrow, Nana Tess."

"Okay, baby. Drive careful. You been savin' yo' money, building you' nest egg lack I been telling you?"

A twinge cinched her heart. It wasn't so much the question—Nana asked her that at least once per month—it was the tone. "Of…course."

"Good girl. Always wanna have yo' own, baby girl. No matter how good the man is. Wanna be able to stand on yo' own two feets. Don't forget that."

"Is everything all right, Nana? You're sounding funny."

"Hush, girl. You read too much inta everythang. Go 'head now and get yo' supper. I know you ain't eaten yet, wit yo' skinny self."

Tyler grinned, feeling a bit better. "I'm not skinny. I'm just right for my height."

"Humph. So you say. See ya tomorrow."

"'Night, Nana. Rest well."

"You, too." The dial tone hummed in Tyler's ear.

Nana Tess never said goodbye. She'd just hang up the phone. *Click.* Said it made things too final, as if you weren't going to see each other again. Even when company came, she'd walk her guests to the door, tell them to have a nice day, and shut it behind them. Those who didn't know her thought she was just "plain old rude." In reality, Tess Ellington was one of the most mannerly people Tyler had ever known.

Everything that Tyler was, at least to a degree—her beliefs, her behavior—was because of what had been instilled into her by Nana Tess during those two precious years and the intermittent visits in between. The only path upon which they forked-in-the-road was prayer and the church. Even now, at eighty-seven years young, Tess found her way to Sunday service. Tyler, on the other hand, had lost her faith in the higher power years ago, when she'd cowered in the dark corner of her bedroom, unable to help her mother. She'd prayed then, hard, like Nana had taught her. But it didn't help. Her mother had died, anyway. She'd prayed to have a family to love and keep her, and those prayers, too, had gone unanswered.

Finally, painfully, she'd realized that she was the only person she could depend on.

She kept those thoughts to herself. There was no reason for her Nana to know just how deep her faith-lessness went.

Tyler blinked, shaking her head. The thoughts scattered like a flock of startled doves. "No point in standing around daydreaming." She planted her hands on her narrow hips. "I have a new life to plan."

Tyler was up with the sun. Having packed her trusty overnight bag before going to bed, she was ready for the ninety-minute drive out to Gullah after downing a mug of café mocha—her favorite—and a toasted English muffin swimming in butter.

She took the letter and stuck it in her bag. Nana never took anything for granted. She'd want Tyler to read every word. Tyler patted her bag and grinned, then headed out, her step light, her spirit soaring. On her way she dropped the signed acceptance letter in the mailbox and sped off.

Even at 8:00 a.m., it was already seventy degrees and climbing. It wasn't long before she rolled up the windows, foregoing the hot July breeze and the attacks of mosquitoes for the comfort of the air conditioner.

She'd lived in Savannah all her life yet the majestic beauty of the landscape never ceased to give her pause. Mile after mile was a vista of blue and white horizon overlaid on a canvas of lush green. Stately oaks dripping with moss stood in military fashion along the narrow, two-lane dirt road, camouflaging the sprawling plantations that had once held captive thousands of African slaves—now converted into stately mansions. Though beautiful, they were painful reminders of a dark, ugly past.

Birds chattered, soaring overhead, then skimmed over rippling creeks, seeking their morning fare. Pelicans and swans waded in the water, and scurrying little animals ran along the water's edge. Children's piercing laughter could be heard in the distance. Savannah never lost its charm.

There was a part of her that loved the slow, comforting security of Southern life. Another part of her longed to meet the challenges of a fast-paced city like New York. The prospect of the two selves colliding was scary. Would she fit in? How and where would she live? Would her savings be enough to sustain her until she found a job?

She exhaled a nervous breath. There was so much to do, and she only had a month to get everything accomplished.

Tyler's spirits took a sharp nose-dive when Nana Tess opened the door. For several seconds Tyler stood in shocked disbelief. In less than a month she had deteriorated to half the woman she had been. The sparkle in her dark brown eyes was the same, but she appeared to have gotten smaller both in weight and height. Her movements were slower and more cautious, almost as if she had to program her body to respond to her brain's command on a delayed reaction.

Fear gripped her. How many times had she pleaded with Nana to move in with her, come to Savannah? Certainly when she was an energetic adolescent she had been too much for a woman of Nana's ill health to handle. Yet, even when Tyler was grown up, Tess had insisted that she was fine on her own and that Tyler needed to make her own life, not worry about a sickly, old woman.

Nana was all she had in her life that represented love and security. She was her one link to who she was. She couldn't lose her, too.

Nana Tess's warm smile bloomed, and the lines around her mouth smoothed when she rested her gaze on her granddaughter. The weariness that weighed down her body seemed to lift, drifting away, light as a honeysuckle breeze.

"Baby girl." She stretched out her long, brown arms and Tyler found her way into them, inhaling the scents of lavender and Goldstar powder. Her stomach shifted as the comfort of the familiar enveloped her, momentarily obscuring her fear.

She pressed her face against Nana Tess's thick natural hair, the rough and soft texture of the graying plaits touched by the unmistakable scent of Dax hair pomade. Tyler closed her eyes and smiled. For a moment she was a little girl again.

"Come on in here, chile."

Tyler stepped out of her grandmother's arms and followed her stilted gait into the sprawling country kitchen that still held a potbellied stove. The mouthwatering aroma of sweet potato pie topped with homemade whipped cream permeated the air.

The two-decade-old butcher block table was laden with bowls of sliced fresh fruit, scratch biscuits, Virginia ham, and light-as-a-cloud eggs, straight from Tess's henhouse.

"Know you be hungry. Go wash yo' hands and set."

Tyler walked across the hand-scrubbed, oak-paneled floors to the stained double sink, washing her hands, then drying them on the faded yellow-and-white plaid dish towel that had seen too many washings. It hung by the sink—touched by the slight breeze blowing in from the opened window—the sheer, shorty curtains dancing erotically in and out, bringing with each rise and fall the aromatic blend of green grass, fresh earth and sunshine.

Tyler joined Tess at the table, linked hands with her and said the blessing.

"Eat now. You 'bout thin as a beanpole." Nana Tess chuckled.

"You're looking pretty thin yourself, Nana." A note of caution laced her tone. She spooned eggs onto her blue-rimmed plate followed by a thick slice of ham, then filled a bowl with sliced fruit. She eyed her grandmother.

"Tryin' to keep my girlie figure." Nana Tess put an infant-size portion of food on her plate, and Tyler's worry scale moved up another notch. Tess had always eaten like an overworked farmhand.

"That's not it, Nana. And you know it." Tyler slammed down her fork. "What's wrong?"

Tess avoided Tyler's probing stare, keeping her gaze focused on her plate. "Nothin' for you to fret about. Hear? Just eat and tell me 'bout this news you got."

She was sure something was wrong with Nana. Something she wasn't sharing. How could she even think about moving away to New York now?

"It really wasn't important. I got some new assignments at work, that's all."

Nana Tess angled her plaited head, placed her fork with a clink alongside her plate and stared at her granddaughter.

"Always knows when you lyin' ta me, Tyler Ellington."

"And I know when you're lying to me, Nana."

The two women held their stares and Nana thought how, at that moment, Tyler reminded her of her daughter, Cissy. Cissy was always determined, hardheaded and wanted things her own way. *Couldn't stop her from nothing once she'd made up her mind, from booze to men. Humph, look where it led her.* Where would Tyler's willfulness lead her? She'd tried so hard to instill the good things in Tyler whenever she could, but the child had such a hard life. It still pained her to even think about what her granddaughter had gone through. So they didn't discuss it. Ever. It was a part of their pasts that was best left in the past.

Tess exhaled a weary breath. "I ain't been well, baby. But nothin' to worry 'bout. Cain't hold down my food too good, and I ain't been sleepin' well."

Tyler opened her mouth and Tess held up her slender hand to halt the interruption.

"Knows what you gonna say, and the answer is no. You ain't movin' in here wit me, and I ain't comin' to Savannah. And…I been to see the doc."

"What did he say? The truth," she warned.

"Said…that I'm gettin' old."

Nana Tess laughed, but Tyler thought there was an emptiness that had never been there before. "What else did he say, Nana?" Tyler's heart pounded and the tightness in her chest was cutting off her breath.

"Said…I gotta watch what I eat. Git mo' rest and thangs." She reached across the table and patted Tyler's clenched hand. "Nothing to worry 'bout." Tess's gaze rested on Tyler's face. "Now." She took a breath. "What's yo' news?"

Tyler debated about telling her, knowing that once she did Nana would insist that she go to New York to pursue her dream. But if she gave up her chance she would never forgive herself, and neither would Nana. So she told her.

"Tyler, it's just what you been dreamin' 'bout. I'm happy fo' ya."

Tyler grinned. "It's a great opportunity, Nana." She leaned closer and cupped Tess's hands between hers. "Nana, I won't go if you're sick. I wouldn't be able to keep my mind on why I was there, for worrying about you."

"Now you listen here. Since you was a little bitty thang all you talked 'bout was writin' stories and makin' movies lack on the TV. Every time I looked 'round you had yo' head in a book or was writin' somethin' that came into that pretty head o' yours. Humph." Her dark eyes drifted away for a moment, seeing things from long ago. "I used ta think you stayed in that made-up world of yours 'cause the real world had done you so wrong. But you all growed up now, and this is what all those years of hidin' yo'self away and workin' has come ta. Cain't let you lose that, chile, 'counta me. You done lost enough already. I'll be fine wit you gone. Just knows I won't be if you stays."

Tyler inhaled a long breath, fighting back the tears that threatened to flow, biting down on her bottom lip to keep it from trembling. *Her Nana.* She knew she couldn't fight her. Nana Tess would make her life miserable if she stayed.

"All right. I'll go. But I'll call every day, and I want you to keep your doctor appointments."

"Don't you be callin' here every day. Once a week is fine." Tess grinned and patted Tyler's cheek. "I'll get that handsome young man up the road to check on me." She gave Tyler a wicked wink.

Tyler tossed her head back and laughed. "Nana Tess, you are incorrigible. I want this man's name and phone number before I leave."

"I was hopin' you'd say that." She cackled.

"Not for me, silly. To check on you. Make sure you're doing what you're supposed to."

"It's a start."

Tyler just shook her head and rolled her eyes.

"Now, what all you got ta do 'fore you leave? And where you gonna live?"

The weekend sped by so quickly it seemed that before she was anywhere near close to ready it was time to head back to the city. But she felt good, as she always did when she came to the island. Visiting with her grandmother, being taken care of and feeling needed, combined with the familiar comfort of the old house and the secure hush of the area, all served to rejuvenate her, even though she never let this life cross her other.

She was just putting the last of her clothing in her overnight bag when Tess tapped on the partially open bedroom door.

"Got company downstairs. Young man I told you 'bout. Stopped by for a visit. Come on down and say hello."

Tyler anchored her hand on her hip, her springy curls bouncing with the snap of her neck.

"You're not trying to pull a fast one, are you, Nana?" She wagged an accusing finger in Tess's direction.

Tess's wood-brown face was the picture of wide-eyed innocence. "You know me better'n that."

Tyler's eyes narrowed and she pursed her lips. "That's exactly what I mean." She blew out a breath through her nose. "I'll be down in a minute."

"Good." Tess turned slowly and made her way along the hall, holding on to the hand-carved wood railing that braced the upper floor leading to the stairs.

And if Tyler's hearing wasn't going bad, she'd swear she'd heard her grandmother chuckling.

Tyler appeared a few moments later in the doorway of the kitchen—where much of the entertaining in the South took place—and spotted Nana looking as happy as a sixteen-year-old as she openly flirted with the man whose broad back faced her. His milk-white shirt stretched across his back, standing out in sharp contrast against his almond-toned skin.

Nana's gaze rose over the man's head and rested on Tyler's face. "Come on in, chile, and introduce yo'self."

She stepped across the threshold just as the seated gentleman turned in her direction.

His smile was slow and steady, building in intensity, like daybreak spreading over the horizon, his full top lip etched with a thin mustache. He stood as she drew near and she found herself looking up into pitch-black eyes haloed by a thick veil of lashes that gave him a dreamy look. He extended his hand.

"I feel like I already know you," he said, his voice as slow and sweet as blackstrap molasses. "I'm Sterling Grey."

She placed her hand in his and was surprised to discover that it was softer than her own. Must be because of the type of work he did, she thought, remembering that Tess had mentioned that he took pictures or something like that.

"Nice to meet you, Sterling. My grandmother has been singing your praises."

He chuckled, ducking his head, appearing momentarily embarrassed, but quickly recovered.

"She does a good job of telling a tale. Is that where you get your imagination? She said you write stories."

His gaze seemed to look beyond her practiced surface to the unsettled waters beneath. She was momentarily disconcerted, and it suddenly grew warmer than usual in the sunny kitchen.

She swallowed. "I guess I never thought about it."

She stepped closer and took a seat at the table. "Nana says you're a photographer."

"Trying to be." He smiled.

"What does that mean?" She noticed the way his eyes crinkled around the edges when he grinned, and the tiny dimple in his left cheek. Something vague but familiar touched her insides. She blinked and the sensation vanished.

"I'm just beginning to make a name for myself, starting to get some bigger assignments," he answered in the smooth drawl. "Actually photography started out as a hobby in high school. I took a couple of classes and really liked it. Started taking pictures of everything that would stand still." He chuckled. "And I knew I had the bug. When the guys in school were chasing women, I was in my homemade darkroom developing pictures."

She looked at him for a moment, her thoughts drifting. This was someone who obviously focused on his goal and went for it. She could tell by his tone, the light in his eyes, that he had a passion for what he did. She felt the same way about her writing.

"Maybe I could show you my work sometime," he said, easing into her thoughts.

She nodded. "Maybe." She cleared her throat. "Nana said you're going to be looking out for her while I'm away. I told her I'd stay in touch with you. You can keep me posted."

"Sure. When are you leaving?"

She blew out a breath, leaned on her forearms, her fingers entwined on the table. "I'm going to have to go to New York in about three weeks, start looking for someplace to live, register for classes, look for a job."

"Hmm. Sounds like you have your hands full." He grinned. "Know your way around New York?"

She shook her head, and the enormity of what she was embarking upon filled her like a glass under a running tap. She'd never been outside Georgia in her entire life. She'd read about New York, heard the stories, dreamed about going. But…

"Maybe I can make some calls, have some friends of mine check things out for you."

Her eyes narrowed slightly. Why would he do something like that? In her experience, no one did things without expecting something in return. "You would?" She almost asked "why" but didn't. Nana might just smack her for being rude.

He shrugged. "Sure. It's no problem. I spent a year there trying to land a photography job, and met some really nice folks in the process."

"Why'd you come back?"

Sterling chuckled, and pointed a warning finger. "Not due to lack of talent. Just too much competition. Too much of everything in that city. Too many people, cars, buildings…noise." He appeared to cringe at the memory. He shook his head, then looked at her. "Anyway, I'll make some calls."

"Thanks, I'd appreciate it."

"Now that ya'll got that settled," Tess interjected, "Tyler, you need to be gettin' on. You got a long drive and work tomorrow."

"Trying to get rid of me?"

"Of course. So I kin be alone wit dis fine, young man."

Sterling grinned, leaned over and kissed Tess's wrinkle-free cheek. "You're the one for me, Ms. Tess," he teased, giving her a wink. He turned to Tyler. "I'll help you with your bags."

Tyler pushed away from the table and stood. "I'll be right back." She trotted up the steps and into her room. Looking around, she checked the closet, dresser and adjoining bath to be sure she didn't forget anything. Satisfied, she crossed the plain wood floor—covered in the center by an almost threadbare rope rug of pale blue and cream—to the bed and zipped up her suitcase. She turned toward the door and her hand flew to her mouth, barely stifling her gasp.

"Sorry. Didn't mean to scare you. Just thought I could help."

She let out a breath of relief as he stepped into the room and took her bag.

"Come on before your grandma gets suspicious." He grinned.

He was almost too helpful, she thought, handing him her bag.

Tess slowly got up from the table and Sterling rushed over to help her, holding her arm. "All set?" she asked, sounding somewhat winded to Tyler.

"Nana, are you all right?" Tyler came to her other side.

"Of course, chile. Just a bit tired. I'ma take a quick nap. I'll be fine."

Tyler looked at Sterling over Tess's head. He nodded his assurance.

"I'll call you when I get home." She gathered her grandmother in her arms and was stunned again by her frailness. She kissed her temple. "You take it easy," she whispered into her hair. "I love you, Nana."

"Love you, too, chile. Now go on."

Tyler gave her one last hug, walked toward the door and out into the blistering, late-afternoon heat.

Stopping at her car she turned and looked up at Sterling. "Please watch out for her. She's the most important person in the world to me."

He opened her car door and put her bag on the backseat, then faced her. "I will. Don't worry. She'll be fine." He reached into his shirt pocket and pulled out a small, white card and handed it to her. "Here. Call me anytime."

She looked at the card. Sterling Grey. Freelance Photographer. His number was listed below his name.

"Thanks." She stuck the card in her purse and got in the car.

Sterling closed the door and leaned down.

She lowered her window, her hand resting on the lowered glass.

"You have a safe trip to New York." His eyes grazed her face for a hot minute. He placed his hand atop hers. "I'll get your number from your grandmother and let you know what I found out."

"Thanks." She turned the key in the ignition. The engine roared to life.

Sterling stepped back from the car and pushed his hands down into the pockets of his snug jeans.

Tyler waved one of those Ms. America waves and sped off, spitting up grass and dirt in her wake.

When she'd driven a short distance, she stole a glance in her rearview mirror, catching a final glance at Sterling. Nice, she thought. And that thin mustache gave his mouth a hint of mystery. Her hand still tingled from when he'd held it.

She sighed and stepped on the accelerator. No sense in fantasizing. He was nice and all, but relationships weren't in this deck of cards, especially with someone who knew from where she really came. Every man she'd been in a relationship with—she could count them on one hand—hadn't been worth the effort it took to learn their names. Besides, she didn't have time. She had to concentrate on her future, and a man wasn't in it. At least, none that she could see.

Too bad, though. He seemed nice.

But they all did in the beginning.

Chapter 2

Travelin' Shoes

> *On this marginal date: Client has adapted to up-
> heavals/change in environment by her ability to
> remain internally aloof from outside influences
> and people. Repressive tendencies continue...*

"So when were you planning on telling me?" Lauren
took a bite of her crab salad and gave Tyler the evil eye.

"Take it easy. I didn't want to say anything before I was
sure." Tyler blew out a breath through her teeth and took
a sip of iced tea. "You know how you are. You would've
been on me like crazy glue until I got an answer."

Lauren bit back a smile and rolled her eyes, trying
hard to hold on to her miffed attitude. "You're damned

right." She paused a moment. "Still. I thought we were friends, sisters. I would have been cheering for you."

"Yeah." Tyler lowered her gaze. "You're right, and I'm sorry. I should've said something."

"Ummm. Now that you're sufficiently guilt-ridden…" She leaned across the café table and grinned. "Tell me everything."

Tyler told her how she'd seen the announcement in *Scriptwriter* magazine requesting a twenty-page essay on any topic which the writer believed could be translated into a screenplay.

"So what was your story about?"

Tyler swallowed and stared down into her glass, then at Lauren. "Just about a young girl who spent her life in foster care after her mother was killed."

Lauren nodded. "That's a hot topic for you, Ty." She angled her head to the side. "You write about it like you experienced it yourself."

"Are you telling me, or asking me?" Tyler could feel her defense mechanisms locking into place. Her heart thumped. In the blink of an eye she could conjure up the sea of faces of those who had played "guardian" to her over the years. She'd spent the better part of her adult life trying to put that dark part of her life behind her. The only time she ever let the shadows out of her closet was in her stories, where she could pretend that the lives she showcased belonged to others.

"Just making an observation, Ty. I can only go by what you tell me since you've never let me read a word." She frowned. "What's bugging you? I mean, we've been friends for five years and sometimes, hell, I don't even know who you are. There's just this whole side of…whoever you are…that you keep locked up." Lauren leaned closer and lowered her voice. "I'm you're friend. Not your judge, Ty."

Tyler could feel her insides quaking, the heat rising from her stomach and spreading through her limbs, just the way it did whenever anyone claimed to care about her, to love her, to be her friend. They'd say they'd be there for her. They weren't. She'd be alone and someone new would step in. Her head began to pound. Her world was constantly shifting beneath her feet. Would she ever be able to trust anyone with the truth, with her feelings? Could she tell Lauren what her life was really about, that she wasn't raised in a wonderful house, didn't have great parents or an enviable education, and that she'd never been wanted? If she did, would Lauren still be there? It wasn't worth the risk…the loss. Having Lauren know Nana Tess was one thing. The rest—better left unsaid.

"I'm…sorry, Lauren. I…you are my friend." She reached across the table and took Lauren's hand. "The best one I have…and…I want to keep it that way." She took a deep breath. "So, you going to help me make some plans, or what?" She forced a smile and pushed aside a wayward curl from her right eye.

Lauren smiled in return and squeezed Tyler's hand. "When are you going to give them your notice?"

"Right after lunch. I wish they'd give me an extended leave, but I know that would never happen."

"Speaking of which, what are you going to do for money and a place to live?"

"I have some money saved…and well, over the weekend…"

She told her about Sterling and his offer to talk to his friends in New York who would hopefully find her a place to stay.

"Hmm. So what does this dark knight look like?"

Tyler grinned. "Not bad."

"Well, you can just leave homeboy's name and phone number with me, where they'll be safe."

"Ha! But will *he?*"

"That's never been a problem."

"For you."

Both women laughed.

"So…what's he like?"

Tyler gave a half-moon smile "He seems nice. Looks to be in his midthirties. He's a photographer, lives near Nana, and *she* loves him."

"Too bad you won't be around long enough to check him out thoroughly. I can't remember the last time you told me you were seeing someone."

"Nothing to tell." She took a gulp of her iced tea.

"Maybe your love life will pick up in New York." She took a forkful of her salad.

Tyler squeezed more lemon into her tea. "That's not why I'm going."

Lauren looked at her from beneath thick, mascaraed lashes. "That's just one of the perks, my sistah."

Tyler shook her head and smiled.

The following week Sterling was working in his basement, which he'd converted into a darkroom, developing his latest roll of film. The one rectangular window was completely covered with a black curtain, shutting out any illumination. The combination of near darkness and the level below ground provided a perfectly natural air-conditioned environment. Clotheslines hung from one end of the square room to the other. Every few inches a photo was hung to dry.

Using special tweezers he lifted one sheet from the tray of developing solution and dipped it into another until a hazy image began to materialize and become clear. The picture of Tyler hanging clothes in her grandmother's backyard appeared.

He'd been walking along the creek when he'd spotted her. She'd looked just as if she belonged there in the middle of nature, with that wild hair and earth-tone coloring. He could almost make out the song she was humming as she dug in and out of the wicker basket to hang the clothes. Her long, brown legs were bare, glistening in the early-morning sun. The white shorts she wore gleamed against her skin.

She hadn't seen him, and his photo caught her in all her natural, candid glory. She'd stood, eyes closed against the blazing sun, arching her back—her round, full breasts clearly defined beneath the soft cotton of her lime-green T-shirt—and raised her hand to wipe away the sweat that trickled down her temples to her cheek, disappearing on the back of her hand.

He held up the photo and smiled. That he'd moved down the road from her grandmother was a sheer stroke of fate. What it would mean only time would tell.

But she must never know who he really was. She didn't seem to remember. At times, he wondered if she did remember him. Maybe she was just as good at this game of charades as he was. He looked at the picture again. No, she didn't remember. He would have known. It would have been in her eyes, as it had been in others.

He turned away from the developing trays. No one could know. He'd worked too hard to cover the ugly trail of his past. People tended to attribute guilt by association. Humph. He'd had enough of that to last him a lifetime. Everything was always fine until they made the connection. He'd learned to live with it, to start over, make a life that he was happy with and proud of, cutting off everything and everyone from his past.

Almost everything.

He'd taken a chance coming back to Savannah, back to where it all began. But living out on the island provided him with the anonymity he craved.

Sterling looked at the picture again. Tyler Ellington seemed to be the kind of woman he'd always wanted in his life. According to Ms. Tess she was hardworking, levelheaded and independent. Tess'd never talked about Tyler, the little girl—although there was enough that he already knew, more than he wanted to. She'd only spoken of Tyler, the woman.

Hmm. She'd blossomed into a beautiful hothouse flower after all she'd been through.

The distant ringing of the upstairs phone pierced his thoughts. He hung up the picture of Tyler to let it dry and trotted up the wooden plank steps. He caught the phone on the fourth ring.

"Hello?"

"Sterling?"

"Yes. Who's this?"

"Hi, it's Tyler. Tyler Ellington."

His brow wrinkled in surprise. "Hi. Something wrong?"

"No. Sorry to bother you…um, you sound out of breath. Did I…catch you at a bad time?"

He chuckled at her not so subtle attempt at quizzing him. "Actually, I was in my darkroom…developing some pictures."

"Oh."

"So, to what do I owe the pleasure of this call?"

"I just wanted to say thank you…for looking after my grandmother."

"You did that already," he replied, his tone teasing.

She was quiet for a moment. "Oh, I guess I did. I, uh, also called because I was wondering…if you'd spoken to your friends in New York? I'm going to be leaving sooner than I thought, and well—"

"Sorry. I haven't had a chance."

She pursed her lips in disgust. *Figures.* Folks were always making promises, saying they were going to come through for you, be there for you. Humph. Should have known better. "Listen, don't worry about it, then. I'll figure something out on my own."

The sharp edge in her voice cut right through him. "I'll call as soon as I hang up. When are you leaving?"

"I got a letter today. I need to register for classes next Monday. I'll have to leave Friday. I figure since I was going up there anyway, I would check out some places to stay."

"I'll try to see what I can work out. How's that?"

"If it's not too much trouble."

"No," he blew out. "It's not too much trouble. It's just that I've been really busy trying to put a job together."

He paused. "I'm sorry." He wasn't quite sure what he was apologizing for, but it seemed the right thing to do.

Now she felt stupid and petty for acting so nasty. He wasn't obligated to do anything for her. "No apology necessary. I shouldn't have snapped at you. I guess I'm a little more stressed out than I thought," she added by way of an excuse, when in reality, allowing herself to depend on someone, if only for a moment, had more to do with her mood than anything else.

He smiled. "Now that we have all that out of the way…is there anything else I can help you with— packing, chauffeuring you to the airport?"

Tyler laughed, feeling the tightness ease in her chest. "I don't have that much to pack, and though your offer of a ride to the airport is tempting, my friend Lauren already offered."

"Can't say a man didn't try. But, if you change your mind, give me a call."

"Thanks. I will."

"Will you be stopping by to see your grandmother before you leave?"

Is that what he really wanted to know? Or did she just want to believe he was asking if he'd see her again? "I'm going to try. This is a pretty hectic week for me."

"I can imagine. I know what it was like for me tying up loose ends…moving."

"Where did you live before you moved out to the island?"

He swallowed. "Here and there. I…traveled a lot before I finally decided to settle down in Georgia."

"Oh." Was he being evasive, or was that just her imagination? She took a breath. "Well…I won't keep you."

Sterling leaned his long, muscled body against the frame of the door. "You're not keeping me. I'm beginning to enjoy our conversation."

Tyler smiled to herself. "Is that right? Was that before or after I apologized?"

"Definitely after."

Tyler laughed and the soft sound warmed him, just as it had on so many lonely, frightening nights.

"What kind of pictures do you take?" she asked, pulling him back to the present.

"Mostly commercial photography for magazine and newspaper ads."

"Really? That sounds exciting. Get to meet any interesting people?" She leaned back against the pillows on her bed and bent her knees.

"Hmm, let's see, I've met some models, a few athletes. But most of my work is for food and liquor ads. Some clothing ads, but not much."

"Still sounds like fun."

"It can be. But it's a lot of work. You can't imagine how long it takes to make a plate of pasta look good." He laughed.

"At least it can't storm off the set in an artistic huff."

"No, just wilt." He chuckled, enjoying the repartee. He pulled up a chair and straddled it, bringing the image of her smile into focus. "So what kind of things do you write about?"

"Mostly short stories, family stuff."

"That's what you're going all the way to New York to do?"

"No. Well…not exactly. I want to write screenplays."

"Hey, now that's where the money is."

She grinned. "So I've heard. Some scripts from first-time writers have gone for a quarter of a million dollars."

He whistled. "I'm definitely in the wrong business. But maybe when you make it big you could do a brother a favor and cast me as the dashing hero."

"Where there's faith there's hope, Mr. Grey."

"Keep hope alive!" he said in a great imitation of Jesse Jackson.

They both laughed.

"Well, I'd better go. I need to sort through some things before I turn in."

He took a breath. "It's been nice talking with you, Tyler. I wish you weren't leaving so soon. We could have gotten the chance to know each other…better."

Tyler's stomach did a little dance. "Well, I'm sure I'll be back and forth. Maybe when I get settled…you can come up for a visit."

"Maybe I can." He cleared his throat. "I'll make those calls for you and let you know…say, tomorrow?" That would give him the perfect reason to talk with her again.

"Sure."

"Then I guess I'll speak with you soon."

"Good night."

"Good night, Tyler."

Slowly she hung up the phone, the deep resonance of Sterling's voice still humming in her ear. The more she talked to him, the more that strange sensation that she knew him filled her. But that wasn't possible. He'd said he'd traveled most of the time, and had just settled in Georgia.

She shook her head. Guess it was just a feeling.

* * *

"Girl, if you don't step on it you're going to miss your flight," Lauren fussed from Tyler's living room.

"All right, all right. I'm coming. I just don't want to forget anything."

Tyler emerged from her bedroom, pulling her wheeled, paisley suitcase and lugging a matching garment bag on her shoulder.

Lauren gave her the once-over. "Believe me, if you left anything it's 'cause it was nailed down."

"Very funny."

Just as they reached the door the ringing phone stopped them in their tracks.

"One second," Tyler said. "Could be important," she added, noting the lines of aggravation framing Lauren's eyes.

Lauren huffed in mock annoyance. "I'll meet you downstairs. I'm parked right out front."

Tyler ran to catch the ringing phone.

"Hello?"

"Now you're the one who sounds breathless."

Tyler smiled, letting Sterling's easy drawl soothe her frazzled nerves.

"I was just running out the door. Literally."

"I won't keep you. Just wanted to catch you before you left, wish you a safe trip, and make sure you had Tempest and Braxton's phone number."

"I have it. Thanks. I spoke with her last night. She said they're still renovating the apartment, but it's liveable for as long as I need it." She let the bag fall from her shoulder onto the floor.

"They're both great. I'm sure you'll like them. With

her being an interior designer and him an architect they're always running across great finds in the city."

"She said the apartment is near the school. It's in a building they just purchased. In the *village?*"

He chuckled. "Yeah. Greenwich Village. You'll love it. Are they meeting you at the airport?"

"Yes."

"Great. Well…have a safe trip. I'll keep an eye on Nana."

"Thanks again, Sterling."

"No problem. You just get rich and famous. That'll be thanks enough."

"Yeah, okay." She giggled.

"Take care, Tyler."

"I will." She hung up, took one last look around and dashed out of her apartment.

"Headin' to the big city, huh, Ms. E?" Wes asked, helping her to the car with her bags.

"Yep. Today's the day, Wes."

"Well, I'll look after thangs for ya and git yo' mail."

"Thanks, Wes. For everything." She gave him a hug. "I'm going to miss this place. If it hadn't been for you I would have never gotten in."

"It weren't nothin'. Nice girl lack you deserve a nice place. So what if we did a little jugglin' to get it?" He cackled, following it with his trademark cough.

She'd asked him once why he'd gone out of his way for her. How could he ever tell her why? Even now, after all this time. *Naw, ain't no reason for her to know. Some thangs just best left unsaid.*

He watched her put her bags in the trunk. He was

sure going to miss Tyler, more than she'd ever guess. He'd tried to treat her like the daughter he never had, letting her replace the family he'd lost.

Yeah. Sure gon' miss her.

"Well." She turned to face him. "All set." She planted her hands on her hips. "You take care, Wes. I'll send you my address as soon as I'm settled, and let you know where to send my things."

"Don't you worry 'bout it. Take yo' time. Thangs kin stay long as you want," he drawled.

She gave him a quick peck on the cheek. "Take care, Wes."

"You, too, Ms. E. And say hey to the 'Duke' for me."

Tyler chuckled and ducked into the car.

"He's such a nice old man," Lauren commented as they pulled off.

Tyler smiled, thinking how she'd miss Wes. He'd been her only friend in the building from the day she'd moved in. He'd always gone out of his way to help her—carry her bags, collect her mail—and he always had a funny story to tell her when she came home from work looking down. She remembered that one blazing afternoon he had a long, cold glass of freshly squeezed lemonade waiting for her when she'd come home from her workout at the gym. Yes, she was going to miss him.

"Well, girl, they're calling your flight."

Lauren forced herself to smile, and Tyler knew her heart was breaking even though Lauren put on a good front. Lauren was taking the separation much harder than she was. Rootlessness and leaving the people and places that she'd become attached to were the way of life for her, and she'd stopped allowing herself to feel the bonds of closeness. It stopped mattering. But for Lauren, Tyler was the closest person to family that she had. With both her parents dead and no siblings, she was virtually alone in the world. Sure, she had a string of meaningless men and spent a sinful amount of money on things she couldn't afford. But it was all a facade to cover up all the holes in her life. Tyler knew it, had spotted all the signs the moment they'd met. They were kindred spirits. And even though Lauren suspected that there was something dark and painful in her past, she had never pushed it or forced her to talk about it. That's just how things were between them. They were friends—at least she was as much of a friend to Lauren as she was capable of being.

"Don't be standing there looking like you're gonna change your mind or something. Second thoughts are written all over your face." Lauren brushed a wayward tear from her eye. "Besides, you quit your job." Her voice cracked. "You stay here and you won't have anything to do come Monday."

They both smiled, and suddenly were in each other's arms, hugging, laughing and remembering.

"I'll call," Tyler promised, pressing her face against Lauren's damp cheek.

"Me, too."

They hugged one last time.

"Go," Lauren urged, wiping her eyes.

Tyler bent to retrieve her carry-on bag and, remembering her grandmother's pet peeve about goodbyes, said dry-eyed, "See ya."

"Absolutely."

* * *

As the 747 soared above the clouds and all that she had ever known became mere specks on the ground below, she thought about her future, the opportunity that awaited her, the chance to finally find a way to tell the story that had haunted her life for twenty-six years. Maybe for the first time in her life change would be a good thing.

Chapter 3

Over the Rainbow

On this marginal date: Client continues to exhibit cautious behavior, though minimal improvements have been noticed. Has begun to engage more verbally....

The three-hour flight was more exhilarating than tiresome. The closer the giant bird came to its destination, the faster her adrenaline flowed. She was really doing it, fulfilling her dream. Starting a new life. *Again.* She quickly shook off the disparaging thought. This time would be different. It had to be.

The captain announced they would be landing at Kennedy Airport in approximately eight minutes. "The temperature is a balmy eighty degrees, folks. Please observe the seat belt sign and remain seated until we have taxied to a full stop at the gate. Thank you for flying American Airlines. Welcome to New York."

Her stomach tightened. She peeked out the window. The patchwork of the New York City landscape unfolded before her. What were only colored lines and tiny boxes moments ago became intricate highways, rows of houses, waterways and more cars than she'd ever seen.

Before she could catch her breath she was being swept along the tidal wave of humanity all surging for the shore of freedom.

Alternately rising on her toes to peer over heads, between bodies and bags, Tyler tried to spot Tempest and Braxton. Redcaps hustled back and forth, hailing cabs and moving luggage, while stern-faced security officers gave everyone suspicious once-overs.

Walking forward, her eyes like two metronomes, moving back and forth, scanning the faces until they rested on a smiling, waving couple who looked as if they belonged on the cover of *Beautiful People,* if there were such a magazine.

Tempest was absolutely gorgeous with a creamy brown, flawless complexion that looked to be devoid of makeup save for a glossy caramel color on her lips. She wore her inky black hair in the classic wrap style, which fell casually to her shoulders, brushed away from her smooth brow. Against her burnished brown skin was a bronze tank top and matching palazzo pants in a soft, shimmery material that gave the impression of silk without being so. Her only jewelry was a thin gold chain around her neck with one to match on her right wrist, and a brilliant diamond on her ring finger that could easily be spotted in the distance.

Braxton simply took her breath away. He was well over six feet of hard, Hershey chocolate muscle. She could tell from the ripples beneath the pale-green T-shirt that he wore under his mint-green linen jacket and matching slacks. His bare feet were encased in soft brown leather loafers. She suddenly felt tacky in her bargain shorts and T-shirt.

They stepped out of the waiting crowd to meet her. "You have to be Tyler," Tempest said, greeting her with a beautiful smile. "Sterling gives the best descriptions." She gave her a quick hug, which threw Tyler off. She'd heard New Yorkers were cold and impersonal. Tempest turned toward the stunning man behind her. "This is my husband, Braxton."

He appeared to blush at the unabashed adoration that filtered his wife's voice and put a sparkle in her eyes when she looked up at him.

He grinned, leaned down and gave Tyler's cheek a chaste kiss while gently squeezing her shoulder. "Glad to meet you." The lullaby cadence of Southern roots threaded lightly through his voice.

"Virginia!" Tyler grinned.

Braxton chuckled. "Good ear. Born and raised."

"Thank you both for this. I really appreciate it."

"Don't even worry about it," Braxton said, reaching for her carry-on and slinging it over his left shoulder. "The apartment was empty. We hadn't decided what we wanted to do with it yet." He shrugged. "And here you are. Perfect match."

"Let's grab your luggage and get out of here. I know

you must be starving." Tempest wrinkled her nose. "Plane food is always awful. I fixed a great brunch and it's waiting."

The ride into lower Manhattan was larger-than-life. Everywhere she looked buildings punctured the cloudless sky, scaling across the horizon in every available space. Mighty bridges spanned the waterways, supporting countless cars and trucks. As far as her eyes could see there was something to behold.

When she realized her mouth was open she felt just like a hick tourist in awe of The Big Apple.

"So…what do you think so far?" Braxton asked, looking at her through his rearview mirror.

"There's so much of everything."

The couple laughed. "That's for sure," Tempest said. "But you get used to it after a while. Before you know it, you'll feel right at home."

Maybe, she thought, but doubted it. No point getting attached to anything. Everything always changed.

"Well, here you are." Braxton unlocked the door to the apartment in the three-story brownstone and Tyler stepped in.

The first thing that hit her was that gleaming parquet floors ran throughout the one-bedroom apartment. Floor-to-ceiling windows topped with stained glass looked out onto the tree-lined street, bracing both sides of the living room. The centerpiece was the brick fireplace that stood center stage against soft, cream-colored walls.

Hi-gloss mahogany was everywhere—doors, window frames, closets and a breathtaking mantelpiece in the center of her bedroom, which was complete with a queen-size bed in a teal-colored lacquer finish, matching dresser and tables.

The kitchen was a chef's delight in a cheery pistachio and lemon yellow, reminding her of a summer fruit drink. It was fully equipped with a microwave, dishwasher, frost-free refrigerator and a washer/dryer. Too bad she wasn't much of a chef, much to her grandmother's dismay. "*Nevah keep no man ifn ya cain't feed 'em. Probably why you so skinny.*" Her Nana's words echoed in her head and she fought back a smile.

"I take it you like the place?" Tempest stepped up beside her.

Tyler grinned. "Love it, is more like it. I can't imagine what more you two could want to do with it."

"It's her." Braxton pointed an accusing finger at his wife. "She always wants to do 'one more thing'," he singsonged.

Tempest stuck out her tongue. "If he had his way we'd demolish and rearrange the locations of all the rooms," she countered with a grin.

"There's always room for improvement."

"My sentiments exactly," she purred, insinuating herself in the curve of his arm until she was snuggled against him.

He leaned down and kissed her forehead. She tilted her face to meet his lips.

Tyler suddenly felt like a voyeur as she witnessed the blatant passion that ran like hot wires between them.

What did it take to feel that way? To love someone so much, so completely, that you didn't care who knew

it? Had her mother ever felt that way? Her grandmother? Would *she?*

"We'll let you get settled. When you're ready come
on downstairs and eat," Tempest said, putting a halt to
her wandering thoughts.

She blinked. "Oh. Sure."

Braxton dug in his jacket pocket and handed her a
set of keys. "For the front door and the apartment."

She took the keys and they left with their arms
wrapped around each others' waists.

She took a long breath and looked around. She was
in New York, in her own apartment. Maybe, finally, her
life would come together.

Her first weekend in New York went by at breakneck
speed, just like the people, and every moving object that
inhabited the melting-pot island.

Tempest and Braxton gave her the grand tour of the
eclectic neighborhood, with its specialty shops, cafés,
boutiques and gourmet supermarkets that carried everything from plants to fine wine and everything in between.

She stocked her refrigerator and purchased linens, a
few dishes and a small television with a built-in VCR.
On Monday she'd have her phone turned on. Tempest
said she'd take her to the auction house where she purchased furniture for her clients so that Tyler could pick
out a dinette set. She would have her living room furniture sent up from her apartment in Savannah.

By Monday morning she almost felt like a New
Yorker. That was until she reached the university
campus and was swallowed up in the mass of register-

ing students, most of whom looked young enough to be her little sisters and brothers.

Oh, Lord, what was she doing here?

"You look lost."

She turned with a start, nearly colliding with an exquisite specimen of a man in a black T-shirt who stood directly behind her.

Her gaze connected with his chest to slowly rise, resting a moment on his dimpled chin and his full bottom lip, up to a sculpted nose that flared slightly at the nostrils, toward his eyes that were coal black yet sparkled as if inset with diamond studs like the one in his left earlobe, and to lashes that looked as soft and silky as mink. His chocolate brown skin was smooth, save for a narrow scar on his right cheekbone which gave his near-flawless features a dangerous rugged appeal. His dark hair was cut close and twisted into short dreadlocks, brushed back and away from a brow that appeared to never have had a worry.

The heat of his long, lean body wrapped around her, raising the temperature in the air-conditioned building.

He dipped his head just a bit, his dark eyes widening in question before she realized she'd been staring.

She swallowed and tried to smile. "Oh…sorry. I was just trying to figure out where I had to go."

"What classes are you registering for?"

"I'm in the film division."

The right corner of his mouth curved. "Then you're in luck. So am I, and you're in the wrong building. If you want to hang out for a minute, I'll show you where it is."

Every kidnap, murder and rape story she'd ever heard about New York manifested itself within her, she being the victim. He looked safe and was gorgeous enough to eat, as Lauren would say. There were hundreds of people around….

"Okay, if it's not too much trouble."

His gaze flashed over her for a hot second. "Hey, if it was, I wouldn't have offered. Be right back."

He strolled away with a smooth, easy stride that seemed to carry a secret, hidden beat, his entire body moving in perfect rhythm.

She watched him as he joined a group of men and women who all acknowledged him in varying levels of enthusiasm; the men giving him one-arm hugs and high fives, the women bold embraces and more than "just a friend" kisses.

He talked to each in turn, giving the appearance of being the head guru as everyone nodded in agreement to whatever he was saying.

He tossed his head slightly over his shoulder and several pairs of eyes looked in her direction. The male glances mirrored approval, while the women registered something akin to "the once-over."

Where was the hole she could jump in? If she wouldn't have looked like a complete idiot, she would've walked away. Instead, she tried to look interested in the sheet of paper in her hand. Mercifully, he said his goodbyes and returned to her side.

"Sorry about that. Ready?"

Very, she thought, but said, "Sure."

He moved easily through the maze of people, sign-up tables and cubes of offices. "What's your name?"

"Tyler."

He nodded as if in approval. "Miles Bennett. Where you from?"

"Savannah."

"Yeah? Cool. You sound like you're from somewhere in the South. What made you come up here to school?"

Did she really want this perfect stranger to know all her business? She'd already seen that his popularity quotient was in the upper stratosphere, and now every few feet someone was either waving or giving him a shout-out of "Hey, Miles." He'd probably tell everyone he knew that she was a scholarship student. In other words, lucky and poor.

"Change of atmosphere."

He grinned as if he had some sort of secret, then glanced down at her for a moment. "Don't talk much, do you?"

They exited the building and crossed a small park, filled to near bursting with what looked like every nationality known to man.

He pointed to a building on the opposite side of the park. "It's right over there." He picked up his stride and she doubled hers to keep up with his pace.

They continued on in silence, his last statement reverberating in her head. She swallowed. "What did you do…before you took up film? If you don't mind my asking."

"Naw. I got my degree in business management about five years ago." He shrugged. "Wasn't for me. I was pushing paper and dealing with all the bureaucratic bull." His smooth brow knitted and his eyes took on a faraway look. He shook his head. "Couldn't take it.

Always knew I wanted to do something with movies, so I decided to come back to school last year."

"How is it?"

His eyes lit up. "It's phat. Love it. This is definitely my thing." He held open the glass door and she stepped through. "Registration is right down the hall."

"Any suggestions for a screenwriting instructor?"

"Yeah. *Yeah.* Chase was great. Had him last semester. That's what you're going for? Screenwriting?"

She nodded.

He looked down at her and smiled. "Maybe we'll get a chance to work together. Now that I know you can talk."

"Maybe," she said, noncommittal.

"Back to the one-word answers, huh?" He shrugged. "You'll be okay from here?"

She glanced quickly around. "Sure. Thanks."

"No problem. See you around, Tyler."

She smiled, turned and walked down the corridor, then stopped when she heard him call her.

"What's your last name…in case I wanna look you up?" He grinned, his long body leaning casually to one side.

"Ellington."

He slowly nodded as he spoke. "Yeah, like the Duke." He turned and pushed through the glass door.

Not another one, she thought and headed toward registration.

Registration took less than an hour. She was registered for Screenwriting 1, Intro to Film, and Black Images in the Media. Finished, and with no real agenda for the afternoon, she decided to take a short tour of the neighborhood.

She could feel the energy of the university community all around the sprawling campus. It was an entity unto itself—there, but separated from the surrounding area, much like she felt most of the time—there, but detached, never truly part of what was happening around her. Not really, anyway. At least it was safe.

Before she'd realized it she'd strolled off the campus grounds and onto the strip lined with coffee shops, computer cafés and bistros. A myriad of people were milling around, wandering in and out of the shops, in every gender combination, making her brow rise on several occasions.

Stomach-grumbling aromas drifted out of the eateries, making her realize how hungry she was. Doing a mental "eenie, meenie, miney, mo" she chose one that had outside seating.

She walked through the open wood and glass door and up the reception podium.

"How many?" a petite Asian waitress asked, all smiles and enthusiasm.

"One."

"Would you like to sit inside, or out?"

"Outside."

"Follow me." She grabbed a menu and practically skipped around the tables and out.

Was everyone always in a hurry here? Tyler followed the waitress's path, walking between the tables and the flow of customers when she spotted Miles at a corner table, in nose-to-nose conversation with a striking-looking Hispanic woman. She looked like one of the women she'd seen earlier.

He didn't even notice her.

She took the seat she was shown, mindlessly listened to the specials for the day and tried to concentrate on her menu while taking surreptitious glances inside. *Wonder what they're talking about?*

Chapter 4

Just As I Am

He almost did a double take when he saw her walk through the door, looking lost again, but Maribelle had him in an eye-lock, and the last thing he wanted to do was get her started. She had a hot temper that could flare up at the slightest provocation. He'd spent the entire last semester trying to get next to her, and now that he had he wasn't about to blow it, especially over some woman who hardly wanted to give him the time of day. That fact alone made her suspect. He sneaked a quick peek. She wasn't bad, though, in an understated sort of way. Maybe some other time.

"So…what are we going to do with the rest of the day?" Maribelle asked, leaning a bit closer across the table.

Maribelle, enrolled in the drama program, considered herself a budding actress. Since Miles's student film had gotten such rave reviews at the screening the previous semester, she suddenly saw herself as the next Selena. He knew the deal. What the hell, maybe they'd both get what they wanted.

Miles grinned. "Whatever you want. How's that?"

"How about a ride in that fancy black Jeep of yours… for starters?" Her dark eyes danced with mischief.

He smiled, thinking fast forward to the night ahead, then wondered if it was worth all the trouble. How come he'd never noticed her lisp before? "Sounds like a plan." He took her hand and pressed it to his lips. "Whenever you're ready."

Slowly she stood, sure to exhibit all of her assets encased in her micromini, hot pink shorts and a belly-baring top that struggled valiantly to contain its precious cargo.

"Be right back." She turned away and headed for the ladies' room, with every pair of eyes riveted on her.

Miles almost laughed out loud, knowing that every man in the place would give the last of whatever they had to be in his shoes. What was really funny, though, was that being "The Man" wasn't all it was cracked up to be. For whatever reason, for him it all came too easily. Always had. So he took whatever came his way. It was almost expected—from his parents to his male friends to the women who drifted in and out of his life like the tide. Did that make him a bad person? Sometimes he wasn't sure. Ever since he'd been a kid, things were just handed to him without any real effort on his part. His parents conditioned him to it. For as long as he could remember....

"Miles, Honey, your dad has something to show you," Cecilia Bennett said, standing in the doorway of his bedroom.

"Bet your pop got you a dirt bike this time," his best buddy, Greg Lewis, whispered.

"Yeah. You're lucky, Miles. Your folks are always giving you stuff," chimed in Tony, his next-door neighbor, who might as well have moved in because of all the time he spent in Miles's room.

Reluctantly Miles got up, pulling himself away from the Saturday-morning cartoons, stepped out of the toy department bedroom and followed his mother down the stairs to the kitchen, with Greg and Tony hot on his heels.

"Hey, there, Son." Malcolm Bennett was beaming as if he'd just closed another big development deal. That was usually when he bought him stuff.

"Hi, Dad."

"Come on outside. I have something to show you."

Miles stuck his hands in his pants pockets, easily keeping up with his father with his already long, twelve-year-old legs. Greg and Tony followed close behind.

They stepped out onto the professionally manicured backyard lawn, which had turned into a depository for the overflow of toys that could no longer remain in his room. The two-car garage was equipped with an over-hanging basketball hoop, a moped lay idle on its side near an array of discarded sports balls and a brand-new, shiny black ten-speed racing bike was propped on its kickstand.

He wanted to feel excited. He didn't.

"I saw you looking at it in the magazine. Thought you might like it."

Miles forced himself to smile. That was his third bike in less than a year.

"Enjoy it, Son." His father patted him on the back and walked away.

How many bikes could he ride?

Miles blinked away the images, and the café came into focus. He took a breath, angled his body in the chair, then draped his arm across the back and looked outside.

She was gone.

"Looking for somebody?" Maribelle asked, easing back into her seat.

"Who could I be looking for when I have you?"

"You don't have me…yet." She pointed a long, pink nail in his direction and smiled.

Miles chuckled, trying to regain his enthusiasm. "Is that right?" How long did she really think that was going to last? He stood. "Come on. Let's take that ride."

It was close to ten. The big-screen television was playing low in the background, right along with the stereo that could easily rival those in a recording studio. He paid no attention to either.

Maribelle had left hours ago, and he felt no different or better than he had before her arrival.

Seminaked atop his African-print comforter on the king-size bed, his hands clasped behind his head, he stared up at the whitewashed ceiling. Thinking.

Had to be something to do. He wasn't tired and he didn't feel like being by himself. He could have let

Maribelle stay. She'd wanted to. He didn't. Told her he had things to do. Hmm. That was funny. What things?

He sat up just as the phone rang.

He picked up the cordless, digital phone that flashed the phone number of the caller. He smiled and pressed the Talk button.

"Hey, man, what's up?"

"That's why I was callin' you." Greg chuckled. "You the one who has his finger on the pulse."

"Yeah, yeah."

"You know it's true, my brother. So, where's the party?"

"Live jazz down at the Bluenote."

"Sounds good. Bringin' anybody?"

He thought for a moment of all the women he could call at the last minute who would say yes. "Naw. Not tonight."

"You feelin' okay?" Greg joked. "That doesn't sound like my man."

Miles forced up a chuckle. "Had a rough day. Know what I mean?"

Greg snickered. "Oh, it's like that. She have any friends?"

"Didn't ask."

"Well, don't forget your buddy. So, you wanna hang out or what?"

There wasn't anything else to do, and he and Greg hadn't hung out in a while. Maybe he'd get lucky and find someone who could hold his interest for longer than the time it took to get her phone number.

"I just need to jump in the shower. Give me about an hour."

"Sounds good."

"You want me to swing by and pick you up?"

"Definitely. Females seem to have a thing for that Jeep of yours. I'm gonna have to get me one."

Briefly he thought of Maribelle. "Yeah. See you in a few."

He pulled himself up from the bed and padded barefoot across the hardwood floor to the bathroom.

Maybe tonight would be different, he thought, turning on the shower full blast.

Maybe.

Chapter 5

Hey There, Lonely Girl

> *On this marginal date: This worker observed client in new environment. Seems detached and uninterested in surroundings. Refused to participate in household activities. Remained in room. Situation bears watching. Relocation may be necessary....*

Tyler slipped on her robe and went into the kitchen hoping to find something simple that she could fix to eat.

Tempest had convinced her to buy all sorts of delicacies and she hadn't had the heart to say no. She'd been so good to her since she'd arrived.

Both she and her husband had alternately invited her

to join them for dinner for the past week. Most nights she declined, preferring to stay in her apartment reading or writing. Besides, she didn't want to impose.

She'd even gotten bold one night and ventured out, strolling along the avenues listening to the music wafting out of the cozy village nightclubs. She'd almost gone into one club until she spotted Miles crossing right in front of her, with a woman latched on to his arm.

She started to turn around, but not before he saw her. For an instant their gazes connected. His registered surprise. He smiled at her over the woman's head, then walked through the doorway of the club.

It was obvious he was just another player, she thought, drifting into the ebb and flow of the late-night strollers. It wasn't even the same girl she'd seen him with a week earlier at the coffee shop—the one he'd seemed so interested in at the time.

What did it matter, anyway? She pushed the memory aside.

Deciding on a platter of cold cuts and Ritz crackers, she took the tray and returned to her bedroom.

Sitting Indian-style on the bed she picked up the remote from the nightstand and pointed it at the television, then programmed the sleep-timer for two hours.

She wanted to be sure she was asleep before the television went off. She hated the dark. The absolute quiet. She always kept her bedroom door partially cracked, allowing the light from the hall to seep in, offering her a path—a way out.

Stupid. She knew that. Wasn't quite sure what she was afraid of.

She pointed the remote at the television and turned

up the volume. Settling back against the pillows, she made little cracker sandwiches with the cold cuts. *Seinfeld* was just coming on when the phone rang. She peeked at the antique bedside clock she'd purchased at the auction house. Eleven o'clock. "Who in the world could this be?" she mumbled, picking up the receiver.

"Hello?"

"Hi, it's Sterling. Hope I didn't wake you."

Her heart began to race. "Did something happen to Nana?"

"No. No. Nothing like that. Nana's fine, and as fresh as ever."

Slowly she began to relax. She couldn't imagine any other reason for him to be calling. "How are you?"

"That's what I called to find out. How are things for you in the big city? Did you get the classes you wanted?"

"Yes, I did. My first class is Wednesday." She set the tray aside, sat up and waited.

He cleared his throat. "I won't keep you. Just wanted to say hi and see how you were doing."

"I appreciate that. Um, how are things with you? Any new projects?"

"As a matter of fact, yes. I may be coming to New York in a few weeks if this deal works out. I, uh, was hoping maybe we could get together while I was in town."

Her thoughts rushed to her grandmother. Who would look out for her if he was in New York, too? "How long will you be here?"

"No more than two days."

"Oh. Well, sure."

"Have you gone out much since you've been there?"

She thought about her one aborted trip into the village. "No, not really."

"That'll give me a chance to show you around."

"When do you think you'll be coming? With my classes and all—"

"I'll give you a call and let you know when I firm up the details." He paused. "Is everything all right, Tyler? You sound…I don't know…strange. I mean, if it's a problem for you I can just make my trip and come on back. You don't have to feel obligated to see me."

Briefly she shut her eyes. Why couldn't she just accept people without always looking for a hidden motive? Here he was trying to be nice and she was acting like a real witch. "No, it's nothing like that. I guess I'm just tired."

"Get some rest, then. I'll talk with you soon. Okay?"

"Sure. Good night."

"Good night, Tyler."

Slowly she hung up the phone. Give yourself a chance, Tyler. Isn't that one of the reasons you came—to try to start fresh, do things differently? She closed her eyes, and a hazy picture of her mother slowly materialized. She was smiling, dressed in one of the fancy gowns that she wore when she sang—the red one. She was saying something but Tyler couldn't make it out. Her mother was turning away from her, heading for the door. Tyler tried to go after her but her feet felt as if she had on lead boots, and she couldn't move fast enough. The door opened, closed, and her mother was gone. The room was dark. She was alone.

A shiver ran through her and the vision faded, but the sense of being alone remained.

Chapter 6

Just Give It a Chance

Funny, he'd thought about that Tyler chick ever since he'd seen her that night in front of the club. At the last minute Greg had wanted to bring a date, and since Miles had no intention of being a third wheel, he invited a woman he'd dated a few times. Otherwise, he'd have been alone, like he'd intended in the first place, and he would've invited Tyler to join them. She looked as if she were hunting for something to do, and she wasn't with anyone. Actually, he'd been thinking about her off and on since they first met. She just kept turning up at the wrong times.

Maybe he'd have a better shot at getting to know her now that classes were in session. He hoped she took night classes. She probably did. Most of the "returning" students, those who'd realized later in life that they'd made a wrong career turn, generally took night classes so they could work during the day. Not that working was an issue or a concern for him.

He turned on his computer and pulled up the file containing the revision of his latest screenplay. If this one went over as well as the last he knew he'd soon be on his way. The writing part of it wasn't really his thing. If he could get somebody to take care of that end, he'd be happy. He wanted to produce and direct. And he would. He could feel it.

His long fingers pecked at the keys, making corrections, switching scenes, adding more visual elements. He knew it would take at least one more revision before he felt confident that it was finished, but it was definitely ready to present to the class. If everything panned out, he wanted to start shooting in the fall.

Most of his free time during the previous summer had been spent knocking out the kinks. Without the added worry of finances to distract him, he was able to devote his energies to his screenplay.

He leaned back in his black swivel chair and stared at the screen. What would people really think if they knew where his money came from? Humph. He'd be right back where he'd always been—with folks being with him because of his connections and inside knowledge.

Pressing the Save button, then Print, he moved away from the screen, rotating his stiff shoulders. He checked his watch. Three hours before class.

He got up, went into the bathroom, pushed aside the

glass door on the shower and turned the water on full blast. Crossing the short space to the sink, he braced his palms on the cool, white porcelain and stared at his reflection in the rectangular mirror. *Wonder if Tyler was starting tonight?* He turned his head right, then left, checking to see if he needed a quick shave. *Maybe they could go for a drink or something afterward.* He opened the medicine cabinet and took out his razor.

He shook his head. *Man, you're getting way ahead of yourself. That woman ain't hardly thinking about you.* He smiled. But maybe with a little persuasion he could change all that—always worked in the past. Steam began to fill the room. He ran some water in the sink and used a sponge to wash it out. Yeah, he'd just have to work at it. There'd never been anyone or anything that he'd ever wanted and didn't get. And he sure as hell had no intention of switching up the magic formula now.

He looked up and his reflection was gone. A cloud of mist stared back at him.

Excited. Scared. Nervous. All of those sensations and some she couldn't name formed a tight knot in Tyler's stomach.

She'd never been to college a day in her life, unless she counted business school, and starting at thirty was an experience all its own. But she'd learned early that education was the key. People respected you, treated you better, if you spoke properly, got good grades, succeeded. Those were the things that had helped her masterfully shadow the ugliness of her past. With the right assets, you could make people believe anything.

Trying to be as inconspicuous as possible she finally found the right building on University Avenue after a few false starts. Following the signs, she took the elevator to the third floor and located her room, which was nothing like she'd imagined.

There was a horseshoe-shaped table with seats all around and a row of chairs with desks attached lined against the back wall. Several students were already seated, and all eyes turned in her direction when she stood in the doorway.

Her eyes darted around the room. She flashed a shaky smile and took a seat against the wall, pulled out her notebook and placed it on the armrest-desktop.

One by one the balance of students filed in, for a total of fifteen by her count. She was relieved to discover that everyone in the class was many moons out of high school, and she was nowhere in the vicinity of being the oldest student.

Movement and the beat of low, male laughter pulled her attention toward the door. Framed like a Rembrandt was Miles, in animated conversation with a man who turned out to be Professor Chase. They shook hands and the professor stepped into the room. Miles glanced in her direction, smiled, pointed at his watch and sauntered off.

She turned away, frowning. What did that mean? He was late? He'd see her later? What? *Maybe it meant nothing, Sherlock.*

Resigned to that possibility, she settled back in her seat and spent the next forty minutes absorbing the mechanics of screenwriting. Intermittently, like an itch that needed scratching, her concentration shifted to thoughts and images of Miles.

Who was he, really? Could he actually be as shallow and self-serving as he seemed? Humph. She knew from up close and personal experience that people were never as they appeared. On the other hand, he came across as basically decent. He was polite, concerned. Everyone seemed to like him. Maybe *that* was the facade.

When she looked around again everyone was closing books and leaning toward the person next to them. *Probably discussing the class.*

Tyler closed her book, draped the strap from her bag over her shoulder, squeezed out of her chair and left, totally unnoticed.

Miles was leaning against the wall talking to a friend, and spotted her the instant she stepped out of the door. His stomach muscles tightened and he suddenly felt as if he were about to explain how he'd wrecked the family car, or worse. What was it about Tyler that sparked his interest? Maybe it was the slow, sultry voice, or her unadorned good looks. Or maybe it was simply because she acted as if she didn't give a damn if he never opened his mouth to speak to her again.

She saw him, too, and almost tripped over the person ahead of her. *Real cool, Ty.* He was talking with a guy who had dreadlocks down to his waist, but he was looking in her direction. He was smiling again. At her. What did he always have to be so happy about, anyway? She started walking. Just because he was standing outside the room she'd been in didn't mean he was standing there waiting for her. No point in making a fool of herself. She kept going.

"Hey, Tyler! Hold on."

She slowed her step and turned, but didn't stop. His

long body moved as slow and easy as a cloud of smoke, filtering in and out of the flow of people, heading in her direction.

She stopped and held her notebook to her chest as if it could somehow protect her from the dark look in his eyes. She breathed a bit deeper. And then he was in front of her, and she realized she had to arch her neck just a bit to look at him.

"Hey. Where you headed?"

"Home. I only have one class tonight."

"Yeah. Me, too." He shrugged and suddenly felt like a nerdy teenager. "Uh, if you're not in a hurry, maybe we could grab something to eat…" His statement hung suspended in the air, like clothes on a line.

She swallowed. She didn't need this. Why was he singling her out? She was certain he had an assortment of available women to choose from.

"I don't bite." He grinned a little-boy grin and she felt her heart thump. "Ask anybody."

She couldn't stop her smile.

"If you have something else to do, it's no problem."

She really didn't. What harm could it do? "All right. Did you have some place in mind?"

"Let's take a stroll up West Fourth. See if there's anything that strikes your fancy."

She nodded and wondered as they left the building what she was letting herself in for. One thing was for certain—she had no intention of being another notch on his belt.

As usual, every few feet there was someone vying for his attention. This time he included her in his greetings and brief conversations. In the short time it took them to get out of the building and to the all-night coffee shop, she felt she'd been introduced to enough people to fill two phone books. She didn't remember one name.

"You're a very popular guy," she commented when the waitress showed them to a table.

He shrugged with a half smile. "Just people I meet doing films, in classes and the neighborhood. Everybody wants to be a star." He chuckled.

The waitress came to take their order.

"See anything you like?" he asked.

She took a quick look over the menu, which seemed a bit expensive. Just in case he wasn't paying, she ordered a Caesar salad and a Coke.

"Sure that's all you want?" He looked across at her from beneath minklike lashes.

"Uh-huh. I don't eat much." *Did he think she was skinny, too?*

"A woman after my own heart." He grinned, looked at the waitress, and ordered a steak medium-well, with fries. He handed back the menu. "Most of the time when I take a lady out to eat she tries to order everything on the menu."

She looked directly at him. "Why do you think that is?"

He hesitated for a moment. When was the last time anyone asked him a question that required a truthful answer? He'd become so accustomed to telling people what they wanted to hear that it was almost second nature. His own thoughts, what was really going on, stayed inside. He looked back at her. "'Cause they think they should. Know they can." He grinned as if his conclusion was no big deal.

For a moment, even with his smile, she would have sworn the light dimmed in his eyes. There was a hollowness in his voice that hadn't been there earlier, and a tone of resignation that surprised her, caught her off guard. He seemed so together on the surface, but in that casual sentence he'd said so much. Then again, maybe that was his style.

Why did he say that—ease open the door, Miles wondered? She still seemed standoffish. But when she'd looked at him there had been something trusting in her eyes and in her voice. For that instant he believed she wanted to know. Before he knew it, *bam,* the words came tumbling out. He didn't need her thinking he was some kind of pushover, but for once he wanted to start off knowing somebody with the truth on his side. So, he'd taken a shot. *Hope it wouldn't backfire*.

Her voice was low, thoughtful. "People tend to treat you based on what they believe about you. Whether it's true or not." She took a sip of water.

"You know that from experience?"

In a flash, a snapshot of her life played before her eyes—how she was never a part of things, looked upon as either someone to feel sorry for, or ignore. Not a permanent fixture in anyone's life, and how hard she'd had to work to dispel the negativity that was associated with the "poor thing" everyone thought she was. She blinked away the memories. "You could say that."

His voice lowered and he leaned a bit closer. "Am I treating you like I have some preconceived notions?"

She caught the subtle whiff of his freshly scrubbed body. A distant ripple ran through her. "Probably. Depends on what you're thinking."

"Hmm. You wanna know?"

She raised her brows. "Sure."

He took a breath. "Well…I think you're kind of shy, not willing, or ready, to get too close to people." He shrugged. "For some reason or other, I think it takes you a while to trust, allow someone to be a friend. How am I doing so far?"

She pursed her lips. "Not bad." Actually he was closer to the truth than she'd expected him to be. Closer than she wanted him to be. Most men just wrote her off as being stuck on herself, or worse, frigid. She hadn't given him credit for feeling or thinking anything beneath the surface. Guess she had her own preconceived notions.

"It's a start. I'm sure you have your opinion of me," he added, seeming to read her mind. "I don't think I'm as brave as you are, though. I'll reserve my roasting for another time."

Their food arrived and Tyler wished she'd ordered the steak. Oh, well, she'd just eat slowly. *And what made him think there'd be a next time?*

"How far along is your script?" Miles asked, cutting into his steak and putting a hefty piece in his mouth.

"Not very. I have the outline done and about thirty pages."

"I'd be happy to help you with it…if you want. I've rewritten enough of them to be a script doctor," he joked. "What's it about, anyway?"

She hesitated a beat. "About a woman who goes in search of her past after growing up in the foster care system."

"Hmm. Heavy stuff." He stabbed a piece of meat. "Do much research?"

It was a casual, innocent question. There was no reason for the sudden quickening of her pulse, the tightness in her chest. But it was there, lurking, waiting for the opportunity to surface. Like now.

"Actually, yes. I…did several papers on the foster care system." She took a forkful of salad. *Why did I say that? Oh, Lord, please don't ask me who I wrote them for.*

"Yeah?" He nodded and took a swallow of Sprite. "That always makes things easier. More authentic."

She gulped and concentrated on her salad.

"So, what's it like in Savannah? I've never been there but I hear it's r-e-a-l Southern," he teased.

Tyler laughed, grateful for the change in topic and the opportunity to talk about something familiar. "Depends on what you mean by r-e-a-l Southern," she answered in an exaggerated drawl.

They both laughed and Tyler realized she was actually enjoying her evening. His company. Herself.

They talked more about school, their career goals and mostly their hopes of seeing their work on the big screen.

"Maybe we could work on a project together," Miles suggested as they stood outside the coffee shop. "You write, I'll direct." He stuck his hands in his pockets and gazed down at her, an almost hopeful look in his eyes.

"Maybe."

He grinned. "That's what I'm beginning to like about you, Tyler Ellington—you keep a guy guessing."

They stood in silence for a moment, caught in an awkward tableau of "What to do next." Couples strolled languidly past them down the narrow, tree-lined street, talking, hugging, laughing, enjoying the final days of warmth. The night sky was clear enough to count the stars, which Tyler inadvertently found herself doing.

"Well, I—"

"Can I give you a ride home?"

They laughed self-consciously.

"I'm parked in the lot."

"No. Thanks, anyway. I can walk."

"I'm sure you can. But how far do you have to go?"

"It's only about eight blocks."

"Wanna work off that hefty salad, huh? Come on. I'll drive you. It's no big deal."

She thought about it for a minute. "If you're sure."

"As a matter of fact, if it'll make you feel better I'll drop you off a block away from your house, so I won't know where you live."

He smiled that smile again, and she could see how easily he could charm anyone.

"Very funny."

"I work at it. Come on. The parking lot is down the block." He wanted to take her hand, but had a strong suspicion that she'd freak. Then he had the overwhelming urge to ask to carry her books. Inwardly he chuckled. *Must be losing it, my brother.*

The black Jeep moved easily in and out of traffic, the music from the stereo providing a comfortable background.

Tyler kept her distance, close to the door. Just in case.

"So, is Eleventh and Fifth where you actually live, or the safe spot for me to drop you off?"

"It's where I live."

"Aah, so you *do* trust me!"

"For the time being."

He glanced quickly at her from the corner of his eye and caught her biting the inside of her lip to hold back a smile. She was cute—pretty, really, and nice. She was a little cautious. She should be. It was a strange city and he was a strange man, at least to her, but he dug her. She wasn't like the women he'd known, who were in and out of his life. They all had agendas. He didn't think Tyler did—at least, not one that involved him. So far. He hoped it would stay that way.

He pulled to a stop in front of the brownstone and whistled through his teeth. "Nice place. How'd you luck out on this?"

"Through a friend."

"Nice friend." Male? Female? He wanted to ask, and knew he shouldn't. It wasn't any of his business, anyway. He hoped it was a woman. He stole a quick glance. She had her hand on the lock. Ready. Did she think he was going to jump her bones? He'd gone out of his way not to give her that impression. Although most women expected that from him, he didn't want Tyler to. What did she think about him, anyway? Maybe he should have let her tell him earlier.

Get a grip, girl. He's been nothing but a gentleman all evening. For once, enjoy. Besides, if he tries to get slick you're right in front of your house. She swallowed, let go of the lock and turned toward him, a faint smile on her lips. "Thanks for dinner, Miles."

The corner of his mouth curved and he felt himself

relax, not really sure why he was so tense in the first place. "No problem. Anytime. Matter of fact, I'd like to do it again. Maybe one evening when you're not busy we could go to one of the jazz clubs, have dinner, listen to some music—"

Her gaze wavered between him and the bag on her lap.

He dipped his head a bit to get her attention. "You don't like jazz?" he asked, his tone teasing.

She bit down on her lip and smiled. "I like it just fine."

"So, when can I see you again, besides in the hallways or passing each other on the street?"

This was it. That thin line that took you from "It was nice meeting you" to "I want to get to know you better." Did she want to cross it?

She looked at him and saw that momentary flash of vulnerability, just a hint around his dark eyes, and it made her want to know who Miles Bennett really was.

He wrote his number on a piece of paper from his notebook and handed it to her. "Call. When you decide."

She nodded.

Chapter 7

Risky Business

> *On this marginal date: The continual trauma of upheaval continues to add to client's level of distrust, reinforced by disappointment. Remains guarded and suspect of any affection.*

"You met someone?" Lauren sounded almost incredulous, and Tyler couldn't be sure if her borderline disbelief was because she'd met someone without her help or the fact that she'd met a man at all.

"Yesss. At school, to answer your next question."

"See. What'd I tell you? Perks, sistah. Perks. What's he do?"

The question took her by surprise. She frowned. What did Miles do? The topic never came up. "Don't know."

"You don't know! That's the first think you ask a brother. He's not one of those New York hustlers, is he?"

"Lau-ren."

"Hey, can't be too careful. I don't want to turn on the television one day and see you hiding your face behind your trench coat."

They burst out laughing, visualizing the image.

"Wooo, that was a good one." Tyler laughed, pulling herself together.

"He dress nice?"

"Yes."

"Got a nice car?"

"A Jeep."

"There ya go."

They started laughing again.

"Dressing nice and having a Jeep doesn't mean anything." *Did it?* The few guys she'd dated, she'd met through Lauren on some level or the other. She'd always had the inside info beforehand. Suppose he *was* a hustler? No. Miles didn't seem the type. But then again, what did she know?

"Well, just check it out. Is he cute?" she continued, her interrogation mode in full swing.

Tyler smiled, remembering Miles's easy manner, quick wit, casual but clearly expensive clothes; the way his eyes teased when he spoke. It wasn't so much that he was handsome in the classic *GQ* sense—he wasn't, not really. But with all the pieces put together, Miles Bennett exuded a charismatic aura that made him a work of visual art in motion.

"Cute isn't a word you'd attach to him. He's—"

"All that," Lauren filled in with a wicked chuckle.

"He's *something* like that," she countered, thoughtful. Miles wasn't someone who could be summed up in a word or the latest phrase. Generally she could put a tag on a person five minutes after meeting them. She'd sat opposite enough social workers and psychologists to be able to hang out her own shingle after years of being "in the system." She couldn't seem to do that with Miles. Instinct had made her try. At first glance he appeared as a polished, smooth, rappin', black Don Juan. A closer look revealed something more genuine.

"Anyway, if it's for you, it will be." Lauren took a thoughtful breath. "Ty, be happy. Give yourself a chance. Whatever's been dogging your trail, leave it in Savannah."

Oh, God, how she wanted to. She wanted to wake up with the sun beaming down on her and truly feel the glory of a new day and not feel that nagging fear that whatever she had, whatever she felt, believed in, trusted, could be taken from her on a whim—*in her best interest.*

She swallowed back the tightness in her throat, pushed cheer into her voice and spouted the words she knew Lauren needed to hear. "That's the plan, sis. That's the plan."

Miles hung up the phone. Actually, he slammed it down. The sound of Greg's laughter still rang in his eardrums.

Yeah. Ha, ha. Greg thought it was really funny. He didn't. Right up to now he couldn't figure where he'd gone wrong. He was polite, funny, remembered to hold chairs, open doors. What more did she want? What was her problem?

He stomped across the bedroom, not sure if he was angry at himself for caring, or at her for dissing him. Who'd she think she was, anyhow? Just some cute Southern belle trying to work him. That was all.

A whole week and not a phone call. He still couldn't believe it. He picked up the pile of dirty laundry from the foot of the bed and jammed it all into the black nylon laundry bag. He looked around. The place was a total mess, but the cleaning lady would be there in the afternoon.

He looked around again. He hated her to think he was a total slob. Getting up from the end of the bed, he started picking up the remnants of his week. Glasses, dishes and flatware had mysteriously found their way from the kitchen to his bedroom. Clothes discarded after use lay in various locations throughout the spacious loft; on the backs of chairs, across the couch, on doorknobs.

Typically, this wasn't his style. Most of the time he was pretty neat. This had just been a bad week in general. He'd been up every night until the sun rose, reworking his script. In between, he'd kept thinking about Tyler, wondering why she hadn't called, which threw off his concentration on his script, which got him even more pissed off. And the vicious cycle continued.

As he put the last dish in the dishwasher he came to the following conclusion: he'd make it his business to see her tonight. One way or the other she would be *in* his system, or *out*.

Shutting the dishwasher door, he straightened. A frown drew his thick eyebrows in a bunch. He wasn't used to feeling like this, and he didn't like it one damn bit.

* * *

After an exhausting, not to mention fruitless, day of job hunting, Tyler exerted every iota of energy she had left to prepare for class.

Her feet ached from walking blocks on end, up and down train station steps and rerouting herself the innumerable times she'd walked in the wrong direction. You would think that the people who lived in New York would have a general sense of where things were, she mused. Unfortunately, and at her expense, she chose those souls who either had no clue, or felt no guilt about sending her on a goose chase, or didn't speak English and didn't understand what the devil she was asking, anyway.

Just thinking about it now made her head pound, even as the bubbles from her hot bath rose and tickled her nose.

She closed her eyes and slid farther down into the steamy water, allowing the heat to massage her weary limbs.

"Calgon, take me away."

The chill woke her. When she opened her eyes the remaining bubbles were flat on the surface of the cool water. She sat up with a start, not knowing how long she'd slept. Hopping up out of the tub, she was seized by an attack of goose bumps. She stepped out of the tub and grabbed a towel from the hook on the back of the door and dashed out to her bedroom. She stared in disbelief at the bedside clock. 6:10! Her class started at 7:00. She still had to get dressed and get there.

The race was on.

* * *

Fifteen minutes flat, and she was ready. She grabbed her bag and notebook from the dinette table and a piece of paper floated to the floor. Bending, she picked it up. Miles's phone number stared back at her. A hot flush spread through her stomach.

She sighed and stuck the number in her pocketbook. She'd wanted to call him, take him up on his offer to go out. She'd told him she would call. She hadn't, and she wasn't quite sure why. He probably thought she wasn't interested. He had enough women beating down his door. Probably didn't notice she hadn't called, anyway.

Working up just enough of an attitude to satisfy her lack of assertiveness, she rushed out the door and hoped she could hail a cab on the corner.

Miles was in a hurry. If he worked it right he could catch Ms. Tyler before she went to class. Give *her* something to think about.

However, his well-laid plans came totally undone by an irate Maribelle Santiago, who looked as if she'd been staking out the entrance to the university for just that moment.

"I wanna talk to you, Miles." Her dark eyes that could spit fire as quick as passion zeroed in on him like high-powered lenses.

Man, he was almost scared, but just for a New York minute. He put on his most engaging smile and eased up alongside her.

"Hey, Mari." He brushed her cheek. "How are you?"

"Don't act like you care how I am," she snapped, her

usually undiscernible accent thickening with the rise of her temper.

He stepped a bit closer, cutting them off from the probing eyes and ears of passersby. Nothing like a lover's spat to spark a hot workshop discussion session in an otherwise snoozer of a class.

"I do care." His voice was hushed, intimate, in the hope of soothing her.

"Then why haven't I heard from you?" Her tone had suddenly shifted from woman scorned to little girl plaintive.

Now he was starting to feel bad—worse. "Aw, come on, Mari. I've been busy. You know how it is."

"Oh, it's like that, huh? You been sniffin' behind me for months. Now that you got what you been huntin' for you don't want to be bothered!"

Inwardly he cringed. Her voice had risen to just a notch under a screech, and he felt a major scene unfolding. This was not good. He had to get her somewhere quickly, calm her down and try to explain. What he was going to say was still a mystery, but he'd figure it out. First things first.

He took a quick look around and his gaze ran right into Tyler's. He couldn't begin to describe the array of expressions that danced across her features and swirled in her eyes. Then, as after a sudden storm, her features cleared. She gave him a nondescript smile, the kind you give to strangers on the street as a courtesy, and walked right by him, just close enough for him to catch the subtle scent of soap-and-water clean and perfume he couldn't name.

Damn!

She kept walking, that old familiar sinking sensation

weighing her down. Should have known better, followed her basic instincts. She pulled in a lungful of air. Why had she even allowed herself to think he might possibly be, on the off chance, different? She'd seen where he was coming from since day one. What she'd witnessed just confirmed what she'd already know. So why the twinges of disappointment? Simple. She'd made the mistake of giving someone the benefit of the doubt.

Tyler pushed open the door of the classroom and stepped inside, the gears of self-preservation locked in place, shutting Miles out.

He'd already blown it. Why not go for the touch-down? His eyes creased at the corners as he looked at Maribelle—who was still ranting and raving about how he'd used her—and was stunned by what he saw. *Himself.* A taker. Maribelle saw something she wanted, thought she could get it, and went for the gold—as he had on so many occasions. Now she was upset that "all that glitters," didn't.

"Mari, listen," he cut in, putting his hands on her shoulders. "I'm sorry for the way things went down. But the reality is you knew the deal going in. You figured a little sleepover with me would cement you a spot in front of the camera when I start shooting."

She planted her hands on her hips, started tapping out an impatient beat with her foot, but would no longer meet his gaze.

"The bottom line is, Mari, you offered, I took. That doesn't make it right, just reality." He took a breath. "You don't want me. Never did. You only wanted what you thought you could get, and so did I."

She rolled her eyes and pouted. "Yeah. So now what?" Her gaze rose up to meet his.

"It's whatever you want it to be, Mari. We can be nasty or act like we have some sense. You want to try out for the screening, no problem. Just no guarantees. If we decide to get together again it's all up front. No strings. No tricks. No games."

A slow half grin lifted the corner of her mouth. "No special privileges?"

He shook his head. He almost laughed. She was still trying. Had to give her that.

She looked him over for a minute. "I don't like it. But I'll live with it."

"Cool."

She stretched out a long, false nail and ran it down his chest. "We were good together." She stepped closer. "You can't deny that, Miles."

"Won't try to."

She grinned and gave him another long, smoldering look. "See you around, Miles." She blew him a kiss.

"Definitely."

Maribelle turned, pushed through the glass doors and strutted down the hall.

He exhaled a breath of relief. For a moment he leaned against the pillar, briefly shut his eyes and ran a hand across his face as if he could somehow wipe away the past fifteen minutes. He straightened, took a look around and headed inside. 'I'm getting too old for this."

Tyler settled down and focused on what the professor was saying, but images of Miles and that woman kept interfering with her concentration. And to think she'd planned to take him up on his offer. A slight shudder ran through her. At least she'd avoided the embarrassment of making a fool of herself.

She pulled out the first thirty revised pages of her script and pushed Miles to the back of her mind.

The class was breaking up, everyone pairing off or leaving in groups. Tyler had gathered her things, preparing to leave, when the professor asked her to wait. The few remaining students gave her curious looks before departing.

Tyler stood nervously in front of the professor's desk waiting for him to finish his conversation with a student. To her those few minutes seemed an eternity, and as every second ticktocked she relived other moments like this when teachers had told her how much they loved her work, how talented she was and how much they were going to miss her. She'd go home—wherever home happened to be at the time—her steps heavy, her heart racing with fear, to be told she was being sent to another foster home. And the lady with the flaming-red hair would come and take her away.

"Ms. Ellington. Ms. Ellington?"

Tyler blinked and the past receded, the room coming into focus. Professor Chase was smiling up at her from his seat behind the desk.

"That fertile mind of yours must be working overtime. Please have a seat. I want to talk with you about your script."

She pulled a seat toward his desk and sat, waiting for the other shoe to fall.

"I was going over the work you submitted last week." He pulled out the pages of her draft from his bulging, beige folder and quickly scanned them again. He placed them on the desk, removed his horn-rimmed glasses from the tip of his knobby nose, and looked directly at her. "You have the makings of a very powerful story, Ms. Ellington. I see you've already done a great deal of work. You're leaps ahead of the rest of the class."

He paused, and she was certain he was on the verge of telling her she needed to be somewhere else. Start over again.

"I have a proposition for you. I'd like to work with you on this to get it in shape for the competition in the spring. If you win, you'll have the opportunity to have your script produced and screened."

She could almost breathe again as she tried to unscramble her thoughts and take in what she'd been told.

"You want to work with me?"

"Don't sound so surprised. Your talent and the power behind your scenes and dialogue are all incredible. It would be my pleasure to see this script take off."

She swallowed. "I don't know what to say."

"Say you'll think about it and get back to me next week." He stood. "I worked with Miles Bennett last year and his script won, with him directing." He picked up his folder and tucked it under his arm. "Perhaps the two of you should meet. He could tell you how it worked for him. Help you make a decision."

Miles.

"I'll talk to him."

"No. I mean, that won't be necessary."

"Well, just think about it. It would be to your benefit."

"Thank you, Professor."

"Don't thank me yet. See you next week, Ms. Ellington." He walked out, leaving her alone with the sweet smell of possibility lingering in the air—with the exception of Miles.

She started toward the door. Maybe, just maybe, all the work, the years, the frustration, would finally pay off. Her words, her emotions, would be there for everyone to see. To experience. And maybe, just maybe, the wheels of bureaucratic hypocrisy that professed to protect those who could not protect themselves, that ground and rolled over her life, would be seen for what it truly was—a mindless, emotionless abomination in the guise of righteousness.

"Still here?"

Tyler looked toward the door. She wanted to roll her eyes, but didn't bother. It wasn't worth the energy.

Miles stepped partially into the room. "Anything wrong?"

Tyler walked past him. "No."

He followed her out the door, walking beside her down the corridor.

"How was class?"

"Fine." She walked a bit faster.

"Back to one-word answers again, huh?"

His light tone and nonchalant stride suddenly incensed her. Brakes seemed to sprout from her shoes. She almost heard them screech as she came to an abrupt halt. "What exactly do you want, Miles?"

Not again. He couldn't handle another irate woman tonight. "Why do I have to want something?"

"Everybody wants something." She started walking.

"Maybe I'm just friendly. Is that a problem?"

She glared at him over her shoulder. "Only if you let it."

Tyler pushed through the exit door and out into the warm September evening, leaving Miles in the wake of her Escape perfume.

He deserved it. Tyler stepped out into the street, barely remembering to look both ways before crossing the busy two-way street. Miles Bennett was a player, and she had no intention of being one of his many instruments. Then why was she so ticked off?

Miles sat amidst the usual after-class crowd in the local hangout, nursing a bottle of imported beer. Conversation bounced around him but his ever-ready banter was missing. He had nothing to offer—at least nothing this group would be interested in hearing. Then again, they probably would love to hear how he'd been read by not one but two women in the same night.

He still couldn't believe it. Nothing like this had ever happened to him before. *Must be losing it.*

"Hey, Miles, you hear about that film program with the high school kids?" Greg asked.

It took him a second to register what Greg was asking, and he wondered again how Greg—who wasn't a student but wanted to be with the crowd—always had so much inside information. The group was so used to him that no one every noticed that he wasn't in any of their classes. He took a swallow of beer to buy some time.

"Yeah, yeah, a little something. Why?" Actually he hadn't heard a thing. He'd been so involved in his own projects and trying to keep his personal life in order, he hadn't had the time. But yet, couldn't let the fellas know he was out of the loop.

"They're workin' on a short film, or somethin'," Greg added.

"Really?" asked Leslie, one of the women in Miles's film class. "Maybe I need to sign up. I can't get any of my stuff done."

The group laughed in agreement.

Greg straightened in his chair and Miles knew from Greg's take-charge body language that he was geared to get up on his soapbox. Wonder what the angle was gonna be tonight? Miles slouched in the hard, wooden seat and stretched his long legs out in front of him, hiding a smile behind the neck of the beer bottle.

"That's the major reason why it got started," Greg began. "The black man—"

"And woman," Leslie chimed in.

"And woman. Has minimal representation in the film industry. Sure, we got Spike, Singleton, the Hudlin brothers and a few others, but it's not an industry that we think about making a career in—that we get a break in. Especially behind the cameras, where we can tell the real deal, our way."

"I hear ya, brother," Miles said in agreement, and signaled the waitress for another beer. He knew all too well that the establishment wanted the control, the voice and the vision, crafting what the world saw and believed. The only way to change the world's perception of black people was to be the one in control. One movie at a time. He intended to become a card-carrying member of the private club.

"But how is this program going to help the cause?"

asked Ojo—a long, lanky Nigerian majoring in drama—in his clipped, precise tone.

Miles took a sip of his beer and picked up where Greg left off. "It's just like everything else, man. You catch them while they're young. Show them the possibilities. Let them know they can make a difference." *Give them something I never had,* he thought, *some direction, a reason for doing the right thing*. Maybe he *would* get involved. Give *himself* a reason.

A heated discussion on the film industry and its impact on viewers swirled around him.

Yeah, he would check it out. He'd stop by Professor Chase's office in the morning, see if he still needed instructors. Yeah, why not? Give him something to do besides worry about the women who weren't in his life. Somebody needed to make a movie about that.

Chapter 8

Familiar Things

> *On this marginal date: Struggle to avoid attachment continues, both on personal and interpersonal levels. Subconsciously, however, the need for connection, to belong, persists—battling with the conscious. Conflict of emotion could have deep and long-ranging effects.*

On the short walk home Tyler thought about the conversation with her professor and the possibilities that awaited her, the chance he was offering. But when she put her key in her apartment door and opened it, she was suddenly overcome with a powerful sensation of homesickness. It was as if she'd stepped into some unknown world.

Want of the familiar enveloped her. Her eyes searched the space as if seeking a place where her lost-at-sea ship of emotion could dock, find a safe harbor. Suddenly she wanted her own bed. To get up in the morning, get in her own car and drive wherever she wanted to go without getting lost. To walk down the hall of her job and meet Lauren for lunch. To visit Nana Tess on the weekend.

She didn't think she'd miss home, thought she'd gotten beyond feelings of loss and aloneness. She worked hard to keep those feelings at bay. Those feelings that could sneak up on her, silent as a breeze, and betray her.

As she flipped the switch on the kitchen wall, the magazine cover room—thanks to Tempest—became bathed in a soft white light, giving the room, with its canary yellow and pistachio walls, gleaming cabinets and kitchenware, the illusion of daylight. By degrees she felt the tightness in her chest and the flutters in her stomach ease.

She wasn't really hungry, but she didn't want to go to bed on an empty stomach. Opening the fridge, she searched the neat shelves for something light and quick. Settling on a tub of prepared chicken salad, she fixed a thick sandwich and poured a glass of apple juice.

Chicken sandwich in one hand, glass of juice in the other, Tyler opted to eat in the living room. She pushed the buttons on the stereo and the smooth, crooning sound of Luther Vandross's "A House is Not a Home" floated through the air, wrapping around her as she curled up on the couch.

"It's only what you make it," she said, taking a bite

out of her sandwich, the poignancy of the words suddenly having a more personal meaning.

She rested her head against the couch cushion and closed her eyes. What she needed to do was give Sterling a call. It was too late to call Nana Tess, but at least she could vicariously get a taste of home through Sterling and an update on her grandmother at the same time.

Unwrapping her legs, she got up from the couch and walked into the bedroom, where her one phone was located. She took her phone book out of the nightstand drawer and looked up Sterling's number.

Hope he's home. She sat on the side of the bed, punched in the numbers and waited. As the phone rang her heart beat a bit faster and she realized she really *wanted* to speak to him, hear his voice. Not just to hear about Nana Tess, but…just because.

Sterling's slow, easy voice came across the line.

"Hi. It's me, Tyler."

Sterling leaned back against the cushion of his couch, a smile spreading across his mouth. "Tyler. Good to hear your voice. How's everything?"

"Not bad. Still pretty hectic."

"I know what you mean." He crossed his legs at the ankle. "How are classes?"

A flash of Miles streaked through her mind. "Actually, I have some great news." She told Sterling about the talk with her professor. "I'm thrilled. Sterling, I still can't believe it."

"You should be thrilled. You get the support of your professors, you're halfway there. But, don't forget our deal."

Tyler frowned. "What deal is that?"

"You know, the one where you cast me as the dashing leading man in your hit screenplay."

Tyler laughed. "Oh, that deal."

"Ha. See how easily we forget our friends when we get famous?"

"I'm far from famous."

"But well on your way. Just hang in there."

His voice was so soothing as he told her about his latest photography project, it almost made her forget the unsettling sensations she'd experienced earlier, as well as the incident she'd witnessed with Miles and the woman. *Almost.*

And then she realized they'd been talking for almost ten minutes and she had yet to ask about her grandmother.

"How's my Nana?" she asked when there was a break in conversation.

"She's good. I was over there earlier. We had lunch together."

That made her smile. "Is she eating? Still complaining about being tired?"

"She ate a bit while I was there. Didn't say anything about not sleeping, though."

"Hmm. I'm gonna give her a call in the morning. I'll be able to tell just from what she doesn't say."

"You and your grandmother are really close, huh?"

She could feel the tightness in her chest again, slowly cutting off her air. "Yes. We are." The next question out of his mouth would be about her family. Where were they? Where did she grow up? What schools did she attend?

The questions never came.

"You're lucky," he said.

His comment threw her. She hesitated a beat. "Yes, I suppose so." Luck? That wasn't something she'd ever associated with her life. Far from it. He kept talking, but her thoughts shifted, trying to find a time in her life when luck had played a part.

"…Well, how 'bout it?"

"Huh?"

"Friday. Dinner."

She stumbled over her musings to catch up with the turn of the conversation. "Friday?" Fragments of what he'd been saying began to fall in place. He must have said something about being in New York. "Sounds fine."

"You didn't hear a word I said."

"Of course I did. You'll be in town Friday and you want to go to dinner."

"Not bad for someone who wasn't paying attention."

She chuckled in embarrassment. "Okay. You got me. Sorry."

"What didn't you hear?"

"The part about why you'll be in town."

He quickly told her about his appointment with an ad agency and the possibility of working on a major advertising campaign.

"That's fabulous, Sterling. Good luck."

"Thanks. So, is it a problem?"

"Not at all. I have no plans."

"Great. I'll take you to some of my favorite spots."

"Where?"

"Let it be a surprise."

"But what do I wear?"

"If that's one of those woman trick things to get me

to tell you, forget it. Wear whatever you like for a night on the town."

"Thanks a lot, Sterling."

He chuckled. "Not a problem. Hey, this is long distance, Tyler, and even though I'd love to keep talking to you you don't need to run up your phone bill."

"You're right. So…I'll see you next week."

"Definitely."

"Have a safe trip."

"Intend to. Goodbye."

"Good night."

Later in bed, with the television watching her, Tyler realized she was looking forward to seeing Sterling. There was something about him that put her at ease, made her feel safe. She'd felt that way from the moment they'd met. It was rare that anyone had that effect on her. And she wasn't sure why Sterling did.

She set the sleep-timer on the television, peeked to be sure she'd left the hall light on and the door cracked, then turned on her side, the sounds of honking horns and squealing sirens in the distance lulling her to sleep like the fountains beneath her bedroom window in Savannah.

Maybe she was getting used to things, after all.

Maybe.

Chapter 9

Gotta Have a Plan—That Works

By the time Miles put the key in his apartment lock his mood had lifted considerably. The scene with Mari and then Tyler walking up on him had more of an effect on him than he'd realized. There was a time when he wouldn't have cared one way or the other. He wasn't quite sure why he gave a damn now. He just did.

He dropped his knapsack on a chair in the entryway and stepped out of his sneakers. Why was that woman always walking up on him at the worst times? First it was the coffee shop, then outside the club, now tonight. Man, what must she be thinking?

Didn't make a difference anyway, and there was no sense in stressing it, he decided.

He walked into the bedroom and began taking off his clothes. Halfway down the buttons on his shirt, he stopped. Tyler had gotten to him. Without even trying. That's all there was to it. And he wouldn't just let it go. Not like this.

A hot breeze tiptoed through the open bedroom window, barely ruffling the curtains, then died a natural death before it got halfway across the room.

Sterling lay on his bed staring up at the slowly spinning ceiling fan, bare from the waist up, his hands tucked behind his head, contemplating his upcoming trip. Maybe he could find a way to extend his stay in New York, spend some time with Tyler and do some catching up with Braxton and Tempest.

If he organized everything he could probably swing it. The only hitch was he'd have to find someone to check on Nana Ellington, just in case. He felt responsible for the old lady. Even though she swore she could take care of herself, he felt he couldn't be too careful. Maybe Tyler knew someone. He'd give her a call in the morning.

Closing his eyes, he replayed their earlier conversation. She'd sounded happy, but there was still that cautious note in her voice, the brief bouts of hesitancy. How well he understood. The early part of his life was spent in a state of suspension, never certain of what tomorrow was going to bring.

But things had gotten better for him—after a while. Still there were times when flashes of those days would strike him as sharp as lightning bolts. Some scars just never healed completely. Get hit by enough bolts of lightning, and survive, you learn to be careful.

He turned over and switched off the bedside lamp. No sense giving the mosquitoes an easy way to find him.

Just as he settled down and closed his eyes, the phone rang.

Groaning, he picked up the receiver.

"Hey, man, it's Nat."

His stomach muscles clenched. Calls from his brother generally mean trouble. "Hey, little bro'. Didn't expect to hear from you. Where are you?" *Nowhere near,* he hoped.

"Just passin' through on my way to Charleston. Thought I'd give you a call."

Why, he wanted to ask, but didn't. Sterling propped himself up on his elbow. "How long you gonna be around?"

"Just till tomorrow. Thought we could get together for a minute."

The last time he'd seen Nat had been six months ago when he had to bail him out of jail. Hadn't heard from him since. Nathaniel had stayed in and out of trouble with the police for years. Petty stuff, but trouble nonetheless. He'd stopped counting the times he'd had to get Nat out of jail. When they saw each other last, Nat swore he was going to get his act together.

Funny how fate had dealt them the same hand but each had taken a different turn in life. Nat became a statistic. Sterling had stood on the fringes, but refused to succumb. And there was one man to blame. Their father.

"I'm pretty busy, Nat. Maybe some other time."

He spewed a short laugh. "Yeah. Sure. Seen the old man lately?"

Sterling heard the soft whisper of Nat's breath through the receiver and knew he'd just lit a cigarette. He could almost see the smoke curling upward toward the ceiling.

"No. Don't intend to."

"I saw him when I got into town. He asked about you."

"Yeah? What'd you tell him?"

"What *could* I tell him?"

"Keep it that way."

"He ain't getting' no younger, man."

"And I should feel bad about that?"

"You should feel somethin'. He's your pops."

"I don't have a father. Haven't had one since I was twelve. And I don't understand why you give a damn one way or the other. Look at what he did—to both of us."

"Man, that was a long time go. People make mistakes, Sterling. He paid for his."

"He'll never pay enough."

"Holding a grudge is nasty business, man. It'll eat you alive. You need to let it go. I have."

Thoughts and images tumbled through his head. Feelings that he struggled to keep submerged bubbled to the surface. Old wounds of anger, those sores that refused to close completely, seeped open—burning.

"I gotta go, Nat. Take it easy."

"Yeah. Think about what I said, man."

"Sure."

Sterling pushed out a long breath through his nose. Nat didn't know what he was talking about. Or maybe it was a simple case of like father, like son. Nat probably understood because he was no better than the man who helped give him life.

He turned on the light, sat on the edge of the bed and stared at the floor, then covered his face with his hands. Maybe Nat could find a way to forgive, but he couldn't.

"Professor Chase! Professor." Miles picked up his step and hurried down the university corridor.

"Miles." The professor smiled, taking his glasses from the bridge of his nose. "What can I do for you?"

"I was wondering if you need more instructors for the film class for the high school students."

"Actually, we do. Unfortunately, the positions are reserved for third-year film students."

"Oh." The thought that he wouldn't get it hadn't occurred to him. He was disappointed. "Hey, no problem. Just a thought. Thanks, Professor." He turned.

The professor stopped him with a hand on his shoulder. "Why don't I see what I can do? You have more talent in your little finger than some of my graduate students." He leaned a bit closer, lowering his voice. "Let me check a few things and I'll let you know."

"I'd appreciate that."

"Come see me in a day or so."

"Will do. Thanks." He started back down the corridor, feeling better. One thing out of the way. Now if he could get some conversation rolling with Tyler, he'd be in business.

He pushed through the glass exit door and out onto the campus grounds, cutting across the park to the lot where his Jeep was parked. His class didn't start for hours, and he'd promised his folks he'd drop by.

He dreaded these trips. The scenes. His father insisting that he "get back on Wall Street, where someone of your caliber belongs, and give up this filmmaking nonsense."

Stopping at a red light, he tried to recall a time in his life when his folks ever took anything he said, or wanted, seriously. They always gave him what *they* believed he should want and anything he said to the contrary was dismissed as lacking merit. He'd long ago stopped bothering to try.

The light turned green. Nope, no time came to mind.

When he pulled into the winding driveway of the Bennett Long Island estate his mother, Cecilia, was reclining on a lawn chair, perfectly positioned beneath a towering weeping willow. His father, Malcolm, was teeing golf balls across the impeccably manicured lawn.

They both turned at his approach. Then everything seemed to unfold in slow motion. His mother removed her sunglasses. Her photographic smile, which never seemed to reach her eyes, spread across her rich, red-tinted mouth. His father casually leaned on his golf club, his dark eyes shaded by the brim of his standard white cap.

His mother's pet poodle, Tiffany, ran rings around his legs, barking furiously as usual. Miles had the overwhelming desire to kick the stupid dog up into the tree and demand that they finally get a "real" dog. But, of course, he didn't.

He put on his best smile, bent and gave his mother a perfunctory kiss on her rouged cheek, heartily shook his father's hand, and he was filled again with the sensation of being swallowed whole.

"Glad you could make it, Son," Malcolm said, taking a white handkerchief from his back pocket and wiping his damp brow. "I have some important people stopping by later that I want you to meet."

"I really can't stay long—"

"But we haven't seen you in weeks, Miles," his mother complained. "You could at least stay for dinner."

"I have a class tonight."

"Class! This is much more important," his father said.

"To who?" He struggled to keep his voice even, but he could feel the hot coals begin to heat his belly.

Malcolm glared at his son. "How do you think you've gotten what you have today?"

Here it comes.

"That fancy black Jeep you run around in. A loft apartment in the heart of New York City. A bank account that could choke a horse. Huh? How? By taking film classes?" he spat, his blatant disgust for something he felt so inconsequential spewing from his lips like a geyser.

"Maybe by working for it," Miles shot back.

"Yes. A job that I made sure you got. And you threw it right in my face. Is that how you show your gratitude?"

"Malcolm, please," Cecilia said, putting a soothing hand on her husband's arm.

Always the peacemaker, Miles thought, wondering again why he subjected himself to this ordeal. "I'm going inside for something cool to drink." He turned and walked toward the house.

Malcolm heaved a heavy sigh. "I just don't understand him, Cecilia. We've given him everything. Everything anyone could possibly want. I got him that job on the floor of the stock exchange. People would sell their mothers for a chance like that. He was one of the best brokers this town has seen. And what does he do?" He didn't wait for an answer. "Throws it all away to make movies!" He shook his head in frustration. "I still can't believe it."

"Maybe it's just a phase, Mal."

"A phase! Miles is thirty-three years old. Pretty late for phases."

She patted his arm again. "Just give it some time. I'm sure it will pass." She put her sunglasses on and leaned back in the recliner.

"Pass," he hissed, adjusting his pants over his slightly protruding belly. Then he returned to practicing his golf swing.

Miles stood in the too-perfect-to-be-used kitchen, his palms braced against the cool stainless-steel sink.

When were things ever going to change? When would they see that he was his own man, or at least making a helluva effort trying?

He'd given up the front of being the corporate whiz kid executive. It wasn't for him. But he'd been so bombarded with images of who he should be over the years that "their" reality and his had somehow merged into a murky picture of Miles Bennett. At times he was no longer sure of who he was, where he wanted to go. Maybe that's why he was drawn to the fantasy world of filmmaking, the world of make-believe.

"Miles."

He turned slightly toward the sound of his mother's voice, putting his smile in place.

"Aren't you coming back outside?" she slid her arm around his waist.

"In a minute." He kissed her forehead.

"Don't let your father get to you, Miles. You know how he is. He, both of us, only want the best for you."

"As long as 'the best for me' is what Dad says it is. Right?"

"That's not fair, Miles, and you know it."

"You're right. It isn't." He watched the satisfied look ease across her face and knew that his sarcasm had gone completely over her perfectly coiffed head. "Listen, Mom, I'll have to take a rain check on dinner." He checked his watch, more for effect than time. "It's an hour back into the city and I need to stop by my place before I go to class."

"Your father will be terribly disappointed."

"I'm sure he'll get over it, and you'll make my apologies to whomever I was supposed to meet." He bowed his head and kissed her cheek. "See you in a couple of weeks."

"Call," she said as he walked back out into the yard.

Cecilia stood in front of the sliding glass doors watching father and son. So much alike, and Malcolm didn't even see it. But maybe he did, and that was why he tried so hard to steer Miles clear of the pitfalls *he'd* dropped into.

She couldn't say anything, though. She had fallen into her own pit—a pit of passivity. It was just easier that way.

As usual, his perfunctory trip to see Mom and Dad had ruined his disposition. By the time he'd returned to the city he was in a foul mood, which escalated by degrees when he saw the revision notes his professor had boldly displayed in red on his script.

Walking down the hall, reviewing the notations in the

margins of the script, he would have walked right past Tyler if she hadn't stopped him. That alone made him suspicious.

"Hi, Miles."

He frowned as he slowed his step and stared into her eyes.

"Hey, how are you?"

She smiled, just a little, and he couldn't begin to imagine what was on her agenda.

"Not bad. I wanted to talk to you. If you have a minute."

This was a switch. "Sure. What about?"

"Professor Chase really liked my script and he was telling me that he worked with you last semester on yours and it got screened."

"Yeah—" *Where was this going?*

"He said...maybe you'd be willing to tell me how it worked, things I need to do."

Bam. There it was. *Now that she needs my help she's willing to talk to me. Figures.*

"Sure. No problem. When did you want to do this?"

She shrugged. "Whenever you have some time."

"You know what, Tyler? I don't have any time. But I'll make some. Just for you. How about Friday at six? Is that good for you?" He knew his temper was getting the best of him, his sarcasm running in high gear, but he couldn't stop. Didn't want to. He was fed up with being used for someone else's benefit. And it was about time somebody knew it. Ms. Tyler Ellington just happened along to catch the fallout.

She raised her chin, just a notch. "Sorry I bothered you. I'll work it out. By myself." She turned away, wishing lightning would strike, a flash flood would wash her away, the earth would open, or some other natural disaster would befall her to eclipse this humiliating moment.

It had taken her all day and half the evening to gather up the nerve to approach him. She knew she shouldn't have, but she'd stupidly convinced herself to take the chance. Look what it had gotten her.

He watched her walk stiffly down the corridor, head held high, and suddenly the balloon of disgust and frustration burst.

"Tyler!"

She didn't stop, but he knew she heard him. Everyone else in the corridor did, too.

"Tyler!" He took off after her, walking fast but not too fast, still trying to be cool. No need to get the rumors flying that he was running after some woman.

She pushed through the exit door and practically ran down the stairs.

He was hot on her heels.

"Tyler, wait."

She rounded the stairs, pushed open the glass door and went out into the street. She darted across the park.

"Tyler. Please. I'm sorry."

She heard the hitch of sincerity in his voice, the hurried pace as he attempted to catch up to her. He'd been close enough to reach out and touch her. Stop her. He hadn't.

She hesitated. Almost stopped. Didn't. She picked up her pace and kept going. It was better this way.

Miles slowed. Stopped. Watched her walk away. He let out a breath.

"Damn."

Chapter 10

Just a Dog Day

By the time she'd walked the eight blocks to her apartment, her heart was still hammering. Anger? Embarrassment? Exertion? She couldn't tell.

Tyler put the key in the lock and tiptoed up the stairs. The last thing she needed was Tempest and Braxton poking their heads out, just to say "Hi." She couldn't bear the thought of them seeing her now.

Flipping on the lights, she went straight to her bedroom and sat heavily down on top of the floral print spread. Her eyes burned from the strain of holding back tears.

She'd wanted him to reach out and touch her, stop her from running, let her know that it was really okay to ask for help. Maybe he would have, if she'd let him. But she hadn't, too afraid that he wouldn't.

Instead of going to the usual hangout, Miles headed straight for the parking lot and jumped in his Jeep. He was definitely not in the mood for shop talk. Not tonight.

The Jeep screeched as he rounded corners and darted around what he considered "slow-moving vehicles." He'd been a first-class jerk. Tyler didn't deserve what he'd dished out to her. She'd been on the short end of the aftereffects of a miserable day.

From the little he knew about her she wasn't the aggressive type, and it must have taken a lot just to ask for his help. And what did he do—ground her pretty nose in it. Man!

He pulled into a parking space and looked across the street at her building. For several moments he just sat there, not exactly sure why he was there in the first place, or what to do since he was.

The lights on the second floor were on, and he wondered if that was her apartment. Maybe he should blow the horn. Naw. Not in this neck of the woods.

Taking a breath, he opened the door, paused for a moment debating his options, then trotted across the street.

Tyler opened her purse and pulled out the slip of paper with Miles's phone number. She stared at it for so long that she memorized it.

Reaching for the phone, debating whether or not to call, she picked up the receiver and punched in the first three numbers. The sound of a car door slamming stopped her in midstroke.

"What am I doing?" She quickly returned the receiver to its base, thankful for the diversion. She'd let a momentary sensation of neediness—weakness—cloud her good sense. That had always meant trouble. Any time she'd let her guard down, allowed herself to feel, she invariably regretted it.

"No more regrets, Tyler Ellington. No more," she whispered.

Pushing herself up from the bed, she went into the front room and turned out the lights, sure to leave the one on in the hall leading to her bedroom.

In the bathroom, under the beat of the shower, she let the steamy water massage the knots of uncertainty from her body. If only the same could be done to her mind, she thought. But she'd be all right. She'd be fine.

She rubbed lavender-scented soap across her skin. She'd do what she must for herself. By herself. She didn't need anybody. Never had.

Just as Miles's foot hit the bottom step the lights on the second floor went out, almost as if the very act had slipped the off switch. The stately brownstone, with its high, arching windows, was enveloped in a veil of near darkness, allowing the viewer to almost make out the shadows of hanging planters in the windows, the twinkle of crystal from the parlor floor chandeliers and the gleam of polished wood captured by overhanging streetlights.

He stopped. Squinted as if that would clear the picture and make way for movement and activity. Nothing.

"Figures."

Maybe he should ring the bell, anyway. Whoever had just turned out the lights couldn't possibly be asleep already. What if Tyler wasn't even home?

He looked up at the window again. Hoping. For what?

Damn. What was he doing here running after her, anyway? Now he really felt stupid. What if she were home and decided to look out her window or came walking up the block and saw him standing there like some clown?

With that thought he turned and jogged back across the street, jumped in his Jeep and sped off.

About two blocks away, his pager went off. Checking the lighted dial he saw Greg's number, and the short message to drop by.

It was only ten-thirty. It wasn't as if he had something to do in the morning. Still, he couldn't figure out how Greg functioned at work with the hours he kept.

Hey, what the hell. He made a sharp U-turn and headed for Greg's apartment on Twenty-First Street. Maybe a sit-down with his man was what he needed to take away the sting of his less than stellar day.

"If you went all the way over there, why didn't you ring the bell?" Greg stared at Miles as if he'd totally lost his mind, and wanted to add "stupid" to the end of his question.

"That's the same thing I've been asking myself. Tell the truth, I don't even know why I went over there."

Greg took a long swallow of beer. "You know." He eyed Miles over the neck of the bottle.

Miles stretched out his long legs in front of him and slouched down in a black leather couch almost identical to the one in his loft. His gaze slid around the room and he noticed Greg had purchased the same painting of the Black Messiah that hung in his own living room.

"It's not like that, man," he finally said. "She's…I don't know. She's different."

"Yeah, she won't give you a play." Greg chuckled, then caught the scowl on Miles's face and knew he'd stepped over the invisible line of engagement. He held up his hand. "Hey, sorry. But on the real side, man, why bother? From everything you told me, she's not even your type. Plus, she seems bent on giving you a hard time. So what's the problem?"

Miles stood. "If I knew what the problem was I wouldn't be sitting here talkin' to you."

"I say, step to the plate and tell her what's on your mind—whatever that is—or back off and forget it. She's either gonna go for it, or tell you to take a walk."

Miles stood, jammed his hands in the pockets of his black Tommy Hilfiger jeans, pacing the hardwood floors. Slowly he nodded. "Yeah. You're probably right."

"When's the next time you plan on seein' her?"

"The only time we run into each other is after class."

"Call her."

Miles cut him a look.

Greg burst out laughing, nearly spilling his beer. "You didn't get her number. I don't believe you, man. You're definitely losin' your magic touch, my brother." He kept laughing.

"Glad you think it's funny." Matter of fact, Greg thought everything was funny, especially if the mishap happened to him. It was almost as if Greg enjoyed his misfortunes. He looked at Greg through narrow slits, and at the moment, he didn't like what he saw. "Listen, man, I gotta roll." He picked up his black leather knapsack from the couch and walked toward the door.

Greg jumped up. "Hey, come on, Miles, man. I was only jokin' around. You just got here. Chill a minute."

"I have things to do. I wanna work on this script tonight," he kept going. "Later."

"Yo, uh, Miles." Greg hurried behind him.

Miles turned, hand on doorknob. "Yeah?"

"I need a loan, man. Nothing big." He chuckled. "Bills got ahead of me. You know I'm good for it."

"What're we talkin' about?"

"Around a grand."

"A thousand dollars?"

Greg nodded and almost looked as if he were shuffling his feet.

So that was the real reason for the call. His jaw tightened. "I don't have it on me. I'll get it to you tomorrow."

"Cool. Cool. No problem."

Miles looked at him and Greg seemed to shrink before his eyes. "Call me in the afternoon."

"Yeah. Will do."

Miles opened the door and stepped into the hushed royal-blue carpeted hallway, the scent of rug shampoo still pungent in the air. Rent for a studio in the building could easily run a thousand dollars a month, and Greg, for some unknown reason, had a two-bedroom. He didn't even want to know how much his rent was. Obviously Greg's salary as a paralegal for a collection agency wasn't enough to support his lifestyle, because he borrowed money religiously.

Miles slung his bag over his shoulder. "Later, man."

"Yeah, later. Thanks again. I'll give you a call on my lunch hour."

Miles nodded, heading for the elevator at the end of the hall. The muted sounds of life behind the closed doors with gleaming gold knobs reached out and tapped him as he passed each of the four apartments. Suddenly he wanted something more than the neatly kept space to greet him when he got home.

By the time he put his key in the front-door lock it was after midnight. The building he lived in, once a warehouse, had been gutted and modernized to encompass four loft apartments—one on each floor, his being on the top. He rarely saw his neighbors, and the only noise he ever heard came from the big German shepherd on the second floor who barked ferociously when anyone came into the building. The old dog's growl followed him up in the elevator. Now *that* was a *real* dog.

He tossed his bag on the couch and kicked off his shoes, shaking off the brief shock of the cool floor on his bare feet, and strolled into his bedroom. He picked up the gray remote control from the top of the hand-carved black lacquer nightstand and aimed it at the thirty-two-inch television.

Some late-night movie in black and white filled the screen. He wasn't much interested in watching anything, just in having some background noise—to fill up the space.

The message light on his answering machine blinked an almost hypnotic beat. He ignored it, sure that there was nothing anyone had to say that would change the miserable events of his day.

He sprawled out across the bed. Where was his life going? He had parents who still felt it their obligation to run his life. He had a collection of females he cared little or nothing about, and an alleged best friend who believed that friendship meant sharing everything *he* had—from women to his last dollar. He could almost claim Greg as a dependent on his income tax. And to top that off he'd become totally captivated by a woman who was less than interested in him.

He'd never been an introspective person, just sort of accepted things as his due and never really thought about consequences, because for him there'd never been any. But lately he'd been seeing and feeling things he hadn't before—ever since he met Tyler Ellington, with her quiet, controlled ways, her easy, slow drawl and eyes that looked straight into his soul. What did she see?

He wished he had her number.

Tyler rolled over on her side and peeked at the lighted dial on the bedside clock. One o'clock. She closed her eyes, wishing she'd listened to what Miles had to say.

Chapter 11

A Little Piece for Myself

On this marginal date: Feelings of distrust continue to manifest themselves in client's withdrawal from individuals in power, or those assumed to have potential to impact client's life.

"How's the job hunt going?" Lauren asked, biting into a red apple while she tapped out a report on her computer. The juice dripped from her lips, and she licked it away.

Tyler adjusted the phone between her ear and shoulder while she pressed her peach-colored cotton blouse. "I have an interview this afternoon at a real estate development firm. It's only temporary."

"Hey, temp is better than nothing. Have you talked

with your professors? Maybe they have something at school."

"That's my next step if this doesn't work out. Even though Tempest insists that I don't have to pay any rent, I don't feel right not giving her something. She may say it's okay, but—"

"Yeah, I hear ya. You don't want to wear out your welcome. Are you going to stay there, or look for something else?"

"I'm not sure. It's great for now." She set the iron down and laid her navy skirt over the board. "Did I tell you Sterling was coming up for the weekend?"

"N-o-o-o. This weekend?"

"Yesss. He'll be here Thursday. He has a job appointment Friday morning. Would you mind driving out on Saturday and checking on Nana? He said he would stay for the weekend if someone checked on her."

"Sure. No problem. I know you're gonna spend some time with him while he's there."

"Plan to. He said he wants to take me out."

"Hmmm. Long distance relationships are hard, girl-friend. Believe me, I know."

"Who said this was a relationship? It's just a visit and maybe dinner. That's it."

"Whatever you say. What's happening with you and that guy Miles?"

Miles. "Nothing. I can't be bothered."

"Uh-oh. So tell me, what did he do to get branded with your 'I can't be bothered' motto?"

After a minute of mental debate she gave Lauren an abbreviated version of the previous night's events.

"What's wrong with you? Maybe he was having a bad day. He followed you, didn't he? He said he was sorry. Give the brother some slack. How do you expect to find out what he's really about if you won't talk to him? You have his number. Give him a call."

"I...couldn't do that."

"Why the hell not? Women don't sit around waiting for the man to make the first move anymore. Besides, *you* left *him* standing there. It's up to you now."

Tyler thought about her conversation with Lauren while she nervously tapped her foot, waiting to be called in for her interview. Casually she looked around at the other would-be employees—two men in obviously expensive navy-blue suits with the required burgundy power ties, and a bored-looking, young blond woman who appeared to want to be any place other than where she was—then turned her attention back to the application attached to a clipboard. As much as she hated to admit it Lauren was probably right, she mused, signing her name at the bottom of the page. She'd only caught bits and pieces of Miles's conversation with that woman. She'd surmised the rest.

If she allowed herself to be honest she'd have to concede that she had no real reason to be upset with Miles at all. She'd dredged up all her preconceived notions and poured them over Miles, molding him into a plaster cast of her ideals.

How often had the very same thing happened to her? As much as she spouted her distaste for it, she'd done the very thing she despised.

Fishing around in her bag, she pulled out the slip of

paper with Miles's phone number. She didn't have class tonight, so she wouldn't see him. She studied the already memorized number, then stuck it back in her bag when the receptionist called her name.

An hour later, after a cursory interview followed by typing and dictation tests, she was a full-fledged temporary secretary assigned to the litigation department of Global Network Enterprises.

She was given a quick tour of the floor she'd work on in the thirty-story building, briefly introduced to several of the other secretaries in the pool and hustled over to the personnel department, where she completed a dossier of forms.

"Now, you start on Monday," said Janet Hume, her immediate supervisor, as she walked with Tyler to the elevator. "Eight o'clock sharp. I suppose they told you in Personnel that you get two fifteen-minute breaks and an hour for lunch. Overtime is rare," she rattled on in a tinny, clipped voice. Tyler wondered how Janet had gotten beyond the front door with that voice. "If need be, you may have to stay on occasion." Janet punched the down button and tossed her mane of red hair away from her face.

Suddenly, Tyler felt the air constrict in her lungs. Palpitations swift and as powerful as the flapping wings of a trapped bird pounded in her chest, stirring the sinking sensation in her stomach. She was thrown back more than twenty years, to when the woman with the flaming-red hair had stood in front of an elevator giving her instructions on how to behave with her new family, the cool, white hand gripping hers, keeping her from fleeing. That hand, that woman, seemed to have the power to change her life with a simple touch, her mere appearance.

The wide corridor began to shrink and the air-conditioned building became infused with an unspeakable heat that engulfed her. Perspiration beaded along her hairline.

"You have all that, Ms. Ellington?"

Tyler blinked and the present careened to a stop in front of her. She stared at Janet for a moment and then down at her hand—almost expecting it to be held—before forcing a smile. "Yes. Thank you."

The doors slid open. Tyler stepped into the metal box.

"Looking forward to working with you." Janet turned and hurried off before Tyler could respond. "Do look over the information brochure on the company," she tossed over her shoulder.

The door slid shut.

Tyler took a deep breath of air, pushing away the stomach butterflies that were running rampant.

As the elevator made its descent Tyler roped in her marauding anxieties, refusing to let the faded image of the social worker plague her.

Whatever's been dogging your trail, leave it in Savannah, she heard Lauren caution.

She stepped out into the waning afternoon sunshine, the mighty gold-and-orange sphere beginning its game of hide-and-seek, ducking behind the towering skyscrapers of Manhattan, peeking out periodically from between the pillars of granite, steel and glass.

People rushed past her, car horns honked, sirens wailed in the distance, trains rumbled under her feet. Life pulsed all around her, tried to sneak in beneath her navy-blue jacket and tickle her into submitting to the magic of New York—a magic that no one could ever explain. A person simply had to feel it.

All at once she wanted to be a part of it, a part of something—even something as abstract as a city, a city that would let her exist without knowing she was there.

She moved along with the surge of the crowd and staked out her position on the corner, arm outstretched to hail a cab, daring the woman who'd eased alongside her to take it when it screeched to a stop.

She felt exhilarated, vindicated somehow, when she slid onto the worn leather seat of the yellow speed-mobile and noticed the posted license of the driver. His name consisted of twelve consonants, and she didn't care—at least, not today. Not this moment. Not now.

Tyler sat back, repeated her address to the driver three times and didn't flinch. Actually she smiled.

For the moment, the path behind her was clear.

When she arrived at home there was a message on her machine from Sterling letting her know they were still on for Friday and wondering if she'd gotten anyone to check on Nana.

She called him back, wanting to share her job news and tell him that Lauren would see about Nana Tess, but had to leave a message on his machine.

With that aside, she called Nana.

"Yeah, yeah, that handsome devil told me he was goin' to New York. From what I sees, he mo' interested in seein' you than landin' that job." She chuckled.

"N-a-n-a." She couldn't help but smile. She was anxious to see Sterling, too. "How do you know, anyway?" she taunted, secretly hoping that Tess would reveal some secret.

"He talks 'bout you enuff. Mentions yo' name ev'rytime he comes through the door. Wanna know how you doin', did I hear from ya. Humph, what you think?"

"I think he's just being nice," she said, trying to sound indifferent, trying to ignore the sudden racing of her heart.

"Whatever you say, chile." She yawned.

"You go get some rest, Nana. I'll call on the weekend."

"I'd think you'd be pretty busy on the weekend."

"Not too busy to call *you*."

"All right, then. Good night."

"Good night, Nana Tess. Love you."

"Love you, too. And blessin's on the new job."

Click.

Tyler smiled as she hung up the phone. She could always count on Nana to add a little sunshine to her day.

Sitting in a steamy tub of bubbly water, Tyler thought about how her life was changing, taking a turn. She never put much stock in changes. They were just a way of life for her—grains of sand—nothing to plant roots in, build a foundation on. But this time—she wasn't sure why—she wanted to take a chance on change.

A little bit at a time.

Maybe she'd even take Lauren's advice and call Miles.

Maybe.

Chapter 12

Good Things Come

As promised, Greg called at one o'clock to "remind" Miles about the loan. Reluctantly he tore himself away from in front of the computer screen and peeked out his window at the gloom and pouring rain.

Donning a neon-yellow nylon jogging suit with a hood and one of a dozen pairs of sneakers, he left his apartment, opting for the stairs instead of the elevator, designating the three flights as his exercise for the day.

Poking his head out from beneath the awning of the building he gauged the distance of his dash from the building to his car, guesstimating just how drenched he would get in the process.

Taking a breath, he ran halfway down the block, pressed the button on his handheld alarm and disengaged the locks. Hopping in, he shook off the water and cursed himself for agreeing to come out in this mess.

Traffic was light as he made his way uptown, the windshield wipers swishing valiantly back and forth against the torrent.

He stopped at the bank—chatted briefly with Elaine, his personal banker who made it no secret that she'd like to handle some other transactions for him as well—withdrew the money he needed for Greg and a little extra, then headed to Greg's office on Fifty-Seventh Street.

The rain had eased considerably by the time he reached his destination, but was coming down just enough to get on his nerves.

After a short pleasant chat with Leslie, the receptionist—who he'd briefly dated until it reached a point where she wanted more than he was willing to give—Miles was given the okay to head on to Greg's office.

Greg was in a nose-to-nose conversation with one of the secretaries when Miles walked up on him in the hallway outside his office. Although Miles had always frowned on interoffice liaisons when he worked on Wall Street, Greg never seemed to have a problem with, or see the dangers of, them. Especially now, with sexual harassment suits flying out of courtrooms faster than free cheese, Miles told him more than once to chill. Obviously it hadn't sunk in.

Greg turned as Miles slowed to a stop several feet away. He whispered something to the woman with an auburn weave down to her waist, and sauntered over to Miles.

"Hey, man. Come on in." He ushered him into his office. "Hey, listen, I really appreciate this, man," he rattled, closing the door behind them.

Miles dug into his inside pocket and pulled out a white envelope, handing it to Greg. He suddenly felt like some sort of dealer or loan shark. "No problem."

"Get this back to you as soon as possible."

"Yeah. I gotta run. Check you later."

"Yeah, at the coffee shop, around nine."

Miles nodded and headed out, a sense of futility slowing his step.

He came outside, mildly pleased to see that the rain had stopped, leaving behind a light fog over the city, shrouding the buildings in a thin veil of smoky white. Images of old English movies ran through his head and he smiled, thinking how wild it would be for a modern-day Dracula to come sailing across the rooftops. The perfect kind of day to snuggle up with someone special, talk about stuff that mattered, plan for tomorrow. And he realized that with all he did have in his life, he didn't have something that simple, so basic.

He reached his car just as the meter flipped to "Violation," and spotted an eager traffic cop who was so sure he had a ticket that he would bet his mother. Miles turned to the cop and grinned, a second before sliding behind the wheel.

Beating a ticket by mere seconds was just the little lift he needed. Instead of heading home he decided to head downtown, maybe see a movie, *alone,* get some ideas for his next film.

He turned up the stereo, and Pattie Labelle's "New Attitude" pulsed through the speakers. "Yeah, just what I need, Pattie, a brand-new attitude." He bobbed his head in time to the music.

Rather than trust another meter when he reached

midtown Manhattan, he located the nearest garage and parked his Jeep. He was just crossing Fifth Avenue when he thought he saw Tyler and another woman standing in front of the window of Saks Fifth Avenue.

He stopped, craned his neck just a bit and brought them into focus. Sure enough it was Tyler, with those springy, black curls and skin that reminded him of brandy. She was causally dressed, as usual, wearing a pair of jeans that fit her the only way he liked to see jeans on a woman, and a cute, waist-length leather jacket that hugged her just right. He watched her, not sure whether he should approach her and possibly get dissed in front of her friend or let the opportunity to make some sort of amends slip away.

Tyler looked at the exquisite designer clothes in the window and knew she was out of her league. But how could she tell Tempest, who'd been so excited about showing her the city and finding the perfect outfit for her first day at her new job? Tempest obviously thought she had money. She went to one of the most expensive universities in the city, and the pieces of furniture that she'd had sent up from her apartment in Savannah were all antiques, though she'd found them at rummage or garage sales. It was all a charade and she wasn't sure if she wanted to ruin the image.

"Hi."

Tyler turned toward the sound that dipped down into her belly, and the air rushed to her throat. He was smiling down at her, a soft, easy smile that somehow touched her. He reminded her of a crossing guard, there to protect the innocent, with his bright yellow outfit, and she had to smile. Could Miles be protective?

"Hi."

Tempest turned and looked from one to the other, an inquisitive expression in her eyes.

"Um, Tempest Dailey, this is Miles Bennett. We…met at school. Tempest and her husband own the building I live in."

Tempest stuck out her hand. "Nice to meet you. I was hoping Tyler would get to meet some people. My husband and I stay so busy. I feel guilty not being able to show her around."

He gave Tyler a long, lazy look. "That's what I've been trying to do, but we can't seem to work things out," he said, answering Tempest but keeping his eyes on Tyler.

If Tempest didn't know anything else she knew a vibe, and there were certainly some heavy vibrations going on here. "Listen, I have an appointment in another half hour. I mean, I won't feel the least bit awful if you two pick up the afternoon and I do my thing." She smiled at Tyler, then Miles.

"Not a problem for me, if it's okay with Tyler."

Two pairs of eyes pinned Tyler for an answer.

It's about change, girl, her conscience whispered. "Sure." She turned to Tempest. "You could have told me you had something else to do. I would have understood," she said, her voice underlined with humor.

Tempest shrugged. "Slipped my mind." She looked up at Miles. "Well, though it was brief, it was a pleasure. You two have a great afternoon. Gotta run." She spun away on her three-inch heels and was quickly swallowed up in the crowd lining the famous avenue.

Miles stuck his hands in his pockets, a gold hoop in

his ear this time, twinkling in the barely there light of day. "So, why don't we start from the beginning, forget everything that was ever said or done between us right up to this minute?" He waited a beat. "Well, how 'bout it?"

Finally she nodded.

He smiled down at her, realizing he'd actually been holding his breath. "I'm Miles Bennett—"

Chapter 13

A Tangled Web

Miles had a compelling desire to hold her hand, keep her from being jostled by the crowd as they weaved in and out, threading their way down the street. He hadn't realized until now how petite she was. She couldn't be more than five foot five or six, tops. Guess it was because she'd always worn shoes with a little heel. Today she wore sneakers. He liked it. It made him feel protective. Not that she needed protecting. If anything, Tyler Ellington was a woman who could take care of herself.

He sneaked a peek at her, catching her profile. She was really pretty, with a small nose rounded just a bit at the tip, an oval-shaped face with a soft, palm-cupping chin, a full bottom lip and a top one that looked as if it had been drawn by one of the masters. Finely chiseled cheekbones, just prominent enough to give her face distinction. Her eyes, dark, almost bottomless, brown almonds, seemed capable of looking deeper than the surface, beyond the facade, straight into his darkest spaces. Yet there was a softness, a vulnerability that spoke volumes of pain and things only whispered in the dark.

He wanted to know her, know everything about her. And he wanted to do it the old-fashioned way—slowly.

She sensed him staring, felt his eyes rolling over her. What did he think about what he saw? Why was he interested—a man like Miles Bennett, who had the ability, the charisma, to carry the world in the palm of his hand?

Perhaps that's what made him so interesting to her. Every time she thought she'd had him pegged, he surprised her—like today, wanting to start over. Where was this "new beginning" going?

"Ever been to Rockefeller Center?" Miles asked, breaking into her musings.

She almost laughed. It was as if he'd read her mind and come up with Rockefeller Center as the answer.

"No. I haven't."

"Great. There're a bunch of shops, places to eat. That's where the studio for the *Today* show is located, and the same place where they light the huge Christmas tree," he added offhandedly.

"Really? I'd love to see it."

Her eyes glowed with pleasure, Miles noticed, and he realized how much of what was around him he took for granted. He couldn't remember the last time he'd been to the Statue of Liberty, taken a ferry ride, visited a museum or Lincoln Center. Maybe he could do some of those things with her, see them through her eyes.

Looking at her now, he couldn't figure out why he'd thought she wasn't his type.

They toured the underground environs of Rockefeller Center with its array of everything-in-one-place-you-can-imagine, from fast-food joints to designer outlets.

They settled on the Grotto for lunch, a not too expensive Italian-American restaurant just below street level with a view of the outside.

The homey yet modern decor of red-and-white checkered cloths atop circular wooden tables was spotlighted beneath strategically placed track lights. The tables were close enough to feel cozy with just enough space in between for privacy.

Light, nondescript music played softly in the background, gently soothing the mind and spirit while the aroma of sautéed onions and green peppers, fresh tomato sauce and grilled meat taunted the stomach.

He wondered what she'd order this time. To save her from starving herself he made it perfectly clear that lunch was on him.

She grinned and her right eyebrow arched wickedly. "In that case, I'll have the grilled chicken breast and a large tossed salad." She shut her menu and stared boldly across the table at him. "Scared you, didn't I?"

Miles broke up laughing and wagged a finger at her. "You're funny. Very funny. At my expense."

"I thought that's what you wanted."

She leaned back against the cushioned seat and eyed him from beneath her thick lashes, her arms folded under her breasts.

"Be careful what you wish for," he said in a voice a notch above a murmur. He leaned on his forearms. Closer. "What do you wish for, Tyler Ellington?"

Her heart knocked. His gaze held her, challenged her. In his eyes she saw her dark secrets reflected back at her. And she realized that he wasn't sitting there waiting for a clichéd answer like "Peace on earth, good will toward men." He wanted to hear about her deepest desires, the things she craved most. How could she tell him that she wanted to run back through time and change that life-altering night, that she wanted to be stronger, faster this time so that she could stop it before it was too late.

But it was too late.

"Well come on, tell me," he coaxed, taking a sip from a bottle of his favorite imported beer.

"Peace on earth. Good will toward men," she answered, forcing herself to smile.

"Is that all? No problem." He dramatically raised his arm and snapped his fingers. "Make it so," he mimicked in a fair imitation of Captain Jean-Luc Picard from *Star Trek*.

She couldn't help but laugh. "Not bad. Maybe you're on the wrong career path." She brought the glass of water with a twist of lemon to her lips and took a slow sip.

"We all need something to fall back on," he joked. He took a long swallow of beer. "So—what do you do besides write great screenplays that professors want to produce?"

She ducked her head. "Legal secretary."

"Oh, yeah? I bet you hear and see all kinds of things."

"That's an understatement. Especially in court."

He nodded, thoughtful. He tried to picture her as a secretary; legs crossed, short skirt, notepad on her lap taking dictation from the head of the law firm—and when that slick attorney got up to chase her around the desk, Tyler would haul back with a left hook and land one right between the eyes.

Their meals arrived, cutting off the flow of Miles's wandering thoughts. For a split second he looked at Tyler while she poured Russian dressing over her salad and wondered if she ever had been chased around a desk.

"Aren't you going to eat?" she asked before putting a forkful of salad into her mouth.

"Oh—yeah. Just thinking."

"Believe me, it's too ridiculous to talk about."

She shrugged and began slicing her chicken breast. "So what do you do in your spare time?"

"Write, read old scripts, watch a lot of movies, visit studios." He cut a piece of steak and juice dribbled out.

"I mean as a job."

He grinned. "That is my job."

She stared at him for a moment. "So you're a professional what—student?"

"I never thought of it that way, but I suppose so."

Lauren's warning ran through her head. What did he do for money? How did he take care of his expenses and afford that Jeep? Did he live at home with his parents? No. She couldn't imagine that, but...

Miles leaned closer and looked down at his plate, then across at her. "Not many people know this. Actually only one person, my friend, and I use the term loosely, Greg—"

Uh-oh. She wasn't sure if she wanted to hear this revelation, but her heart pounded in anticipation, anyway.

"After I got my business degree I worked on Wall Street for five years. Made a lot of money for myself and plenty of others. Some of my commission checks were more than the average person's annual salary." He let out a breath. "But that life wasn't for me. I got out while I still had my sanity, and my integrity."

Hmm. She was almost disappointed, having felt certain that he was going to unveil some dark, dangerous secret. More than anything else, she was surprised. Surprised that he shared what he did, and that for all he seemed to be on the outside, there was a lot more to him. And he was actually nice.

"Do you ever miss it?"

"I don't. My parents do." He tried to chuckle.

Tyler frowned in confusion.

He waved his hand as if to dismiss the topic, but said, "It's really too much to explain. To put it simply, they believe I've made a mistake with my privileged life."

He looked away, his features hardening by degrees as he drifted to a place she couldn't go. More was revealed by what he didn't say than what he did, she mused. Miles came from the "haves," she the "have nots." He had controlling parents who would always think "they" knew better. How alike they were in that regard. Her "parents" had been the "system," controlling and manipulating her life into what "they" thought was best.

He toyed with his bottle of beer, pouring it into a tall,

beveled glass. How could he explain and have her understand that everything had always been handed to him? More than he could ever want. And he took. He never questioned or gave back. He went through life believing it was his due. And his parents, friends, teachers and women reinforced it. When he went into film that was the first time in his life that he could control what happened. He could draw the picture, give the direction, make it be what he wanted, not what others wanted from and for him.

He guessed he was lucky that the effects of burnout happened early. That had given him the opportunity to indulge in something *he* wanted.

"What did your folks want for you?" he asked, then noticed the almost paralyzed look on her face. It happened so fast that he wasn't sure if what he'd seen was real or imagined.

She cleared her throat. "My…mother always supported what I wanted to do."

With a trained eye he watched her face as she spoke, the tiny little nerve endings that fluttered just beneath her skin, the barely perceptible waver in her voice. He hadn't imagined what he'd seen moments ago. For whatever reason, family was a touchy area for her. Fine with him. He wasn't too thrilled to discuss his, either.

But what she said next sucked his assessment right down the drain.

"My mother is a nightclub singer, jazz mostly." She took a sip of water. "She travels so much it's hard to keep up with her."

"Yeah?" He nodded in appreciation. "Jazz is my

favorite kind of music. What's her name? Maybe I've heard of her or seen her perform."

"I...doubt it. She does small stuff."

"You never know."

She took another sip of water. "Cissy. Cissy Ellington."

"Hmm." He rolled the name around in his memory banks. He knew he was familiar with just about every jazz singer or musician. Couldn't remember ever hearing the name Cissy Ellington, though.

"Guess you're right. I haven't heard the name." He grinned. "Is she any good?"

"She's wonderful. At least to me."

She put her fork down and tucked her hand under her chin. A faraway look shadowed her eyes.

"When I was little I remember watching Mama get dressed in her sparkling gowns and I'd sit on the floor with my legs crossed Indian-style while she put on her makeup and did her hair. I remember thinking, I have the most beautiful mother in the world, and everybody loves her."

"I'd like to meet her one day."

Tyler blinked, the sound of Miles's voice snapping her out of her fantasy. She licked her lips.

"Maybe."

She focused on her food, painstakingly cutting her grilled chicken into almost perfect, bite-sized pieces. Where had that come from, and why did she say it all to Miles? She hadn't told that lie in years, not since she was in grade school and the children teased her about not having a "real" mother. She'd told them all how famous and fabulous her mother was, and how rich— so rich that she hired people to take care of her daughter while she traveled. She'd almost forgotten how much she herself believed it, needed to believe it, wanted it to be real. Did she want so much to be accepted, seen as an equal, that she'd resurrected her picture-perfect world and presented it as real life?

Oh, God. What had she done?

"How much further have you gotten on your script?" Miles asked.

She could have shouted hallelujah for the change of subject. "I have about fifty pages done."

"Can I take a look at it? I'll show you mine if you show me yours," he added with a sly grin.

Tyler slanted her eyes at him, choosing not to address his last comment. "I suppose so. If you want to."

"I wouldn't ask if I didn't want to, Tyler. I hope that's something you'll finally understand about me." He looked at her for a moment, hoping that what he'd said would touch home. "I figure if I take a look at it I can show you all the things that might pose a problem shooting."

"Fine. Let me know when you're free."

"How about tomorrow evening, I could—"

"I can't. Not tomorrow. A friend of mine from Savannah will be in town for the weekend."

"No problem."

He shoved a forkful of steak into his mouth. What kind of friend? Male? Female? The last time he didn't ask, and it had bugged the hell out of him until he finally met Tempest. He wasn't going to let it sit this time.

"Maybe I can take you and your friend out on Saturday. Show you around." He took a sip of beer and waited.

Obviously he wasn't going to make this easy. "Actually,

he's been to New York before. Lived here for a while." She focused on the remainder of her salad. "We'll probably do something." She looked up. "But thanks for the offer."

His mouth curved halfway on one side in the guise of a smile. *So, it's a he.* "Some other time, then."

Tyler nodded and put down her fork.

Miles checked his watch.

"We'd better get going," he said, signaling for the waitress.

He paid the check with his Gold card and they left.

Conversation was minimal as they drove back to downtown Manhattan, the state of the unusually warm weather for late September and the ruthless city drivers being their topics, which was fine with Tyler. At that point the less said the better, especially after the hole she'd dug for herself. And she actually felt strange telling Miles about Sterling. It wasn't as if she owed Miles any explanations. It was just awkward. She'd never been in a situation like that before. Lauren would think it was hilarious. "Keeps 'em on their toes," she would say. Personally, she could do without the added drama—particularly since she was slowly accepting the idea that she kind of liked Miles.

So where did that leave Sterling? *When it rains it pours,* she heard Nana Tess whisper. And she still hadn't gotten anything to wear for tomorrow night.

"Here you are, safe and sound."

Tyler looked out the window and saw they were parked in front of her building. She'd totally zoned out in the last few minutes.

"That was quick." She unbuckled her seat belt, then

looked at him. "Thanks for lunch, Miles, and the tour. I had a great time."

"So did I. Hope we can do it again soon."

She smiled, but didn't answer.

"If you won't be long I can wait for you, drop you off at school."

Man, did he sound like a wimp, or what? He was practically begging her to spend time with him. That wasn't his style, and he'd have to figure out real quick where he'd lost it. But the bottom line was, he wasn't quite ready to let her go. He enjoyed her company, her hesitant but sincere smile and her intelligence, and she was definitely easy on the eyes.

"That's okay. Really. I have a few things to take care of before I leave."

"Hey, just an offer." How many times could he be told "Thanks, but no thanks" in one day? "So, maybe I'll see you later."

"Sure. May-be." She opened the door and hopped down, then turned to him before shutting the door. "Thanks again, Miles."

He nodded and watched her trot up the steps and inside. Shifting into Drive, he sped away, a feeling of incompleteness settling over him.

Who was this guy she was seeing tomorrow?

Sterling checked the time on the kitchen wall clock, three hours before his flight—an hour-plus drive to the airport. The one downside of living so far out was that he had to drive into Savannah or Charleston for anything major.

Draping his garment bag over his shoulder, he picked

up his portfolio in one hand and his carry-on in the other. After taking one last look around he rushed out the door and put his bags in the trunk of his car.

Nana was on her porch, swaying as gentle as a breeze in her swing. The vision made him smile.

He crossed the wide dirt path that separated the two houses—shaded on either side by a rainbow of trees and flowering plants—and stepped up on Nana's porch. Her eyes were closed.

"Hey, Nana Tess," he whispered.

Slowly she opened her eyes and a slow smile spread across her mouth.

"Hey, yourself. Know it be you. Knows yo' footsteps."

"Thought you were asleep."

"Just restin' my eyes." She sat up a bit in the swing. "You headin' off now?"

"Yes."

"Took care of my bills for me?"

"Yes, Ma'am. First thing this morning."

"Good, 'cause ya know how much I hates messin' wit them bills." She sighed. "Tyler used ta take care of 'em for she went up north. Did a good job, too." She looked up at him. "You don't do too bad, neither."

They both laughed.

"I've got to get going, Nana. Is there anything you need?"

"Well, ifn there was you couldn't do it, or git it. You gots ta go. So get goin'." She swatted him on the arm. "That ole fresh Lauren'n be by here tomorrow. I'll just run her ragged. Do 'er good." She chuckled.

"You're a mean old lady." He bent down and kissed her cheek. "Behave yourself till I get back."

"Aw, shucks, ain't a decent-lookin' man 'sides you in a hunerd miles of dis place." She gave him a wink. "Ain't no choice *but* to behave. You give that grand-daughter of mine a good hug for me." She blinked several times, then looked up at him, her voice having lost some of its vibrancy. "Sho' do miss that gal."

Sterling patted her shoulder.

"Git goin', Boy, fo' you miss you' flight."

"See you in a couple of days."

"Sho' nuff." She started swinging again.

Sterling bounded down the creaky wooden steps. "Bye, Nana Tess," he called over his shoulder.

Tess smiled and closed her eyes.

He wasn't one for speeding, but he was definitely behind schedule and he'd promised himself he'd bring Tyler a present from home. A surprise. He pressed on the accelerator and shot five miles over the speed limit. Had he worked it right he could have picked her up something during the week, but the days had gotten away from him. Now he'd have to stop in Savannah. There was no way he'd bring her an airport gift.

He drove with the windows down, the warm fall breeze bringing with it the sweet scent of rich red earth, fruit trees and chewing-good green grass.

The best place to shop was in the historic district. The prices were a bit high, but there were great selections. He pulled off the highway to the exit for the center of town.

Stopping at the first red light, he ran a mental check-list of gift possibilities. When the light turned green, he looked both ways as was his practice before pulling out into the intersection. When he looked to his left his heart almost stopped pumping in his chest.

Crossing in front of him was his father. A sudden, powerful urge to step on the accelerator and squash him like a bug welled up inside of him from the depths of his soul, exploding in a million tiny lights in his head.

When he looked again the old man was gone, blending in with the crowd of humanity as if he really belonged among them.

Blaring car horns from behind propelled him forward. Mindlessly he eased out and across the intersection.

He drove by instinct, past the clothing shops that strove for trendy with the Southern woman in mind, the florists with their riots of seasonal flowers, and the bakeries with their gooey pecan pies and lip-smacking sweetbread that seemed to stand in the door and say, "Get in here and get a taste."

But all he could see was his father. All he could feel was betrayal and pain. And he felt like doing something he hadn't done in years. Crying.

It had been more than twenty years since he last saw or spoke to him. Through Nat he'd learned that their father had returned to Savannah five years earlier. He'd made it his business to stay out of Savannah when he'd moved back to Georgia from Charleston the previous year. It was inevitable that they'd run into each other at some point. He thought he'd steeled himself against any emotion.

He hadn't.

When his father walked in front of him he felt as if he'd been hit in the belly with a cast-iron ball. Everything he'd kept at bay came hurtling back.

When he looked again, he was back on the highway headed for the airport.

Chapter 14

Easier This Way

> *On this marginal date: Feelings of inadequacy and a need to be accepted are demonstrated by client's proclivity to fabricate and pretend. May not be consciously aware of behavior...*

Tyler tossed her purse on the kitchen counter and walked into the living room. She probably should change clothes and gather up her notes. She should get ready for class. But somewhere between stepping out of the Jeep and coming upstairs she'd lost a burst of energy. She felt deflated, pricked like a balloon.

Flopping down on the couch, she laid her head back and closed her eyes. Her afternoon with Miles played before her. She knew what was weighing her down. Her conscience.

Yes, her mother had been a nightclub singer. She had dressed in beautiful clothes. But she was dead—murdered. And she'd made it sound as if her mother would walk through the door any minute.

But would Miles have understood the truth? She'd never trusted anyone with the truth, not even Lauren. She didn't want to be pitied. She didn't want the sad looks of "understanding," or avoiding subjects when she was around so as "not to upset her."

So she created a world in which the horror of that night didn't exist, and she moved on and through the nightmare.

She had before. She would again.

Always.

When she walked out of class later that evening Miles was waiting for her. He wasn't camouflaged in the midst of a conversation this time. He was there. Alone. Leaning against the wall, looking right at her. He almost looked dangerous with his black, Kenneth Cole T-shirt and black jeans. Today a tiny gold stud twinkled in his ear.

She walked up to him.

"Hi." She smiled.

"How was class?"

"Not bad."

"I thought you might want to hang out for a little while. A few of us go over to the coffee shop, swap stories, eat, talk. How 'bout it?"

"I…was planning to go straight home."

"Something special on your agenda?"

"No. But—"

"Then come on. Just for a while. I'll drive you home."

He gave her that smile that could melt a glacier.

She hesitated, but only for a moment. He'd gone out of his way to seek her out. He obviously wanted to spend some time with her. She wouldn't question the reasons why. Not this time. And, well, she wanted to spend time with him, too.

"Sure. But I can't stay long."

"No problem." He grinned, and she felt that flutter in her stomach again.

They walked out together and suddenly she felt like the air was being pumped back into her deflated balloon.

"Hey, folks," Miles greeted the usual assemblage.

All eyes turned in his direction but stayed pinned on Tyler as they said their hellos to Miles.

"This is Tyler…Ellington. She's in Chase's class," he added, and Tyler thought he said it as if to justify her inclusion.

"Tyler, this is Leslie. We're in film class together."

Leslie gave her a short wave, the kind when you only wiggle your fingers.

"Leslie's dad is one of the producers for ABC television." He winked at Leslie. "But she has dreams of being the first black female Spielberg."

"You got that right," Leslie said without hesitation.

Miles pointed to Ojo, who stood and shook her hand while Miles mentioned that his father was the Nigerian ambassador to the United Nations and Ojo was being trained to be a delegate.

Next up was Greg, who seemed to have some sort of honorary membership in the elitist group by virtue of being Miles's friend.

Miles held out a chair for her, then pulled up one for himself from the next table and straddled it.

"So, what's happening?" Miles asked as he signaled the waitress and ordered a bottle of Corona. He leaned toward Tyler. "Want anything?"

"A soda…Sprite."

"Add a Sprite to that, will ya, Karen?"

"Sure thing, Miles. Anything else, folks?"

Orders were placed for fries, burgers and onion rings, along with refills for their respective drinks.

"Tyler, how do you like NYU so far?" Leslie asked, nibbling on some peanuts.

"I like it. It's just so big. It takes some getting used to."

"Yes. That is exactly how I felt when I first arrived," Ojo said.

Tyler smiled, enjoying the lyrical, precise quality of his voice and the no-nonsense attitude of Leslie, who told the group she was happy that there was finally another woman in the group.

"Now I won't have to battle all the women's issues alone."

Tyler smiled shyly and the guys raised their bottles of beer in mock salute.

"What part of the South are you from, Tyler?" Ojo asked.

"Savannah."

"Beautiful city," he continued. "I've been there several times."

"You've been everywhere several times," Miles

joked. He turned to Tyler and bent his head, but kept his eyes on Ojo. "Ever want to know about any place in the world, that's the man."

Ojo seemed to preen with Miles's compliment, Tyler noticed.

"I've had no choice but to travel," he said by way of explanation. "But that is another story. Why leave all that beauty for this?" he asked Tyler with a wave of his hand.

"I wanted to study film and screenwriting, and heard this was one of the best places for it."

There was a round of nodding heads and murmurs of agreement.

"As long as you don't want anything produced," Leslie complained.

On that note, the group launched into a heavy discussion about university politics, which sounded to Tyler as if Greg knew more about it than anyone. Then it was the dating game, women's rights, the welfare system, plays, movies and black men as second-class citizens.

Tyler listened to the fast-paced conversation, the passion behind the voices, the intelligence in responses, observed the polish in their styles, their casual but expensive clothing, and felt completely out of her league.

They were all people with solid backgrounds, important families, experience in the world. The only thing they hid behind was a camera. Yet, observing each in turn, Tyler realized they were all performers—herself included—each carving out a role they wanted to play.

Leslie, with her cover-girl looks, wanted to be the

Angela Davis for the next millennium. Ojo wanted to disassociate himself from his diplomatic ties and just be a regular guy, but he enjoyed the privileges and prestige they afforded him. Greg simply wanted to be in whatever role secured him the best vantage point, whether as the messenger of inside information or entertainer sharing tales of his female conquests.

And then there was Miles.

On the surface he came across as a self-serving, charismatic gigolo—the leader of the pack, the one who everyone gravitated to, wanted to be accepted by, seen with—yet underneath he was struggling with his own battles of who and where he was in his life, a side of which she'd only gleaned a brief glimpse. He was the greatest enigma of all.

At first she thought she didn't fit into this small world he'd introduced her to. But she did. Wasn't she really a master at the game of charades? *Guess who I am?*

Miles watched her periodically, as the ebb and flow of conversation swelled around her. Through it all she remained virtually quiet, only smiling or nodding her head. He had no idea what it felt like to be left out, but he was sure he wouldn't like it, and couldn't imagine that she would. He wanted her to feel comfortable around his friends, not left on the sidelines, which the crew could easily do if a person couldn't keep up. He found an opening when the chatting segued to music.

"Tyler's mom is a jazz singer," he said, turning to her with a smile of inclusion.

She felt the air squeeze out of her lungs.

Inquisitive faces turned toward her.

"Get out," Leslie said. "That's phat."

Greg leaned forward. "Can she get us any tickets to shows?"

Leslie punched him in the arm and rolled her eyes in dismissal.

"She…just sings in nightclubs. Small stuff." She took a long swallow of her Sprite.

"I wish my mother could sing," Leslie said wistfully. "Woman can't carry a note in a pocketbook."

They all broke up laughing.

"Perhaps we could all see her perform one night," Ojo said.

Her heart began to race. "She…rarely comes to New York. She…mostly plays in the South. And not as much as she used to."

"Hey, maybe one of your screenplays could be about the life of a small-town jazz singer," Leslie offered, excitement building in her voice. "I'd love to direct something like that."

"You'd like to direct anything," Miles tossed in, and ducked just before she tossed a balled-up napkin at him.

Tyler took a breath and forced a smile. She had to get away. She pushed back in her seat. "It's really been great meeting you all. But I have to get going."

She stood, and so did Miles.

"It's been real, folks," he said. "See you next week. Greg, I'll get with you during the weekend."

He put his hands on Tyler's back and she felt a sudden, thrilling heat scuttle up her spine. She almost shivered from the simple pleasure of it.

A discordant chorus of "Nice meeting you" reached

out and touched her. Leslie did the wave thing again, and then she and Miles headed for the exit.

The space on the small of her back grew hotter. She wanted to tell him to take his hand away, but didn't want the little pleasure to end.

But it did.

Just as they reached the door, the woman she'd seen Miles with before sauntered in.

"Hi, Miles," she crooned, blasting him with a smile.

"How are ya, Mari?"

"Not as good as you, I see." She turned smoldering, dark eyes in Tyler's direction.

"Tyler Ellington, this is Maribelle Santiago."

"Hi," Tyler whispered.

Mari didn't respond.

"Take it easy, Mari."

Miles and Tyler started to walk out. Maribelle leaned toward Miles.

"You don't waste any time, do you, baby?" she asked just loud enough for Tyler to hear.

Miles ignored the catty remark and felt the muscles tighten in Tyler's back. "Come on, let's go." He pushed open the door and let her through.

Tyler was quiet on the walk to the Jeep. Quiet even for her, Miles noted, taking cautious, out-of-the-corner-of-the-eye glances.

She wanted to say something about the little scene but figured she should just leave it alone. He didn't seem to be too eager to discuss it himself.

He was trying to keep his temper under control. Mari had a hell of a nerve doing that, and he was going to put her in check the next time he saw her.

He peeked at Tyler again. What was she thinking? Just when he thought they were finally getting on the right track this had to happen.

Miles opened the passenger door and Tyler got in, quiet as a mouse. He turned the key in the ignition, then turned the car off and angled his body in her direction.

"Tyler, listen…back there with Maribelle—"

"Please. Don't explain. That's your life."

"No. I do have to explain. What I said earlier about starting over? I meant that. So I want to clear the air so we have a clean slate. Okay?"

She hesitated, then nodded in agreement. Besides, she really did want to know about him and Ms. Maribelle.

"Yes. Mari and I did…get together. Once. And that's all it was. It was never a 'relationship.' I thought she understood that. I know that might sound callous and indifferent, but that's the way it was. What she said, and I'm sure you overheard, was said for your benefit and nothing more. There isn't anything happening between me and her. I want, yes, I *need* you to believe that."

She looked at him for a moment, trying to see beyond the polished facade, beyond the words. "Why? Why do *you* need *me* to believe you?"

"Because it matters to me what you think, Tyler. And to be truthful, I'm not sure why. I just know that's how I feel. I can't be any straighter than that."

She looked away. She wanted to make room for trust. It was just so hard. So very difficult.

"What if I do believe you?"

"Then we can move on from here. Just maybe take this somewhere."

Her stomach tightened and she felt the warmth of "just maybe" flow through her. "We'll never get anywhere if we just keep on sitting here."

He smiled, feeling a sense of relief, and turned the key.

They talked and laughed on the way to Tyler's apartment, recapping the evening, with Tyler giving Miles her spin on his eclectic group of friends. He was impressed with her insight and on-target analyses. They talked about their writing projects and how strongly they felt about depicting another side of black life on the screen, not what society had been accustomed to viewing. Miles explained to her the grueling process of getting a script off paper and onto film, and how in order to be successful a writer had to have a thick skin to keep from going under from people's criticisms.

"You're going to make a great producer or director one day," he said, making the turn onto her street.

"Why is that?"

"You have a natural talent for seeing beyond coverups, pinpointing nuances in people's personalities. That's what makes a character come alive on screen. Unfortunately not everyone who goes into filmmaking can do that."

"Can you? See beyond the surface?"

He pulled to a stop in front of her building and turned off the engine. He thought about her question and what she was really asking. "I try. I think it's what I do best. At least most of the time."

"What do you see now, Miles? If you look beyond the surface?"

He slowly unbuckled his seat belt and then hers, keeping his eyes on his hands as he spoke. "I see a woman, a very beautiful woman, who keeps a part of her completely to herself. Who has a past that affects everything she does. Someone who is in search of something and isn't sure where to find it." He looked into her eyes. "Someone who, for whatever reason, I want to help find what she's searching for, and maybe find a missing part of myself in the process."

How could he know that? She watched him move closer, cutting off the space between them. Her heart began to pound. How could he see so clearly beneath the layer of make-believe that she'd dressed in? He'd, without trying, reached a place that she hadn't dared to go, and wasn't afraid of what he saw. But what if it were just a line, a way to get her to...

He reached out and trailed a finger down her cheek, a thumb across her lips. He felt her tremble beneath his fingertips. He moved closer, just a little, and felt her warm breath brush across his face. She didn't move and he could see the little pulse flutter in her throat.

Languidly he moved closer until his lips barely touched hers. Testing. He heard her soft sigh and pressed closer, feeling her lips ease beneath his. Gently he cupped her face in his palms and drew her to him, gradually increasing the pressure of the kiss until he felt her lips part.

Tentatively he ran his tongue across her lips, momentarily savoring the flavor, the texture, then dipped inside to sample what was offered. Their tongues danced to all the slow songs they'd ever heard, taking their time, bumping and grinding, making up their own melody along the way.

She pressed her hands against his chest, her fingers

like pins of heat against his skin. He slid his hands across her face to tangle in her mass of springy curls, hair that he'd longed to touch. His heart raced and he wanted to gather her closer, tighter, so that she couldn't get away. Ever. The realization scared him with the power of its suddenness.

So hot. So very sweet, she thought through the haze of feelings that flamed within her. She hadn't expected to feel like this—not from a kiss so gentle yet so full of passion that it frightened her. She wanted more of him, but was afraid of what she'd find, afraid that if she allowed herself to be consumed by feelings, let herself indulge in the job of being wanted, it would be taken away—as it had always been. How could she risk that?

Without warning she pulled away, unable to look at him, knowing she'd see the look of dismissal, the disappointment.

He placed a finger under her chin and tilted her face up, forcing her to look into his eyes. "Whatever it is, Tyler, it's okay." His voice was a note above a whisper, soothing, coaxing. "We can take our time. There's no rush. Not this time. Not for me. Let's just try. That's all I ask."

She swallowed the knot of fear and doubt. Could she? Could she give herself a chance again, especially with a man who seemed to have a pattern of leaving women at the curb, who gathered them as trophies? Was that the kind of chance she wanted to take?

It's all about change, she heard Lauren whisper. "I'm not the best at relationships, Miles." She laughed, a self-deprecating laugh. "I don't have a great track record."

"Then let this really be a new beginning. Neither do I. Maybe we can both change that."

Her eyes searched his face, hoping to find…what, she wasn't sure. "I'll try."

He smiled. "So will I."

"Good night, Miles." She started to get out.

"Does this mean you'll give me your phone number now?" he teased.

Chapter 15

The Simple Things in Life

Tyler walked up the stairs to her apartment, the tingle of Miles's kiss still warm on her lips. She almost felt giddy, as if she wanted to spin around the room with her arms outstretched. And she knew that if she took a peek in a mirror she'd see a silly grin on her face, a flush in her cheeks.

It felt good to just feel good. To let go. Even for a little while.

She took a settling breath. *Get a grip, girl,* she warned herself. It was only a kiss. But hell, she couldn't remember a kiss making her feel like this—this yearning for more. And he still wanted to see her, wanted to try to see where things could go with them. And she believed him—needed to believe him.

Maybe, just maybe.

She touched her lips with the tip of her finger and smiled.

The phone rang.

Maybe it was Miles calling from that cell phone of his.

"Hello?"

"Hey, Tyler. It's me, Sterling."

Reality careened her feelings to an abrupt halt. She'd totally forgotten about Sterling.

"H-i. Where are you?"

"At the airport. Just got in and wanted to let you know. I'm heading over to the hotel. We're still on for tomorrow?"

"Uh, sure."

"Everything okay, Tyler? You sound funny."

"No. I mean, yes. Everything's fine. I'm just getting in from class. I guess my mind was still on my script." She was definitely ad-libbing a script now, she thought.

"Great. I'll give you a call later in the afternoon."

"Sure."

"Well, wish me luck."

"Oh, right. Good luck tomorrow."

"Thanks. Talk to you tomorrow. Bye."

"Good night."

As she hung up a sweeping sensation of guilt surged through her. Why should she feel guilty? She hadn't done anything wrong—so far—except allowing Miles to believe he was getting involved with the woman she wasn't. And how was she going to fix that?

Heavily, she sat down on the couch. Why couldn't life just be simple? For once.

* * *

A half smile curved Miles's lips during almost his entire drive home. What was it about Tyler Ellington that got his juices flowing, had him thinking crazy and acting as if he hadn't gotten his "be a man" degree?

She was definitely not like any other woman he'd dealt with. She wasn't flashy, didn't seem to be out to get him—*just because*. She had her own goals and didn't rely on him to make them a reality. She was easy to be with, intelligent, and most of all she had him thinking about trying to do the right thing. When was the last time he'd been able to say a woman had that kind of an effect on him?

Never.

Yeah. She was special. And he was going to make it a point to let her know it every chance he got.

Sterling unpacked his suitcase and laid his clothes out for his meeting the following morning. He looked around. It felt good being back in New York, though he could only take it in small doses. Knowing that Tyler was there made it better.

He was really looking forward to seeing her the next day and wanted to make their time together a memorable one. He wanted her to think about him when he went back home, wanted to hear the eagerness in her voice when he called.

He sat on the edge of the bed and untied his shoes. How many years had she floated through his dreams, seen those eyes of hers when he closed his, heard the soft laughter that made him feel good inside? Now, maybe he could make this one dream of his a reality.

She deserved to be happy. So did he. Together they could be.

Sleep didn't come easily that night. Tyler tossed and turned, watched television, listened to the stereo, even subjected herself to an age-old remedy of a warm glass of milk.

Finally exhaustion captured her, sweeping her away into a pit of dreams filled with images of Miles, Sterling and her grandmother. Twirling in and out was her mother—a vague, faded image of Cissy wearing that red dress, the dress she'd worn that night. She was singing, but Tyler couldn't make out the words.

They were all pointing at her. She couldn't hear what they were saying, but she knew. They were telling her it was all her fault. Beautiful, talented Cissy was dead because of her.

Then her mother stopped singing and looked at her. Her eyes were only black holes, her mouth a red slash. She turned and began walking away, down a dark tunnel.

Tyler called out to her. Begged her to stay. Cissy kept walking and Tyler cried, pleaded. The vision of her mother grew smaller, dimmer. And the lady with the red hair took her place.

"M-a-m-a!"

The sound of her own voice catapulted her upright in the bed. Her body was drenched in sweat and she shook as if she'd been dipped in a vat of ice.

"What could I have done?" she cried, burying her hands in her face. "I was only four. Only four."

The following morning she awoke with only a faint memory of her dream. She knew it had been about her mother, but she wasn't quite sure what.

By the time she'd finished her shower and drank a glass of orange juice whatever was left of her dream was gone entirely. What she did remember, with vivid clarity, was the kiss she'd shared with Miles. The thought of it made her smile. She took a breath and the scent of him filled her nostrils, the remnants of the unsettling sensations dissipating. She closed her eyes and she could see that little-boy grin. It almost made him seem shy, but to anyone who knew him better. It was all part of the charm.

Tyler was tempted to call him, just to see if he'd respond to her the same way today as he had yesterday.

She didn't get the chance. The phone rang and she had the unspoken hope that it was Sterling saying they'd have to call off their date.

"Morning, sleepyhead."

Her heart beat a bit faster at the sound of Miles's down-low voice.

"I'll have you know I've been up for hours."

"Is that right? Doing what?"

"Things," she teased.

"Oh, *women* things." He chuckled, then grew serious. "I was hoping you were thinking about yesterday. Last night in particular."

A hot flush coursed through her as the memory came alive. "Maybe."

"There you go with those one-word answers again. Maybe? You were supposed to say, 'Yes, Miles, I was thinking about last night. And I want to know when I can see you again.'" He paused. "'Cause that's what I was thinking."

There were those flutters again, wreaking havoc with her stomach. "Really?"

"Yes. Really. So what's your answer? I know you have a hot date tonight with your 'friend,' but I was hoping we could get together tomorrow. Spend the day, maybe see a movie, go to dinner, take a jet plane—"

She started to laugh. "All that in one day, huh?"

"Why not?"

"Can I call you and let you know?"

"I thought you'd never ask."

"I'll call you tomorrow."

"Early," he said.

"Early."

"Later."

The dial tone hummed in her ear.

She hugged the phone to her breasts, savoring the conversation. Maybe things could be simple, after all.

Chapter 16

Some Things Remain the Same

This time her shopping spree was a success. She found something for her outing with Miles the next day and something for her first day at work on Monday. She'd spent the better part of the morning bargain hunting until she found just what she wanted: a simple, burnt-orange jersey knit that fit her just right and looked perfect under her blazer for her date with Sterling, a mint-green suit for work and a cream-colored pants outfit with wide legs and a cinched jacket—for Miles.

She hung her purchases in the closet, then headed for the shower. Sterling had left a message on her machine saying he'd be there by six, with tickets. Tickets to what she couldn't imagine.

She didn't want to be late. It was already after four.

As she slipped on her stockings, with the music from the stereo playing softly in the background, she wished she still felt as excited about seeing Sterling as she once had. It wasn't that she didn't want to see him. She did. He had a knack for making her feel at ease, and that was fine, but for the first time in longer than she could remember she didn't want that sameness. She wanted to be challenged, to take a leap of faith and see what it brought her. Miles did that for her. He excited her, ignited a passion in her that had been dormant. They shared the same dreams, the same goals and ideals. She needed that.

She stood and wiggled the panty hose over her hips, then stopped. Her reflection stared back at her from the mirror across the room. What was she doing, rerouting her life after one kiss? That wasn't like her.

She shook her head, almost as if the act would magically clear her thoughts. When she looked again, her reflection remained the same.

Miles lay sprawled out on Greg's look-alike couch, sipping a bottle of Corona. A tape of *Soul Food* played on Greg's thirty-two-inch television.

He really didn't want to be there, but he definitely didn't want to be sitting up in his apartment thinking about Tyler and her mystery man. Bottom line, whoever he was, he was going back to where he came from, and *he* would still be here.

"So what's happenin' with you and Tyler?" Greg asked, walking into the living room and taking a seat on the matching love seat. He draped his leg over the arm of the chair. "You did take her home last night—" His statement hung in the air.

Miles slid his gaze in Greg's direction. "It's not that kind of party, man."

"Aw, come on, you can tell me. What's she like?"

"Like I said, it's not that kind of party. She's not like the rest of them."

"Oh, I get it. She's holding out on you." He chuckled.

Why was he here? "Is that all a woman is to you, something to get over on? Get something from?"

"What's with you lately, man? Last time I checked you was feeling and dealing the same way."

"Yeah. Well, things change." He took a drawn-out swallow of beer.

Greg looked at him for a long moment, wondering where his main man had gone. "What'd this chick do to you, anyway? Got your head all messed up." He shook his in confusion.

"Maybe she's helping to get it straight. Ever think of that?" he sat up. "I've been doing a lot of thinking lately, man. I can't keep going through life snatching up everything that comes my way without looking at the long term. I want something more than I've been getting and giving." He thought of Maribelle and all the others before her.

"She really got to ya, huh?"

"Yeah. She did."

Greg took a breath. "Then I hope it works out for you. If that's what you really want. Anyway, you being out of circulation leaves more goodies for me."

They both laughed.

Some things will never change, Miles thought.

* * *

When Sterling said six, he meant it. The doorbell rang on the dot.

Tyler gook a quick look in the mirror, patted her curls and then hurried down the stairs, catching a glimpse of him through the glass-and-wood door. She took a breath, put on her best smile and pulled it open.

That slow, dawn-breaking smile spread across his mouth. He leaned down and kissed her cheek, and she caught a gentle whiff of his cologne.

"Hi. It's good to see you, Tyler." She was even prettier than the last time he saw her. An inner glow seemed to radiate from her. He hoped it was because of him.

"You, too. Come on in. I just need to get my bag."

She led him upstairs and gave him a quick tour.

"You really lucked out, Tyler. This place is great." He slid his hands in the pockets of his navy-blue pants as he watched her turn out lights and check windows.

"Believe me, I know. I can't imagine what it would cost if I'd had to find some place on my own. I really can't thank you enough for helping to make it happen."

"I'm just glad it all worked out. Where're Tempest and Braxton?"

"They went out earlier, but they definitely want to see you before you leave." She wanted to ask him if he planned to stay through the weekend, but didn't. "Tempest said to drop by when we get back."

"No problem. I was hoping to see them. But if we get back too late, I can probably stop by tomorrow."

Tomorrow. "I didn't ask what their plans were for tomorrow, and…I won't be here."

"Oh." He looked at her for a moment. "Plans?"

She nodded. "Yes. I'll probably be leaving kind of early."

"I was hoping we could spend the weekend together."

"I know, and I'm sorry. Something came up."

He nodded. "No problem. There's always Sunday."

She smiled. *There was her answer*. "Ready?"

He checked his watch. "Yeah, we'd better get going. Parking is murder."

They walked toward the door.

"Are you going to tell me where we're going now?" she asked, locking the door behind them.

"Nope."

"Are you at least going to tell me about your interview today?"

"Definitely. Over dinner."

"And where might that be?" She draped her bag over her shoulder and her jacket over her arm.

"There you go again, trying to trick information out of me."

"Can't fault a girl for trying."

He partially opened the door of the rented Ford Taurus, but held it, momentarily preventing her entry. He looked down at her. "I want this evening to be special, Tyler. I've been thinking about it for weeks."

She swallowed, not knowing what to say. Before last night, she'd been looking forward to this evening, too. "We'll never know if we don't get it started." She smiled up at him and slid into the car.

They found an all-night parking garage in midtown and walked about two blocks before he stopped in front of the theater.

"I hope you like tap," he said with a grin.

She looked up at the marquee that blazed *Bring in Da Noise, Bring in Da Funk*.

"Sterling, how in the world did you get tickets?" The group at the coffee shop had gotten into a heated discussion about black plays and their themes, and this was mentioned as being one of the better ones. Tickets were pretty impossible to get.

"I have connections, little lady. Come on, the show should be starting in about fifteen minutes."

As they stood in line to hand in their tickets she looked to her left. Standing there, as casual as you please, was Alice Walker talking with another woman. Her mouth dropped open and she tapped Sterling hard on the arm.

"That's Alice Walker," she said in a rough whisper filled with excitement.

"Yep. Sure is." He smiled down at her. "You're liable to see anyone in New York. That's the *one* good thing about it."

Tyler stared in awe as the line moved forward. Well, this evening was off to a swinging start, she thought, the faint strains of doubt slowly easing. *Just relax and enjoy,* she silently chanted.

"The show was fabulous, Sterling," she enthused as they piled out of the theater with the other enthusiastic audience members.

"Yeah. I heard it was good, but it turned out to be better than I expected."

"Thank you so much."

"Don't thank me yet. The night is young."

He took her hand.

Reflex almost made her pull it away. She didn't.

They walked down Broadway, taking in the sights and sounds of the October evening. She was glad she'd brought her jacket, as the air had chilled considerably since they'd left her apartment. Fall was definitely here, with winter on the way.

"So what's next on your secret mission, Mr. Phelps?" Tyler quizzed, using the old cliché from *Mission: Impossible*.

"I don't know about you, but I'm starved. So we're going to take a short walk and have dinner. How does that sound?"

"It sounds as if you have the art of surprise down to a science."

"That's just one of my many talents."

"What are the others?"

"Now, that would take all the fun out of the surprise." His eyes glided over her face. "Why not just relax and enjoy? Let me entertain you."

She smiled. "Why not?"

They wound up at the famous B. Smith's restaurant. Tyler had read about Barbara Smith, ex-model and businesswoman extraordinaire, for years. Her face had graced the pages of many magazines. She'd never thought she'd be sitting in her restaurant.

She casually looked around, not wanting to look too much like an out of town tourist. There was so much to see. Beautiful black men in perfectly tailored suits; gorgeous women with expertly made-up faces captured in the glow of candlelight.

Mouthwatering aromas drifted around them and her

stomach rumbled. Fortunately, they were quickly seated because Sterling had made a reservation.

He'd thought of everything, Tyler mused, pleased by all the thought that had gone into their evening. He had made it special, just as he'd promised.

While they waited for their dinner Sterling finally told her about the ad deal he'd landed.

"It's a small, black public relations firm that wants to put a campaign together depicting positive black images," he said.

"That's definitely a challenge, and long overdue."

"Exactly. I have so many great ideas. I can't wait to get started." He hesitated a moment before he added the next bit of information. "The downside is, I'll have to do a lot of traveling to capture the images I want. With you being here—I don't know how that's going to affect someone looking after Nana."

That reality hadn't crossed her mind. "How long do you think the project will take?" Her mind was racing with possible alternatives, short of her returning to Savannah.

"At least a couple of months. I will be back and forth, though."

"Hmm." She was quiet for a moment. She already felt indebted to him for all he'd done since she'd left home. She couldn't conceive of imposing on him anymore. He did have his own life to live. She'd have to figure something out.

"It'll work out. Just concentrate on doing a great job. I'll talk to Lauren. Between the two of us, we'll make it work." If there were only someone else she could trust—but her sphere of friends totaled one. With

Lauren's hectic love life and her darting and dodging creditors, she already had her hands full.

"Good. I was kind of worried."

"Does she seem okay?"

"She was fine when I left, swinging in her swing like she didn't have a care in the world."

She smiled, envisioning her grandma in the swing, as she'd seen her on so many occasions.

"When do you get started?"

"I signed the contract this morning. I wanted to get going on it when I got back home. I'll probably make Selma my first stop. It has a great, but dark history. I want to show how we've made an impact there. Then I thought I'd head to Florida, then cross-country to California. I need to set up some appointments first, make my flight reservations. I'll probably leave in about two weeks. Do you think that's enough time for you to find someone?"

"It'll have to be. As I said, I appreciate everything you've done, but you worry about you."

Their dinner arrived and conversation flowed around their delicious meal, Tyler's classes and her new job. Although she participated in what was being said, her thoughts were far from the topics. What was she going to do? She didn't want to go back home if she didn't absolutely have to, but for her Nana Tess she would, and she didn't care what that stubborn woman said.

She was just getting started in her new life—making headway and even testing the waters of a possible relationship with a man who made her pulse pound. But what was different this time in her life from any other? Any time she'd thought she'd found a bit of happiness, she'd found out that the slice of pie she'd cut for herself and was on the verge of biting into was snatched away from her. Some things never changed.

"For someone who said the food was delicious you haven't eaten much," Sterling said, pulling her from the turn of her thoughts.

"Oh, everything is fine. Really. I guess I wasn't as hungry as I thought."

Sterling put his fork down on the edge of his plate. "Listen, I know you're worried about your grandmother. So am I. And believe me if I had a way around it, I wouldn't go. If there's anything I can do, just ask. It's not a problem. Maybe I could check into some places that offer visiting services for the elderly."

"Oh, no," she warned. "Nana Tess would have a screaming fit if some stranger came looking in on her. And more than likely scare the poor soul to death."

"You're probably right." He reached across the table and put his hand atop hers. "Don't worry. I'm sure everything will work out. Anyway, Nana is a tough lady."

"She is that," she said softly.

By the time they returned to Tyler's apartment it was close to midnight but the lights on the parlor floor were on, which meant that Tempest and Braxton were still up. Tyler was secretly relieved. Now Sterling could have his visit and she wouldn't feel so guilty about not being around the next day.

When they came into the building Tempest poked her head out, and the next ten minutes were a cacophony of greetings, hugs, kisses and handshakes, with everyone trying to talk at once. They finally all settled down in Tempest and Braxton's apartment for some late-night snacks.

"Your project sounds wonderful, Sterling," Tempest said, passing around a silver platter of pâté, smoked salmon, and whitefish, with wheat crackers.

"Definitely something we could all stand to see," agreed Braxton. "I'm glad for you, man. You've been out there for a while. It's about time you got a break like this."

"Yeah. I'm hoping it'll lead to other things. Really get my name out there."

"I'm sure it will," Tempest agreed. "The work you did for us was fabulous. We still use the portfolio you put together."

"How long are you going to be in town?" Braxton asked. "Maybe we can do something before you head back."

Tyler's heart thumped.

"I had planned on staying until Sunday. I was hoping to spend some more time with Tyler." He glanced briefly in her direction. "But she has plans. I figured I'd see about getting a standby flight and head out tomorrow."

"No. Don't do that," Tempest insisted. "Stay the extra day, and the three of us can paint the town. For old time's sake. And you can still leave on Sunday, as you planned."

"Yeah, man. How 'bout it?"

Sterling shrugged and gave a half smile. "Hey, I don't want you guys going out of your way on my account."

Tyler wondered if that last remark was really directed at her.

"You know better than that. We haven't seen you in almost a year. It'll be great."

He blew out a breath. "Sure. Sounds good."

"Then it's settled," Tempest said. "Where are you staying? We'll pick you up…."

* * *

"I had a great time tonight, Tyler," Sterling said as they stood in front of her apartment door.

"So did I. And...I'm really sorry about tomorrow. I—"

"Don't worry about it. Some other time. When do you think you'll be coming home?"

"Not before the holidays."

He nodded. "I guess maybe I'll see you then."

She looked down at her feet, then back up at him.

"I'll call you before I leave for Selma. You'll let me know what arrangements you make for Nana?"

"Yes. Definitely. I'll start working on that Monday."

"Great. Well, I guess I ought to be going."

They faced each other for a few awkward moments, neither knowing what was the best thing to say or do next.

He wanted to kiss her. Just once. But he didn't think he could stand it if she turned him down, or worse, didn't respond. He couldn't figure her out. He'd thought that something was happening between them. Everything seemed fine until he said he was actually coming to New York. What had changed?

"Have a safe flight," she murmured. "And thank you for a wonderful evening." She rose a bit on her toes and pressed her lips softly against his cheek.

"Sure."

She turned to open her door.

"Tyler—"

Angling her head over her shoulder, she came face-to-face with the desire that glowed in his eyes, startling her with its strength.

She swallowed, almost afraid to answer, unsure of what her response would bring. "Y-es?"

He reached out and stroked her face with the tips of his fingers, a melancholy smile framing his mouth. "Take care."

He turned and walked down the stairs and out.

Tyler let out a shuddering breath, remaining immobile, her hand on the doorknob, until she heard his car start up and drive off.

Slowly she walked inside, closing the door quietly behind her. She felt bad for Sterling. He had expected so much more than she was able or willing to give. She liked him, didn't want to hurt him. He'd gone out of his way to help her, but she couldn't allow that kindness to turn into her weakness.

She tossed her purse on the couch. What happened tonight was what she'd spent most of her adult life trying to avoid: becoming indebted to someone, feeling obligated. It was why she rarely, if ever, asked for help or favors. Nothing in this life was free. She'd learned that hard lesson years ago. No one did anything without expecting something in return.

Walking into her bedroom she saw the flashing red light on her answering machine. She pressed the Playback button and sat on the edge of the bed to listen.

"Hi, Ty. It's me, Miles. Be ready tomorrow about ten. I'll pick you up. Dress warm and comfortably. Later."

She played the message again, smiling at the sound of his voice, thinking about the next day and wondering what he'd planned for them.

What would Miles ultimately want in return?

Chapter 17

The Best-Laid Plans

On this marginal date: Client has had no real male role models to relate to. Impressions have been formed based on previous disappointments, television and newspapers. Adult interaction may cause difficulty.

One thing was certain, Tyler thought as she lay stretched out on her bed, crossing and uncrossing her legs—Miles was no Sterling. It was already ten-thirty and no sign of him.

She aimed the remote control at the television and tried to focus on the newscast. Settling back against the pillows on her bed, she wondered if this was an indication of how things would be between them—him promising and her waiting. She peeked at the bedside clock. Ten-forty. He had five minutes, and then she would get out of her clothes and—well, she didn't know, but she would find something to do.

The doorbell rang.

It'd better be him. She walked to the front window, raised it and stuck her head out. Miles looked up, a satisfied grin on his face and a big, white shopping bag in his hand.

"Hurry up before this gets cold." He held up the bag.

"What?"

"Just come on down, girl."

She shut the window, her heart beating with the rush of excitement. The aggravation she'd felt a moment ago seemed to have vanished as she trotted down the steps to the front door.

She leaned against the door frame, barring his entrance. "Let me see what's in the bag first, before I let you in," she demanded, trying to keep the smile off her face.

"Man, can't keep anything from you." He opened the bag and let her get a little peek and a whiff of what was inside.

Her eyes widened in surprise. "You brought food?"

"Breakfast, to be exact. Now can I come in?"

She gave him a long up and down look, fighting back a smirk. "Beware of strangers bearing gifts." She stepped aside and let him pass, then led the way upstairs.

"Aw, I'm not so strange." He chuckled.

"One man's opinion," she rejoined, opening her apartment door. "You can put that on the counter in the kitchen." She showed him the way and he immediately began unpacking the bag. Soon the table and the counter were covered with circular aluminum dishes with white tops, plastic utensils and an array of condiments from maple syrup to rich brown gravy.

"I wasn't sure what you liked for breakfast, so I got a little bit of everything. We have pancakes, French toast, sausages and bacon—beef, of course. There're eggs, biscuits, grits and a fruit cup for those who are trying to keep their figures." She poked him in the ribs. "Tea, juice and coffee." He grinned. "Hungry?"

By the time they'd finished sampling all the goodies it was almost noon.

"I don't know about you, Ms. 'I don't eat much,' but I'm stuffed, and if I don't get up and get moving I'm going to have to take a nap." He rocked back in the kitchen chair and rubbed his stomach.

"No sleeping," she said, stifling a yawn. "You promised me a day out, and that's what I expect. We'll jog to the Jeep."

Miles laughed. "What happened to the girl with the one-word answers?"

"Here's the plan," he said as he pulled out into traffic. "I thought we'd go to Central Park. It has a great rowing lake. We can rent a boat, enjoy the afternoon, then head uptown to Sally's, a great West Indian restaurant in Harlem, for a late lunch. I'll bring you back home to change, and then we'll go the Village about nine for a show and dinner." He turned toward her. "How does that sound?"

"Wonderful. But what happened to my plane ride?" she teased.

"Woman, you're gonna be hard to satisfy."

* * *

It was a glorious afternoon. The sky was cloudless and the sun beamed down, casting golden rays across the water. The abundant trees were beginning to turn brilliant shades of orange. Everywhere Tyler looked there were signs of beauty, a sense of tranquility. All the horror stories she'd heard or read about Central Park seemed almost impossible to imagine.

And Miles was at his charming best, regaling her with hilarious stories about his escapades in film and the quirky people who thought they could act, his stint as an intern for a cable station which was really a gofer job, and his upcoming work with the high school students.

"Professor Chase pulled some strings for me. I start next week."

"What made you want to do it?"

"Good question." He stared off toward the horizon, the tiny diamond stud in his left ear twinkling in the waning light. "I guess I realized I needed something, Tyler. To find a way to contribute, make a difference, somehow. This gives me the chance to do that."

She looked at him, a faint smile on her mouth. He kept surprising her. Every time she had a doubt, a misguided or prejudicial thought, he surprised her. Just like this morning. She'd convinced herself that he wouldn't show up, but he'd been thinking about her when he went out of his way to bring that feast they consumed. He sought her out even after she'd given him the brush-off. He made her feel comfortable around his friends, and he excited her in a way no man had been able to in the past. She wasn't sure why. There just seemed to be a caged energy that pulsed around Miles Bennett like an aura, and being with him she couldn't help being captured in the essence.

She wanted to let down the barriers, let him cross the line. Trust him. If only she could.

"Maybe you'd like to sit in on a couple of sessions, get a feel for things," he said, easing into her wandering thoughts.

"You think it would be okay?"

"Sure. I don't see a problem."

"I'd love to." She grinned.

"Consider it done." He looked up toward the sky. "We'd better be heading back. The sun's going down and it can get pretty chilly on the lake." His voice dropped to a low throb and his gaze held hers. "Then again, it would give me all the reason in the world to put my arms around you and keep you warm."

A sudden rush of heat flowed through her, and she couldn't imagine what he meant by chilly.

Even after all they'd consumed at breakfast, being outdoors and rowing had worked up their appetites.

Once again, Miles was true to his word. Sally's was wonderful, and all of the waitstaff, especially the waitresses, seemed glad to see him, calling him by his first name in their thick Jamaican accents and hovering around their table making sure they had everything they needed. One would think he was their most valued customer.

Miles had the uncanny ability to charm everyone he came into contact with, apparently without any real effort on his part, she thought. It was so natural—the sparkle in his eyes, the sincere laughter.

As she watched him interact with the employees—

remembering each of their names and something personal about them—and thought back to the night at the café, she realized what made him unique. He made everyone around him feel special, as if whatever they said, thought, or did was important.

Just as he did for her.

He turned to her and smiled, and that cold, dark space in her heart felt just a bit warmer.

"You have about an hour or so to change," Miles said when they'd returned to her apartment.

"It shouldn't take that long." She flipped on the light in the foyer and walked into the living room, turning on the lamp on the end table.

"Cool. Then do you mind if I wait? We can run by my place when you're finished and I can do my thing."

A wave of panic rippled through her. Was this payback time? She fiddled with the dials on the stereo, buying some time.

Suddenly he was behind her and her whole body tensed. He put his hands on her shoulders and gently turned her around to face him.

He looked down into her eyes. "To put your mind at ease, as much as I'd love to make love to you right this minute, it's too soon, for you. And regardless of what you may think or have seen or heard, I'm really not that kind of guy unless I'm with that kind of girl. And you, Tyler Ellington, are not that kind of girl." He leaned down and placed a long, tender kiss on her forehead.

"Go get ready. I'm just going to sit right on that lovely-looking couch, listen to some music and take a short nap." His mouth curved up on one side. "Cool?"

Her heart was racing so fast she couldn't speak. She nodded her head, turned and wanted to run out of the room. She fought down the urge and strolled out as if getting an *almost* proposition was an everyday occurrence in her life.

Miles leaned his head back against the couch cushions, tried to listen to Luther and not the sound of the shower pounding in the next room. He closed his eyes. To make bad matters worse, a vision of Tyler's naked body slick with soap and water danced behind his lids. Every instinct and hormone went on full alert. It took all he had to keep from marching into that bathroom and breaking his promise.

He jumped up from the couch and began to pace, whispering "Amen" when the water finally stopped. But then his imagination shifted into second gear when he thought about her drying off, spreading scented oil on her body, slipping into her clothes.

He should have gone home. So what if it meant an extra trip to come back again? At least he wouldn't have had to go through *this*.

"Ready."

He turned and she stood for the briefest moment framed in the archway. His stomach shifted, then settled. She looked hesitant, expectant, beautiful.

He smiled. "You look…really nice."

"Thanks. Hope I didn't take too long."

"Not at all. Let's go."

On the short trip to his loft Miles kept taking surreptitious glances in Tyler's direction. Had she looked this good when she went out with what's-his-name? Did whoever he was have the same desire for her that he did? He wanted to ask her. He wanted to know if it were anything serious.

He didn't.

On the ride up in the elevator he thought of the erotic scene between Michael Douglas and Glenn Close. *Yeah, Buddy, you've got it bad.* He shoved his hands in his pockets and leaned against the wall of the elevator.

When she stepped inside his apartment her eyes widened. She looked around. "This...is fabulous. It looks like something out of a magazine." She thought of her apartment in Savannah with its used furniture, her grandmother's comfy but weathered home and even her classy, temporary quarters in New York. None of them could compare with this. She wondered what Miles thought of her living conditions.

It was becoming more and more obvious that Miles Bennett was used to comfort, accustomed to the finer things in life, having money, using it and accepting it as his due without question.

She wasn't part of that world. She never would be.

"Want anything before I get in the shower?"

"No. I'm fine. Thanks."

"Make yourself at home. Kick off your shoes if you want." He grinned. "Be back in a few."

She wandered over to black wood wall unit that must have been at least five feet wide. Encased behind smoky glass doors was a stereo system that she wouldn't even attempt to turn on. Lined against the wall in a floor-to-ceiling rack was a movie lover's haven filled with vintage and contemporary video movies, along with some on CD.

Sleek, black leather furniture, stuffed to overflowing, graced gleaming wood floors. Original works by well-known African-American artists Tom Fieldings, Doris Price, Elizabeth Capplett and John Biggers graced the pearl-gray walls. She couldn't fathom how much they were all worth.

Along the far wall was a bookcase with an eclectic selection of books, from literary classics to academics, from sports to Walter Mosely mysteries. She ran her fingers along the spines as if she could somehow acquire some secret knowledge about the owner. Moment by moment she was becoming more intrigued and certainly intimidated by Miles Bennett. She picked up a copy of *Tryin' To Sleep in the Bed you Made,* by Donna Grant and Virginia DeBerry, and before she realized what'd happened—she'd become engrossed in the lives of Pat, Gayle and Marcus.

"See anything you like?"

She spun around. *Yes, she definitely did.* "You have wide tastes in reading." She slid the book back on the shelf.

Miles walked slowly across the room, fastening the clasp on his gold watch. "I guess it comes from drifting from one interest to another over the years, traveling, meeting a lot of people with a wide range of interests." He stood in front of her, close enough to inhale the soap-and-water clean scent that was more provocative on her than any perfume.

He tilted up her chin with the tip of his finger. "I have this crazy urge to kiss you." He lowered his head and stepped a bit closer. "How do you feel about that?"

When he brushed her bottom lip with his thumb her

breath caught in her throat and she felt ripples race up and down her spine—again. He was really good at that. Really good.

He slid an arm around her waist. "I'm waiting," he whispered, a breath away from her mouth. "Tell me it's all right."

Her heart thumped and her body responded though she couldn't.

She raised her head and trailed her hands along his smooth jaw. She heard him moan almost as if in agony, and the very idea thrilled her, thrilled her to know that she could make him feel that way, that he did feel that way.

Tentatively she brushed her lips against his, and it was as if a dam had burst. They clung to each other, so close the air rushed from their lungs, their mouths fused. Their bodies arched and dipped to find the perfect puzzle piece match.

She felt his body responding to her, the growing hardness of him pressing between her thighs. And her own body's reaction startled her. For years she'd been unable to feel all the things she was told she should feel. She'd thought she was incapable of experiencing what other women took for granted. Yet now a hot, wet heat seeped down and out, settling where he moved ever so slowly against her.

A weakness overtook her when his hands began to rove up and down her back and along her sides, caressing her hips. When the pads of his thumbs brushed over the tips of her breasts, the sound of her own strangled cry brought them both back to reality.

Miles broke the kiss but didn't let her go. He rested his head against hers, taking in long lungfuls of air.

"Tyler," he whispered, hugging her to him. "I don't know what you're doing to me, what's happening." He eased back, looked into her eyes and smiled. "But I like it." He let out a breath. "And I think we'd better get out of here before something happens that neither of us is ready for."

He took her hand and squeezed it. "I keep my promises."

They had a front table at the Bottomline, a jazz club in the heart of Greenwich Village. The place was packed with fans of Dianne Reeves, who performed for a solid hour to countless ovations and cries for more.

Miles and Tyler wouldn't talk over the music and couldn't over the roar of noise when the show ended. They held hands instead, and stole little glances when they thought the other wasn't looking, occasionally shouting out comments over the din.

Enjoying the atmosphere, the music and Miles, Tyler realized she was happy—not pretending to be, but actually happy. The thought scared her. Happiness was something she never expected in her life. The moments had always been brief and the endings painful. But looking at Miles, talking with him, being with him, allowing herself to open up just a little bit with him, made her want to try. Even if it did hurt in the end.

Her idyll was short-lived. When she looked up Sterling was standing over their table.

Chapter 18

Just the Way Things Are

"Sterling."

"Didn't think I'd see you again before I left." He turned his attention to Miles and stuck out his hand. "Sterling Grey."

Miles stood. *So this was Mr. Friend from home.* "Miles Bennett."

This was one of those moments a woman always prayed would never happen to her, Tyler thought, completely undone.

"I saw you both earlier, but didn't want to intrude. Braxton and Tempest are at a table on the other side. We were just getting ready to leave and I wanted to say hello."

Tyler finally found her voice. "Glad you did." Now

that was an out-and-out lie. She was never more embarrassed in her life.

"Good meeting you," he said to Miles, who nodded in response. "I'll call you, Tyler."

Miles watched him walk away. Slowly he brought the glass of water to his mouth. *That was civil.* He wanted to be angry even though he knew he didn't have the right. Both of them had a life before they met each other. He had no claims on Tyler as much as he might want to. What he did feel was jealous, and the unprecedented emotion rattled him to the core. And Tyler's silence didn't help matters in the least.

He took another sip of water, watching her profile over the rim of the glass.

What could she say to Miles? She should give him some sort of explanation. But what was there to explain? Nothing was going on between her and Sterling. He was just a friend. Then why did she feel so damned guilty?

"Ready?" He needed to get out, get some air.

His sudden question jerked her out of her malaise. "Sure." What she really wanted to do was run somewhere and hide.

The drive home was spent in relative silence, both caught in their own thoughts and worries. Miles hoped she would say something, anything, about her relationship with Sterling Grey. And he refused to ask.

Miles pulled the car to a stop in front of her door and turned off the engine.

Tyler's heart began to race. She turned to him and smiled an unsure smile. "I had a great time."

He looked down at his hands for a moment, then

across at her. "Yeah." He tilted his chin toward her door. "Guess you'd better be going."

His voice sounded so indifferent, so matter of fact—the same tone she'd heard so many times when her life was being shifted beneath her. She wanted to say something to make it right, make whatever had gone wrong go away. But nothing she'd ever said, no amount of hard tears, ever changed anything.

She felt her insides coming apart. How could she tell him that yes, she was attracted to Sterling and knew that Sterling felt the same way about her, but that the person she wanted to be with was him, because he did something for her she didn't believe Sterling could—made her feel special. How could she say that?

She couldn't. To reveal her inner feelings was the first step to detachment. If they thought you were becoming too attached, off you went. So now she had this sensation that swirled in her stomach, this sense of emptiness, which she'd spent so much of her life trying to avoid. How could she tell him that, either, without telling him why? She couldn't.

Instead, she did what was instinctive. She hurried off to that secret place where things didn't hurt, people didn't disappoint. There she could pretend that everything was wonderful.

"Yes. It is getting late." She opened her door, then looked over her shoulder. "Good night."

"Yeah. Later."

Before she'd gotten her key in the front door, she heard the Jeep roar down the street.

Slowly she walked up the stairs. It was better this way.

* * *

She didn't hear from Miles for the balance of the weekend. She was half expecting that he would call. In the short three months they'd known each other he'd always been the one to make a move to bridge the gap. Maybe he was just tired of the peacemaker role.

Sterling hadn't called, either, since he'd returned to Savannah.

Slipping her feet into black pumps, she stood facing herself in the full-length mirror. She'd convinced herself that the mint-green suit she'd selected for her first day of work would bring her luck. *Maybe she should have worn it Saturday.* She buttoned the jacket and adjusted it over her hips and then ran her fingers through her wiry curls, letting them halo her head and frame her face.

A horn blared beneath her window and she knew it was the car from the service she'd called earlier. She snatched up her purse, checked to be sure she had everything she needed, grabbed her lined trench coat from the hall rack and ran out the door.

Tyler's day sped by, filled with meeting people, trying to remember names and faces, filling out forms, getting adjusted to a new system and handling a bigger workload than she'd ever had at DCH in Savannah. Even when Janet Hume stopped by her desk several times, tossing her red hair back and forth across her shoulder, the overwhelming sense of panic began to lose its strength.

When five o'clock arrived she was exhausted but happy. A sense of accomplishment buoyed her spirits. When she'd left her apartment that morning the residual effects of her feelings about Miles and how things had gone between them were still there, combined with the anxiety of starting a new job. She'd gotten through it. She'd gotten her confidence back.

And she knew what she would have to do when she returned home.

Take a chance.

All day he'd sat in front of his damned computer and couldn't write one coherent scene.

He rubbed his hands across his face, realized he needed a shave and decided he didn't care. He pushed off with his feet and let the wheeled chair carry him to the other side of his home office space. He looked at the phone. He knew what the problem was. *Tyler*. Plain and simple. She was under his skin. And he hadn't been able to get anything right, not even a decent night's sleep, since he'd left her at the curb Saturday.

All he could think about was that she was hiding something from him, not telling him something, for what reason he didn't know. He'd been straight with her about Mari, and everybody else, for that matter. He wanted her to know the deal up front. Why couldn't she give him the same respect, the benefit of the doubt? At least he'd know what he was dealing with.

That's what bothered him—the fact that he was making moves to get involved with a woman who only wanted things one-sided.

From day one he'd been the one to look for her, strike up a conversation, make the calls. And that wasn't even like him. But he'd thought if he wanted his life to change, *he* would have to be about change.

He'd never been interested in the lives of the women he'd dealt with. He hadn't really cared about their innermost thoughts, their goals, what made them happy. He hadn't needed to. But Tyler brought out something in him he hadn't known existed, and he didn't want to do the same old thing anymore. Not with her.

So his approach to Tyler was entirely different than his approach to other women. And she responded. Or at least he thought she had.

But maybe she was the player, and he'd been played.

Miles turned away from the phone, disgusted. Yeah, maybe it was the way Greg said—he was losing his touch.

He got up, stripped out of his gray sweat suit and got into the shower. Maybe a little hanging out was in order.

Tyler was surprised to see a thick brown envelope waiting for her on the stairs leading to her apartment. Picking it up, she spotted the Savannah postmark and the return address of her old apartment. Even though she knew it would be filled with bills and junk mail, she couldn't help the little feeling of excitement at the thought of getting a piece of home.

Sure enough, that's all it was, courtesy of Wes. The treat was his neat, handwritten note.

Hey there,
Know you living the life in the big city. Likely forgot all about us folks down here. But jest like I promise, here go your mail. Been checking on your place. Everything fine. Ready for you anytime you want to come back. Sure do miss

your smile. Be good to see you whenever you
come on home.
Wes

Her throat tightened. The letter was so simple, but it
said so much. It touched her that this man who had be-
friended her and never asked anything in return still
cared about her and kept his promise.

Slowly she folded the letter, tucking it away in the old,
hand-carved jewelry box that her grandmother had given
her when she'd turned thirteen. Pieces of her life played
through her head and all at once she understood that
little by little she'd taken a chance, opened herself up to
be cared about, and hadn't realized it was happening.

There was Lauren, who'd been steadfast from the
moment they'd met. Wes, who'd gone out of his way
for her. Sterling, whose kindness toward her grandmother extended to her. Tempest and Braxton, who
opened their home to her, a perfect stranger, and made
her feel welcome. And no one had really expected
anything in return, except Miles. That was what intrigued her. Everyone else was satisfied with just letting
her be Tyler, whoever that was. Not Miles. Miles wanted
to get as much as he gave. He challenged her to cross
the line, not just accept the fact that the line was there.

Miles wanted to offer her the opportunity to have a
relationship—a real relationship, the kind she thought
she could never have, give and take.

And though she'd worn a thin veil of resistance, it
hadn't stopped any of his efforts. She had always put
the brakes on closeness. Whenever she felt it coming on,
she'd sabotage it, just as she'd been trying to with Miles.

She opened the jewelry box and reread Wes's letter. It was the last push she needed. She pressed the letter to her breasts.

"Thank you, Wes," she whispered.

Miles was just on his way out the door when the phone rang. His first thought was that it was Greg, asking to be picked up, but they'd already agreed to drive separate cars in case either of them landed any action. Maybe that was what he needed to get out of the foul mood he was in.

Quickly he crossed the room and snatched up the phone.

"Yeah?"

She hesitated, almost didn't speak.

"Hello?"

"Hi. It's Tyler."

A sudden tightening gripped his chest. He wanted to say something slick, some quick one line that would let her know she didn't make a difference. He couldn't find the words.

"How are you?"

"All right. Why? What's up?"

"I just… I was hoping we could talk."

He wasn't going to make this easy for her, not again. "We're talking right now. Just say what's on your mind, Tyler. For once."

She closed her eyes, calling up a picture of him: the way his eyes crinkled at the corners, his smile with that perfect mustache teasing his top lip, the smooth, easy stride that made him appear as if he didn't have a care in the world, the dark, haunting eyes that could fill with passion as easily as dismissal.

"Whatever you're thinking about me and Sterling, don't."

"Hmm. What makes you think I'm thinking anything?"

"Because you had the same look in your eyes that I did the night we ran into Maribelle."

He bit back a smirk, but wouldn't give her an inch. "Yeah, okay. Go ahead." He leaned back against the wall.

"He's a friend of the family. We went out on one date. We, unlike you and *Mari,* never even shared a kiss."

The little dig caught him right between the eyes.

"Then why'd you act like that when he showed up? Like you had something to hide?"

"It was awkward for me. Maybe for you it's an everyday thing."

Ouch, another good one.

"I've never been in a situation like that before."

"He wasn't looking at you as if you were just a friend," he probed.

Tyler took a breath. "I know. He'd like to be more than friends. Is that what you want to hear?"

"That part was obvious. What I want to hear is how you feel about that."

"It's not what I want."

The words flowed through him releasing the tension he'd built up inside. "What *do* you want, Tyler? And don't tell me peace on earth or any of that bull."

She smiled. "I think I'd like to keep trying out what we got started."

"You *think?*"

"Yes. It's what I think—very strongly. How's that?" Laughter bubbled in her voice.

"I *think* I'm gonna have to work at it until you can say, 'I *know* it's what I want.' How does that sound?"

"I'd say you had your work cut out for you."

"Don't give me a hard time, woman. Don't try it."

They laughed, and before they realized what happened they'd been on the phone for two hours. Miles had carved out a spot on the floor, right beneath where he'd stood when he answered the phone. His pager had gone off so many times during their conversation he'd finally turned it off.

They talked about her new job, the difficulties he was having with his screenplay, getting hers in shape for the professor and still holding down her job, his goal to open his own studio within the next two years.

As he listened to her soft, lilting drawl, heard her laughter, shared his thoughts, his dreams, he realized what they were sharing was intimacy, and it was erotic foreplay. He felt himself grow hard, not so much from the want of her physically, as from the fire she sparked in his mind, the drive that her probing questions gave to his ambition.

He knew that if—no, when—they did make love it would be something neither of them had ever experienced before. Yeah. He was going to do just as he'd promised himself. Go slow. As the saying went, the best things come to those who wait.

He just hoped the wait wouldn't be too long.

Chapter 19

Tell No Lies

Tyler finally heard from Sterling. He called before he went away, and they talked for a long time. He said he understood that she didn't feel the same way he did, that maybe she would one day but if she didn't he hoped that wouldn't stop them from being friends. She'd insisted that it wouldn't, and promised she'd be down for Thanksgiving.

With Sterling away in Selma, Lauren promised to check on Nana on the weekends, which took a load off Tyler's mind. She'd even called Wes, who sounded thrilled to hear from her. He said he would gladly check on Tess if Lauren ever ran into a problem. Tyler said she didn't think that would happen but promised to give Lauren his number just in case.

As much as she was enjoying the attention from Miles, the success with her job, the progress of her screenplay and the new order in her life, she couldn't shake the feeling at a level just below the surface that it was all temporary.

Miles was waiting for her outside the building where she worked, just as he had for the past few weeks. On the nights they both had class they went straight to the university. Even on the nights when he had class and she didn't, he still waited for her, dropped her off at her apartment, then drove over to school.

She sat in when he ran the classes for the high school students on Saturday mornings, and was amazed to watch the patience he exhibited with each budding filmmaker, sharing his experiences, techniques and anecdotes about the business. This allowed her to see an entirely different side of Miles, one he rarely, if ever, demonstrated to anyone—other than her. The thought made her smile.

Tonight was a free night and they'd decided to take in a movie, see if they could pick up any tips.

"You decide what you want to see?" he asked, giving her a quick kiss and checking his rearview mirror before pulling out.

"How about that new Samuel L. Jackson movie?"

"Sounds like a plan." He gave her a sidelong glance. "Something bothering you?"

He was really getting good at reading her moods. Almost too good, she thought. Well, no sense in avoiding the inevitable.

"There's something I wanted to talk to you about."

"Let's hear it."

"I...I'm going home for the holiday."

He looked at her again and a million thoughts ran through his head—the first being about Sterling Grey.

"You didn't say anything about going home. Thanksgiving's in three days. You're just getting around to saying something. Why all of a sudden?"

"There are things I need to take care of." She'd yet to tell him about Nana Tess. It wasn't that she was ashamed of her grandmother, how she lived, that she couldn't read or write. Well, maybe that *was* a bit of it. But how could she talk about Nana Tess without telling him everything else—all the things she didn't want to say, the things she didn't want him to know? She knew that once she got started everything would spill out. And she didn't ever want to see "that" look in his eyes, hear the pity in his voice. It was easy to fabricate a mother who was no longer around to refute anything she said. But Tess was proof positive of another side of her life. For Lauren, and even Sterling, to know Tess was one thing. Miles was a different story.

"What things?"

His tone sounded accusatory, as if he were challenging her reason for going, which immediately put her on the defensive.

"Why do I have to explain to you why I'm going home? I'm just going. I—"

"Forget it, Tyler. That's what you have to do, then do it. Don't fish around for reasons to give me."

He stepped down on the accelerator. *Things to do.* Yeah, right. He'd really thought they were making progress, getting to know and understand each other. Trust each other. He didn't push her. He'd kept his promise to himself and to her to take it slowly. But there was a part of Tyler he couldn't reach, no matter how he tried. And he was really beginning to wonder if all the trying was worth it.

"I'll only be gone for the weekend."

"Whatever."

She couldn't remember what the movie was about. All she could concentrate on was the indifference that radiated from Miles like a sunbeam. Oh, he was pleasant, his usual attentive self. But there was a distance between them and she knew if she tried to cross it she'd fall into a pit of no return.

So she kept her silence. As she always had.

For the next two days, Miles shifted from anger to disappointment to jealousy. What other reason could there be for her to just up and leave like that except to see that guy? If the trip was about nothing, then why was it so hard for her to tell him what that nothing was? He'd be damned if he'd ask her again.

He turned on his side and looked at the time on the bedside clock. She had a three o'clock flight. At least she'd told him that much. Guess she wanted a ride to the airport. *Yeah, right.*

They hadn't seen each other since the night she dropped her bomb. When she'd called he'd told her he was working on his screenplay and would get back to her. He didn't, because he knew if he did it would be something, and he didn't feel like dealing with it. He hadn't even picked her up from work. Hey, she was a big girl. She could find her own way home. Shouldn't have gotten into the habit of doing that, anyway.

He knew he was acting like a real ass, but he didn't

care. For the first time in his life he'd made every effort to play it straight. He wasn't fooling around—lying, cheating, wheeling, dealing. He'd gone out of his way to be there for Tyler. She didn't seem to understand that. Or maybe she did and it didn't make a difference. He'd gone against every rule, every instinct he'd lived by, everything that had always worked for him in the past, and look what it got him.

A woman he didn't even know.

Tyler wanted to call and say something, anything, before she left. At least a half dozen times she'd picked up the phone and dialed the number. But she'd hung up before it began to ring, thinking she could and then realizing she couldn't put herself through the minefield that Miles had planted around himself.

She'd warded off his rebuffs by corralling the feelings she'd allowed to escape. His short sentences were met with her one-word answers. His absence with her silence. The break in the rituals that had become a part of who they were together, she chose to ignore.

She'd done it all before. It was second nature.

But this time it was starting to hurt a little bit. Just a little.

Just enough.

Chapter 20

You've Got To Give a Little

On this marginal date: Attempts at socialization have resulted in greater detachment. Fear of loss precipitates behavior and lack of ability to form permanent bonds. Resulting in superficial and/or temporary liaisons.

When Tyler stepped off the plane the first person she saw was Lauren, grinning and waving and looking as stylish as ever in a "somebody famous" outfit.

"Girl, it's good to see you!" She squeezed Tyler in a bear hug, then held her at arm's length, giving her the once-over. "New York hasn't changed you too much. Still look the same as ever. Simple and coordinated," she teased. "But on you it looks good."

"You just have a way about you, Lauren," Tyler said dryly.

"Makes me special. Now, come on before I get a ticket." She hooked her arm through Tyler's and they made their way out of the terminal.

Lauren chattered almost nonstop from the moment they got into the car until they reached Nana Tess's house an hour and a half later. The most Tyler had to do was nod and say "Hmm" or "Really?" and Lauren was on another roll. This was fine with her. It didn't give her too much time to think about how things had disintegrated between her and Miles.

Maybe she could have told Miles. It seemed he'd been up front with her about his life—past, present and future. She wanted to trust him….

"So how are you and that guy Miles doing? Still working things out?"

"Something like that."

Lauren glanced at her from the corner of her eye. "What's that supposed to mean?"

"Exactly what I said. Something like that."

"In other words, you blew it with him. Am I right?"

"I didn't blow anything."

"What's it with you, Tyler? I mean, as soon as a man even looks like he's going to get close to you, you find a way to sabotage things. Either you stop returning phone calls, start looking for things wrong with him, or let working, writing, whatever, interfere. You shut down and shut them out, for whatever reason. And we may be friends, but I can't say *I* really know you, Tyler. Sure, I'd go out of my way for you, I listen to your ideas, share my life with you, but you know, I've never really felt the same thing coming from you. It's all been one-sided."

"That's not fair, Lauren."

"You're right. It isn't," she said, a hitch in her voice. "When have you ever shared anything with me that actually meant something, Tyler, given something of yourself to me, or to anyone for that matter? You don't even trust me enough to let me read your short stories. You just *tell* me about them."

Tyler caught movement from the corner of her eye, heard the muffled sniffles and knew Lauren was crying. But what could she do? This was who she'd always been. She'd never quite understood until now how she actually affected someone else. Was Miles feeling the same sense of futility? Did everyone?

"Lauren, I…I'm sorry. I—"

"Don't apologize, Ty. Guess I'm just feeling sorry for myself. Forget it." She sniffled. "Jason and I broke up."

"Oh, I'm sorry."

"Hey, no biggie." She sniffled again.

They pulled onto the red dirt road of her grandmother's house, each caught in their own thoughts but putting on their best faces when Tess opened the door and stepped onto the sagging porch.

She was always stunned that her girlhood vision of Tess's house outshined the reality. Each time she came the house seemed to have slipped into a deeper state of disrepair. The roof, tired from years of baking under the Georgia sun, hobbled to one side. The once yellow frame structure was a weary, dingy moss color from decades of rain, heat and lack of paint. There was a rotted section on the bottom plank steps that reminded her of a toothless grin.

Everything creaked and groaned, like arthritic joints swollen from overuse and age.

But to tell Tess Ellington she needed to move or have repairs was as useful as talking to a pet rock.

"Ain't nobody comin' in my house touchin' nothin'," she'd said. "I done lived here for sixty-odd years and I like it jest fine!"

End of discussion.

Seeing Nana Tess standing there, as weathered and frail as her battered house, Tyler was reminded of everything she'd built in her life trying to escape—educating herself as best she could, working hard to lessen her Southern drawl and the use of slang, fighting to be the best student, the best worker, to be praised and accepted.

Yes, she adored her grandmother, and yes, there was a sense of comfort, a sense of security about the house where she'd spent part of her youth. But Tess and the house in Gullah also represented a reality of her life that she couldn't share. How could she ever bring a man like Miles into this world? A man who had never known poverty, illiteracy, doing without, struggle, shame?

She couldn't.

She stretched her arms out to her grandmother and held her close, silently asking for her forgiveness.

When she became wrapped in her grandmother's strong, loving hug and inhaled lavender and Dax pomade, none of that mattered.

At least for a while.

"Ya'll come on in. Come on," Tess ordered, giving Lauren a squeeze before they all went inside.

Tyler and Lauren did as they were told and were rewarded with a small feast of golden fried chicken, whipped potatoes and snap peas.

"Knew ya'll be hungry. Go get washed and come eat. Then you can tell me all 'bout New York."

"It's busy. Big. Exciting," Tyler said, spooning a second helping of potatoes onto her plate. "There're just so many people."

"The main thang, you gettin' what you went there to git. Don't worry 'bout nothin' else. Hear?" She pointed a finger at Tyler.

"I hear, Nana Tess."

"Sterling promised to join us for Thanksgiving dinner tomorrow. Ain't that nice?"

Tyler felt her stomach tense. They hadn't spoken since he called to say he was going away. And though he'd said they could still be friends, she honestly felt that he hadn't taken it all that well. She didn't want tomorrow to be an exercise in tension.

"Doesn't he have family?" Tyler asked; the thought suddenly occurring to her. Why *was* Sterling having dinner with them?

"Don't seem to. Never heard him talk 'bout no kin."

Hmm. How strange. Maybe that's why she felt as if she knew him—in spirit. They were both orphans, but at least she had Tess. Was there anyone out there for Sterling? Maybe that was her real reason for staying away from Sterling. He knew from where she came. There was nowhere for her to hide.

"Hope you brought yo' overnight bag, Ms. Lauren,

'cause you and yo' friend gon' be up half the night cookin'!"

Lauren leaned over and kissed Tess' cheek. "You know I'm staying, Nana. We're going to teach that granddaughter of yours to cook if it kills us."

Tess leaned back in her chair and cackled with laughter. "Then ya'll better hurry it up. Cain't afford to lose a precious minute!"

Tyler made a face at them both and they all bubbled with laughter—that good old-fashioned kind of laughter that is remembered long after the melody has faded.

Sterling looked out his kitchen window, partly obscured by the curtain. He'd heard the car pull up to the house, the sounds of female laughter. He caught a brief glimpse of Tyler as she crossed from the car to the house, her movements cautious, almost hesitant, as if seeing the place for the first time.

But in that instant of hesitation he captured another mental picture: neck slightly arched, slender arms outstretched, that wild hair gently touched by the rustling breeze.

He smiled just a little and let the curtain fall back in place, imagining the three happy and laughing women inside the rambling old house.

Family.

Something he'd longed for and had been denied. He couldn't count his brother, and to him his father didn't exist.

Maybe now that Tyler was back away from the influences of New York and the man she'd decided to spend her time with rather than him, he could help her to see how things could be between them—if she'd just give them a chance.

They were cut from the same cloth, he and Tyler. What better way to stitch together the threads of their lives than together?

The New York Knicks waged a losing battle against their arch rivals, the world champion Chicago Bulls. Miles and Greg were stretched out in Greg's living room with their mouths open after a move Michael Jordan had just put on John Starks. The Chicago Center crowd was going wild.

"Man! Did you see that?" Greg shouted, falling back on the couch. "I don't even know why any player bothers to try to stop Mike. Big waste of time."

"You know they're gonna play that one back." Miles took a sip of beer.

"What's up for the holiday?" Greg asked during the commercial.

"No plans."

"Yeah? Why?"

"'Cause I don't have any."

"You mean you and Ms. Tyler aren't hookin' up for the long weekend?"

"No."

"She blow you off?"

Miles cut his eyes in Greg's direction. "What's that supposed to mean?"

"It means for weeks you don't have time for nothing but her. Now that she's out of the picture for a minute, you're stretched out on my couch watching the game."

Miles expelled a short, nasty chuckle as he stood.

"We can fix that right now. 'Cause you know what, man?" He made a show of looking around the apartment. "I have the exact same tube in my crib. The same pictures on the wall to look at and the same damn couch to lay on. Your problem is you spend so much of your life trying to be me. This was the one thing you couldn't duplicate. A slice of trying to be real. And that's bugging the hell outta you. You've been so used to getting whatever I had since we were kids—money, toys, clothes, friends—you just can't stand it that Tyler isn't being shared with you, too. Well, check this, like I told you before, it ain't that kind of party. Get a life, man. And I don't mean mine."

He strode over to the closet and pulled out his black leather coat, nearly confusing it with one of Greg's that looked just like his. He almost laughed, but he wasn't in the mood.

"Hey, listen, Miles, man. No reason for the attitude," Greg said as Miles kept walking toward the door. "I was just telling you the deal, that's all. You've changed."

Miles grabbed the doorknob and looked at Greg over his shoulder. "Don't you think it's about time?" He pulled the door open. "Later. And don't forget about my money." He shut the door quietly behind him.

Miles drove around the city for hours, no real destination in mind. For a hot minute he even thought about driving out to his parents' house. Then again, he wasn't that desperate.

By the time he finally decided to call it a night he knew he didn't want to spend the rest of it alone.

He stood in front of his bedroom phone and thought

about what he was about to do. He opened the night-stand drawer and took out his phone book.

Maybe Mari was in the mood, for "old times' sake."

Chapter 21

Cross That Bridge When You Come to It

"Who in the world is gonna eat all this food?" Tyler moaned after hours of stirring, cutting, chopping and mixing.

"Don't matter none who eats it," Tess said from her seat at the kitchen table. "It's in the doin', chile. In the doin'." She popped open a green bean, letting the seeds fall into an aluminum bowl. "It's 'bout gittin' folk, friends, family together. Sharing what we got wit each other, even if it ain't nothin' but a long story. And being thankful you got somethin' to git together about."

Tyler turned toward Lauren, who had her eyes locked on the pie dough she was kneading. Wasn't that what Lauren had been asking all along, and Miles, and even

Sterling—for her to just share a little part of herself, even if it *was* just a long story?

"Pass me some more flour, will you, Ty?" Lauren asked, still keeping her gaze averted.

Tyler reached up into the cabinet overhead, careful of the one hinge that kept it in place and took down the metal tin of flour.

"Here ya go."

Lauren turned and their eyes met. Tyler reached out and Lauren placed her hand in Tyler's.

Tess watched from the corner of her eyes and smiled sadly. *Po' chile got so far to go, and I don't know how much longer I got to teach her.*

Lauren was in the shower pretending to be Chaka Khan, singing "Tell Me Something Good" and wasn't half bad. She was even doing her own backup. Nana was already in bed and the aromas of baked breads, pies, ham dripping in maple syrup, macaroni embedded in three kinds of cheese and the sweetest green beans and collards had just began to settle down for the night, ready to make their big debut tomorrow.

Tyler tiptoed down the creaky hallway steps into the kitchen and picked up the fat, black tabletop dial phone from the corner table, where it had held a place of honor longer than Tyler could remember.

She closed her eyes for a split second, then began to dial. She didn't realize she'd been holding her breath until the phone stopped ringing.

"Yeah?"

"Hi. It's me, Tyler."

That slow, smooth as silk, barely there drawl dragged

through his bloodstream like needed oxygen. He wanted to shout, "Baby, come home. I miss you." He didn't.

"Hey, Tyler. What's up?"

She never knew how to answer that question and realized long ago that no one really expected an answer.

"How are you, Miles?"

"All right. And you?"

She wanted to shake some emotion into him—yell, scream—anything was better than this purgatory.

"Had a good flight."

"Yeah? Glad to hear it." He leaned against the wall. He wasn't going to make it easy for her. He'd gone about as far as he intended to go with Tyler Ellington.

"Miles—"

"Yeah?"

"I…miss you." There, she'd said it. One little baby step.

His heart thumped. "Miss you, too, Ty."

She released a silent sigh of relief. "Can we talk when I get back? Really talk?"

"We can always talk, Tyler. But I don't want to be the one doing all the talking. Know what I mean?"

"Hmm." She held the phone tighter.

"When are you coming home?"

"I have a noon flight on Saturday. I get into Kennedy at three."

"I'll pick you up."

"I'd like that."

"See you Saturday."

"Good night, Miles. And have a good Thanksgiving."

"You, too."

He leaned back against the wall and shut his eyes. *One more time, baby. We'll try this thing one more time.* He hung up the phone. What he had thought was a need that had to be filled with Mari, just was. He tossed his phone book into the back of the nightstand drawer.

Man, he had it bad.

Slowly Tyler hung up the phone. Her entire body seemed to be floating, as if the weight that held down her spirit had finally been lifted. She practically sailed up the stairs and slipped under the cool cotton sheets. Visions of Miles's smile, the sparkle in his eyes, the deep timbre of his rich voice, kept her company all night long.

When she awoke the next morning she realized she'd slept without the hall light on.

It seemed a hundred people were expected for Thanksgiving dinner the way Tess fussed and gave orders from the instant Tyler's and Lauren's feet hit the floor.

"I'm gonna be too exhausted to eat by the time she gets through with me," Tyler whispered to Lauren.

"Who you telling. Nana Tess ain't no joke."

They both chuckled.

"Ain't got no time for foolin' round. Dinner is three o'clock sharp. Jest like it's been for sixty years." She smoothed the white linen cloth across the table. "Sterling be over soon. Don't want the po' man to thank we got a house fulla women and cain't git one lousy meal together."

The duo rolled their eyes skyward.

"You'd think it was the Pope," Tyler said under her breath.

"He'd better eat every crumb. And he'd better be fine!"

Tyler snickered.

Almost as if summoned by the sheer force of his name being tossed around, Sterling knocked on the door.

"It's open," Tess called out.

Sterling strolled in—his white shirt open just enough to expose a glimpse of his chest and with a pair of navy dress slacks that outlined the muscles of his long legs—and Tyler could have sworn she heard Lauren gasp.

"Happy Thanksgiving, ladies." His statement was meant for everyone, but his gaze looked for and settled on Tyler.

"Hello, young man. Hope you brought yo' appetite." Tess chuckled. "These girls been workin' like the devil."

He crossed the wide kitchen to where Tess sat and planted a kiss on her cheek. "As much as you've been talking about today, Nana Tess, you know I did. Hope you didn't work them too hard, though."

"Little hard work never hurt nobody," she mumbled.

Sterling turned toward Tyler.

That slow, day-breaking smile that was so familiar to her spread across his mouth. "Hi, Sterling."

He walked over to her, gently clasped her shoulders, and bent his head to brush her cheek. "Good to see you, Tyler."

"You, too." And this time she meant it. "This is my friend, Lauren Hayes. She was looking after Nana while you were away. Lauren, Sterling Grey."

"Nice to meet you, Lauren. You must be some good friend."

She smiled and turned to Tyler. "That's what I keep trying to tell her." She stuck out her hand. "Nice to meet you, too. Heard a lot about you."

Tyler wanted to nudge her, and would have if she didn't think she'd get caught.

"I didn't do it. I swear," he joked, holding his hands up in surrender.

Tyler smiled. Maybe the day wouldn't be so bad, after all.

At three o'clock sharp they were all seated at the table holding hands, with Sterling leading the prayer of thanks.

"I'm thankful for the opportunity to be included in this circle of friendship and a part of this day with three wonderful women. Thank you, Lord, for all that is before us, and let your blessing continue to touch us all."

"Amen!" they shouted in unison.

The next hour was filled with tall tales told by Nana, with "Pass this, pass that," the cling and clang of utensils, lip smacking and lots of laughter.

"I can't move," Lauren groaned.

Tyler rubbed her belly in sympathy. "Me, either."

"Well, somebody better git movin' and clean up all this food," Nana said.

Everybody groaned.

Lauren was assigned to find containers for all the leftovers. Tyler washed the dishes while Sterling dried. Nana had mysteriously disappeared, and Tyler would have bet her last dollar that she was fast asleep.

Looking around her, experiencing the companionable activity, she felt a sense of peace. The old cracked walls didn't look quite so bad. The worn but hand-scrubbed floors had a special kind of sparkle. Even those yellow dish towels didn't look so faded anymore.

What would Miles see with his filmmaker eyes? She scrubbed a dish and ran it under water to wash away the sudsy bubbles. Absently she set it in the drain. Would he see what she always saw when she first arrived? She wanted him to accept her for who she was, all of her. To do that she'd have to open doors that had been sealed shut for two decades. And deep in her soul she knew that what lurked behind the doors would never go away again if she let the past slip out. Then the door would always be a wedge between them.

She wouldn't risk it. Not this time. Not when she had every intention of making it work. This was a part of her world she would never share. She couldn't.

"All done," Sterling announced, placing the last dish in the cabinet.

Tyler forced a smile and wiped her hands on the dish towel. "Thanks."

"Ty, I'm gonna head home, girl," said Lauren. "Got some things to take care of in the morning."

"Why don't you stay? I was planning to go by my old apartment tomorrow. We could drive in together?"

"I could take you, Tyler, if Lauren needs to go home," Sterling said.

"No…I couldn't ask you to do that."

"You didn't. I offered."

Tyler glanced at Lauren, who gave her a nearly imperceptible rise of her brows. Tyler let out a breath. "If you're sure—"

"I need to go into town, anyway. Pick up some film."

"You know Nana's going to have one fit when she gets up and you're gone," Tyler warned.

"You two can keep her busy fussing about something. She won't even miss me." She laughed. "But I'll call her tomorrow and make my peace. Definitely don't want to lose my visiting privileges." She turned her smile on Sterling. "Listen, it was good to finally meet you. Ever need any models," she said, winking, "give me a call."

Sterling chuckled. "Definitely."

"Okay, girl, I'm out."

"I'll walk you to your car. Sure you don't want to stay?"

"Positive." She took her bag and her blazer out of the hall closet.

"He seems really nice, Ty," she said under her breath. "And he likes you. You ought to give the brother a play."

Tyler avoided looking her in the eye and opened the door instead. "I want to try to work things out between me and Miles."

"Hey, cool. At least you're trying to work it out with somebody."

"Very funny."

"Wasn't trying to be. Just real."

"Sterling's nice, Ren. Don't get me wrong, but I don't think it could work."

"It's your life. You know what turns you on and what doesn't. Sterling's not the one." She opened her car door.

If only it were that simple. If she could just explain

it. She wanted to, wanted Lauren to stay so they could sit up all night and talk—like girlfriends.

The question bubbled up in her throat. And sat there.

"I'll call you," Lauren said, slipping behind the wheel and shutting the door. She looked up at Tyler through the partially opened window. "It'll work out, Ty. Whatever it is." She gave her a tight smile, started the engine and drove off.

Tyler stood on the dirt road just staring at the car as it disappeared into the glade of trees, wishing that Lauren would turn around and come back. But she knew that wouldn't happen.

Slowly she turned toward the house and Sterling was standing in the doorway, watching her. The light from the hall cast a silhouetting shadow around him. And a sudden flash of a man whose face she couldn't see, stood in her darkened bedroom doorway. A shudder rippled up her spine. She drew her arms tighter around her waist. Her eyes locked on him.

He slid his hands into the back pockets of his slacks and stepped down the plank stairs, his features slowly coming into focus. *Sterling.* The tension that had coiled her body gradually began to ease.

Sterling looked up at the sky, which was just beginning to fill with stars, then settled his gaze on her.

"Still nice out."

She nodded.

They stood in silence for a moment.

"Want to go for a walk?" he asked.

"No. I—"

"Great way to work off all that food you put away."

She cocked her head to the side and gave him a long

up and down look. "I beg your pardon. You didn't do so bad yourself, my brother."

"Hey, I'm still growing. Gotta keep up my strength."

"Any excuse is better than none."

He stepped a bit closer. "Then let's not make any. Walk with me."

She hesitated a beat. "All right."

"So, how long are you planning to stay?" he asked as they strolled along the winding dirt road.

"Until Saturday. Have to be back at work on Monday, and I want to give myself a day to get it together." She thought of Miles waiting for her at the airport.

"How's the job?"

She laughed. "Hectic. They really keep me busy. Are you finished with your traveling?"

"For the time being. I need to lay out the first set of photographs I took and send them up to New York. See if it's what they're looking for."

"Hmm."

"I thought about you a lot, Tyler…since the last time I saw you." He paused a moment. "You don't have to respond, or think up something appropriate to say." He looked down, then at her profile. "I wanted you to know."

He stopped. Took her hand.

Her insides knotted when she looked into his eyes.

"I don't know what's happening with you and that guy in New York. It doesn't matter. I want you to know I'm here. To talk to, be with." He gave her a half smile. "Maybe even think about sometime."

She swallowed, her heart thundering. "Sterling—"

He shook his head. "No excuses. No explanations. Whatever we can be to each other, whenever we can. That's it. That's all."

What was he really saying—that he was willing to share her with another man if that's what she decided to do? She couldn't even fix her mouth to ask the question.

"Come on. Let's head back."

They returned to the house in silence.

She didn't know what to say, anyway. Why in the world would a man like Sterling be willing to settle for what he offered her? Was he really willing to give of himself without expecting anything in return? It didn't make sense.

Then all at once it did. She angled her head in his direction. How often had she done the very same thing, been willing to settle for any piece of attention, affection—just to have it? More times than she could count. She knew what had happened to her. She understood why she kept people at arm's length, why it was so hard for her to give—any more. But what had happened to Sterling to make him feel he had to settle?

To ask those questions of him, to dredge up things in his past, would only make him want to know more about her. To Sterling, she was an educated, career-oriented woman with a solid family, roots and a grandmother who lived on the island because of choice, not because life in the city reminded her of the daughter she'd lost to it.

Yes. That's how it would stay.

"What time do you want to leave in the morning?"

When she looked, they were in front of Nana's house. "Whenever you're ready."

"Say about ten?"

"Sounds fine."

"I'll see you then." He leaned down and lightly kissed her cheek. "Good night."

"'Night."

She watched him walk down the path toward his house until he was swallowed up by the darkness. Moments later, she saw the glow of light peek through.

As promised, Sterling drove her into the city. For the entire ninety-minute ride Tyler thought that at any minute he would resurrect their last conversation, but he didn't. They spent the time listening to an "oldies" station and reminiscing. Before she knew it they were pulling up in front of Midwood Manor.

"You want me to pick you up, or anything?"

"No. Thanks. I'm meeting Lauren. She's coming back with me so she can drive me to the airport tomorrow."

He nodded. "I hope you'll think about what I said last night."

"I…will." She opened the door, needing to get away. She really didn't want to have this conversation.

"Take care, Tyler."

"You, too." She smiled without showing her teeth. "Thanks for the ride." She got out of the car and hurried along the path leading to the entrance. She didn't hear his car drive away, and she definitely wasn't going to look back. The last thing she wanted was to see him still sitting there.

As soon as she got to the door Wes was walking out, smiling as if he'd just hit the lottery.

"Ms. E!" A big grin split his face.

He hurried over to her as fast as he could go and stretched out his arms. Tyler stepped into his embrace and hugged him back.

"Sure is good to be missed." She giggled.

"And you *was* that." He stepped back. "Lemme take a look at ya. See if the big city done changed you any."

He looked her up and down and she could feel the heat rise to her face.

"Still lookin' like a star, Ms. E."

"Only to you, Wes." She grinned.

"How long you here for?"

"Just until tomorrow. I have a noon flight."

"And you took time to visit me." He bit down on his bottom lip. "That makes me feel real good, Ms. E. Real good." He lowered his head and shook it slowly.

Tyler put her hand on his shoulder. "You were always good to me, Wes. From the first day we met. I'll always remember that."

"Jes doin' what needed to be done."

Tyler frowned. "What do you mean—needed to be done?"

"Eh, eh. Nothin', girl. Jest meant I was lookin' out for ya. That's all."

She tried to read his face, see the meaning behind his words. But all she saw was what she always did—a nice old man with a kind heart. She shook off the momentary twinge of unease that breezed through her.

"Still keeping my mail?"

"Sho'. Come on into the office. I'll git it for ya. Thank it's jest a buncha bills and thangs."

"Of course." She chuckled and followed him into the building.

Sterling felt the blood rushing to his head, pounding, pounding. He didn't want to believe what he'd just seen, couldn't believe it. All the conversations with Nat that he'd barely listened to, had tossed off, came rushing back. He'd said their father was working at some big fancy building. He'd never cared to ask. Didn't want to know. Now he did.

He wanted to run down that path, grab her out of that old man's arms and tell her what the man had done— how many lives he'd ruined.

The last time his father had hugged *him* he was ten years old. His eyes began to burn.

Chapter 22

Taking Giant Steps

> *On this marginal date: Patient's trust level remains minimal. Reserves open acts of affection for older adults as if seeking parental acceptance. Still unable to exhibit or maintain intimacy with those in own age range.*

"Had a good visit with Wes?" Lauren asked as she hustled around her apartment, trying to get ready.

Tyler leaned back against the couch and smiled, thinking about Wes. "Yeah. Short but nice. It was really good seeing him. You know he's still holding my apartment for me? Don't know how he's doing it, and he told me not to ask. Said if things didn't work out in

New York and I wanted to come home I'd always have a place to stay."

"Man. Wish I knew somebody like that. He's like the perfect grandfather."

"Guess I got lucky."

"Who you telling." Lauren sat on the edge of the ottoman and pulled on her sneakers, then stood. "All set?"

Tyler stood and stretched her arms over her head. "Yep. Let's get to shopping."

They spent the next few hours browsing through stores, with Tyler looking for some inexpensive accessories for her apartment. Although Tempest had showed her where to get some great finds, they were still totally beyond her budget limits. She settled on some ceramic pottery that would be perfect on the kitchen counter, some hand towels for Nana's kitchen—which she knew would wind up in the basement, in a box along with all the other things she'd bought for the house over the years—and a great see-through shower curtain with drawings of tropical fish for her bathroom. Lauren bullied her into buying some real lingerie from Victoria's Secret.

"Since you're trying to 'work things out' with Miles, you can use the extra ammunition," Lauren whispered in her ear while Tyler paid for her purchases.

She knew Miles had been more than patient with her, never asking, never pushing. They'd gotten close a number of times, and he had always put on the brakes. Sometimes she wondered if she weren't sexy enough, if she didn't really turn him on—if he saw her like other men in her life had seen her—frigid. Did he get what he wanted from other women while he waited for her? How much longer would he wait?

"Come on," Lauren said, halting her wandering thoughts. "I'm starved. And I want to head to Nana Tess's before it starts getting dark."

Tyler absently picked up her package and walked with Lauren out of the mall.

"Ya'll drive careful, now," Tess warned from the top of the sagging front steps.

Tyler felt her heart pinch when she saw her grandma standing there looking so frail, knowing she'd be alone but smiling all the same. All her life Nana had been her only constant, her source of who she was. How unfair it was of her to be ashamed of a woman who gave all she had.

She wrapped Tess in her arms, feeling her eyes fill. She wanted to stay, keep smelling the lavender and Dax, listen to the steps creak when she tiptoed up them, the rooster crow when the sun rose. But she couldn't.

Swallowing down the knot in her throat, she gave Tess one last kiss.

"I'll call as soon as I get home, Nana."

"Chile, you know I be sleep. Call tomorrow."

"I will." She trotted down the steps and headed for the car, turned and waved.

"Bye, chile," Tess whispered.

And as Tyler slid into Lauren's car, she could have sworn her grandmother said goodbye. A slight shudder ran up her back.

"Guess this is it, girlfriend," Lauren said as they approached Tyler's departure gate.

"Thank you for everything, Ren. Lookin' after Nana Tess, chauffeuring me around and…being my friend."

"That's what friends do, Ty." She smiled.

Tyler pressed her lips together and nodded. She hugged her tightly, hoping that one day she could be the kind of friend to Lauren that she had always been to her.

"Talk to you soon, Ren."

"Get it together with that Miles guy. Maybe he's the one."

"Yeah," she said on a wistful note. "Maybe."

Miles stepped out of the shower, wrapped a towel around his waist and peered into the steamed bathroom mirror.

He'd been up for hours, couldn't really remember sleeping. When had a woman gotten to him as Tyler had? And she wasn't even trying. At least he didn't think she was.

Every time he'd shut his eyes during the night he'd seen her dimpled smile, her wild black hair, felt the soft curves of her body that he'd been trying to explore further. But just at the moment when he had her beneath him, whispering how much she wanted to be with him, Sterling showed up and the two of them walked away together.

Must be his subconscious working on him. He'd lost track of the women he'd walked away from, or sweet-talked away from another man. But damn, he didn't want *this* to be payback time.

He had a half hour to get to the airport and for the entire drive his last conversation with Tyler played through his head.

She wanted to talk.

What was she willing to tell him? That she wanted to be with him—*really* be with him? That she was willing to open the door that she'd kept shut and let him in?

That's what he wanted. If he didn't know it before, he knew it now. Maybe her going away and him thinking she was with another guy had done it for him. He wasn't sure. All he knew was that he was getting tired of playing the running game.

But what if she told him she didn't want to be bothered. That she wanted to be with that guy?

Frowning, he turned up the music. He couldn't remember a time when a woman had walked out on him. He didn't even know how to deal with something like that.

He took the exit to the airport and crept along in the sudden bottleneck of horn-blowing traffic. He checked the digital clock. Her plane would be landing right about now. He added his horn to the offbeat orchestra.

By the time he pulled into the passenger pickup lane, her plane had been on the ground for twenty minutes.

He didn't want her standing around waiting, thinking that he didn't show.

Peering between overcoated bodies in hat-covered heads he spotted her the minute she walked through the door.

There she was, looking all lost, just like the first time he'd seen her, and that sensation of wanting to protect eased through his bloodstream again.

Somebody needed to protect him from Tyler Ellington.

He pulled to a stop about five cars down from where she stood, opened the door and stepped out.

"Tyler! Over here." Just as she turned in his direction, he waved his hand over his head.

Tyler felt that rush again—that fluttery feeling in her stomach. The same way she'd been feeling lately whenever she saw him, heard his voice.

She couldn't have stopped the smile that spread across her mouth if she'd wanted to. She waved back, knocked bags and elbows with the other travelers, and sidestepped the redcaps on her way to him.

He came around the front of the car to the sidewalk and stood in front of her.

For the first few seconds everything around her seemed silent, the people disappeared into the background and there was only her and Miles.

"Hi," she breathed.

He smiled, leaned down, placed his hands on either side of her face and kissed her the way he'd been dreaming about kissing her—long and slow. He let his tongue tease her lips, memorizing their softness, the sweet taste of her. And he knew, at that moment, just how much he'd really missed her.

Reluctantly he eased away. "Ready?" he asked as casually as if he always stood in the middle of human traffic and kissed a woman senseless.

All she could do was nod her head, afraid of what she'd sound like if she tried to answer.

He took her bags from her hands and walked to the car. His heart was hammering with every footstep, but he couldn't let her know that she'd gotten to him that way—not over one kiss and a three-day absence.

Tyler followed, a half step behind, her entire body quivering from the aftereffects.

Silently she slid into the car, fastened her seat belt and dared to sneak a peek at his profile, hoping to see something in his expression. He looked as if nothing out of the ordinary had transpired.

Maybe to him it hadn't.

"How was the flight?" he asked. He really wanted to ask how her visit back home was, but he wouldn't. He wanted her to tell him on her own.

"Not bad."

He turned on the music and Marvin Gaye's classic, "Distant Lover," flowed through the speakers. Miles almost cringed.

"How was your holiday? Did you see your parents?"

"Fine and no." He turned to her for a second. "Spent it in front of my computer, working on my script."

"How's it coming?"

"Almost there. Another run-through should do it. As I said, the writing part of it isn't really my thing. But—" He shrugged. He pulled onto the exit to the highway and headed back to the city.

"I though we could stop by my place first. Unless you're in a rush to get home."

"I'm in no rush. I… We have the whole evening."

He glanced at her from the corner of his eyes. *The whole evening.*

Tyler curled her legs beneath her and took a sip from the mug of hot chocolate Miles had fixed. She looked around at the designer furniture and the expensive artwork, and she felt comfortable and not out of place— as she usually did, as if she didn't deserve it. And she realized that for all Miles had—most of which she was

sure he hadn't even told her about—he never flaunted
it, never acted as if he were above it all. If anything, he
seemed to want to distance himself from his affluence
and just be a regular guy.

Miles walked into the living room and adjusted the
volume on the stereo until Phyllis Hyman was singing
just right. He joined her on the couch.

She had yet to say a word about her trip—about
Sterling, about anything of consequence. Maybe, he
thought, the phone call was just another game, a way
to keep stringing him along. When he looked at her
sitting there sipping her hot chocolate, her gaze slowly
roaming the room, thoughtful, he knew better.

He leaned his head back against the couch, draped
his arm around her shoulder and pulled her closer,
letting his fingers trail in her curls.

"Miles…"

"Yeah?"

"When I went back home, I know you wanted to
know why I had to leave, what I was going back to."
She hesitated. Could she do this, really do this? She
took a breath and studied the melting whipped cream
that floated on the top of her mug, allowed the sensation of his gentle fingers to ease the drumbeat of her
heart. If she did this, there was no turning back, yet if
she had any real hope of making it work with Miles she
had to start by being honest. And if he couldn't handle
it, then she'd know he wasn't the man she'd hoped he
was and she knew she could walk away before it hurt
too much.

Slowly she looked up and turned her gaze in his direction, and what she saw in his eyes was an openness

and sincere willingness to listen. He encouraged her with his soft half smile, the slow strokes of his fingers.

She swallowed back the last of her reservations and began the story she'd never told anyone.

"My mother's not in Georgia, not singing in night-clubs. Hasn't been for more than twenty years. When I was four years old…I saw my mother killed…."

As she went on, at moments she spoke with passion, at others with pain and anger, and those instances that sounded as if she were recording someone else's life, Miles lived the heartache and sense of worthlessness with her. While her story unfolded he began to understand her reluctance to trust, her wariness at acts of kindness.

For him, someone who'd always been given every-thing, even things he didn't want, it was so hard to imagine what a life of not having, of being so uncertain about day-to-day existence, could do to a person.

And yet she'd found a way to survive. Maybe that's what made her such a great writer and an even greater person.

Finally, she stopped and looked at him with hesita-tion expecting to see…what, she wasn't sure.

"Tyler, I—"

"I don't want your pity, Miles." She tried to get up.

He held on to her arm. "I may be feeling a lot of things, but not pity. Sit down, Tyler." She didn't move. "Please," he said more gently, "if we're going to talk, it takes two to make that happen. Not you laying out your life, then jetting as soon as I look at you. It can't work like that."

She stared at him for a moment, wanting to summon

some anger, some reason for escape, so she wouldn't have to face him or herself after what she'd said. She couldn't. Slowly she sat down.

He took her hand, which felt like ice. Gently he rubbed it. "I don't feel sorry for you. How could I? You came through all that. You, Tyler. Not somebody else. That takes a lot more courage than I've ever had." He stroked her cheek. "I do feel sorry for myself—for coming across as the kind of person you didn't think you could talk to. And I feel sorry for all those people in your life who never stuck around long enough to experience the pleasure of you. Talk to me now, Tyler. Not just the story of your life, but talk to me about what's inside. I want to know."

"My…my life has been one continuous series of ups and downs. No one wanted me for any length of time, so I began, I guess, believing that if I pretended to be like everyone else I would be accepted, cared about. I wanted to tell you about my Nana Tess, but I thought it would open up areas of my life I didn't want opened, that maybe you'd ask all the questions I didn't want to answer. And I'd have to tell you that Nana Tess can't read or write, that I barely remember my mother, that I turned to a world of make-believe to hide from my real world, and then somehow you would think less of me because of it.

"And when I went back home I realized that what I was doing was hiding the one person in the world who'd always loved and cared for me because I was too ashamed of how she lived, how she talked."

Tears slid over her lids. "I knew I couldn't do that to her. No matter what it did to me."

Miles wiped the tears from her cheeks with the pad of his thumb.

"Baby, you have nothing to be ashamed of and everything to be proud of. You have someone in your life who loves you unconditionally. Not everyone can say that. Your grandmother may not have been able to give you things. But she gave you more than my parents have ever given me with all the toys, money and business contacts they threw my way. All that never amounted to anything compared to what your grandmother gave you with the little she had."

For the very first time in her life the heavy weight of insecurity, of doubt, began to ease like clouds drifting away after a terrible storm.

"You want to know if I feel different about you? I don't."

She tugged on her bottom lip, determined not to cry again.

"If anything, I want you even more, Ty." He cupped her chin and turned her to face him. His gaze swept across her face. "I need you to believe that, if this thing we have between us is going to work." He blew out a breath, trying to form the words he'd never said, or said before but never meant.

"I'm not going to lie to you. I've done my share of bs-ing over the years, using what I had to my advantage. I've been through more women than I can count. But I've gotten to a place in my life where I want to change that. On the surface it may seem that Miles Bennett has it all together—the well-off family, great education, Wall Street background, clothes, a little money. But it's all a front, Tyler.

"I have a family I barely speak to, a six-figure job I walked away from because I hated it, a string of unfulfilling relationships and a circle of friends I couldn't call on if I really needed them. I don't want to live the rest of my life like that. I can't. I want to make a difference, somehow. And I want you to be a part of it."

She reached out and caressed his cheek and he turned his head to kiss her palm. He held her hand to his mouth, brushing it with a kiss so tender it felt like a passing breeze, causing a shock to run up her arm.

"Miles, I'm no good at this—"

"Yeah." He kissed the inside of her wrist. "I know. You told me." He moved closer and gently nibbled her ear. "Neither am I."

His mouth grazed her neck and he let his tongue slide along the tender cord and then sucked the skin, his own need for her escalating with the sounds of her soft sighs.

Tentatively he ran his hands across her shoulders and down her back until he reached the bottom of her waist-length sweater. He slid his hands beneath the soft wool and felt the satin smoothness of her skin.

She clung to him, burying her face against the heat of his neck when she felt the clasp of her bra come loose.

It was going to happen, she thought, as the flame erupted in her stomach when his fingers brushed the tips of her breasts, bringing them to tight peaks. Right here. Today. With Miles.

Her senses spun as he pushed up her sweater and took one and then the other breast to his mouth, gently teasing, taunting, laving them until she shook from the inside out.

Her eyes slid closed. She heard the soft sounds of her own whimpers mix with the deep timbre of his groans. She couldn't believe she could feel this kind of intense need with anyone, and that she could stir it in him. She almost wanted to stop it—stop it before it got too good and then was taken away—but she couldn't, not when his hands continued to burn her flesh, when his mouth awakened every nerve in her body.

Then, just as she'd feared, it ended. Just stopped.

She slowly opened her eyes.

"Not here, Ty. Not like this." He kissed her mouth, then took her hand. "Come with me." Gently he pulled her to her feet and led her into his bedroom.

He was so very gentle. So patient. He even made taking off her clothes an art form. His soft groans of encouragement when she sought to touch him, his whispered phrases about the wonders of her body and how she made him feel, were the aphrodisiacs she'd never had.

And when he took the time to put on a condom she understood in a whole new way that he truly cared about her, that whatever happened from that moment on he would protect her.

Because of that, when she felt his body lower onto hers, the pressure of his penis press against her wet opening and saw his eyes seeking her seconds before he pushed past the entryway, she gave herself to him, totally. She wasn't just opening her body. She was opening a part of her being she'd never shared with anyone. And she wasn't afraid as she rose and fell with all the emotions and sensations that raced through her.

She wasn't afraid.

He thought he knew what he was going to get when he finally found himself buried deep inside of her. It was not as if he'd never been to such a place before, even though it hadn't been with her. But the instant he felt her heat close around him, wrap him in a sheath of incredible warmth, it was no longer just about "seeing what it was like."

Yes, he'd wanted her. And yes, he'd wanted it to be special. But he'd wanted it all before, and it never had been. Not until now. Tyler wasn't clinging to him, moving with him, whispering his name, just because she wanted to impress him with her sexual prowess, as the others had. She meant every movement, every shudder, word, touch. She meant it. And her wanting him, giving herself to him, took him to a place he'd never been with any other woman.

Reality.

Chapter 23

Change Don't Come Easy

"I really need to get home," Tyler mumbled against his chest.

He held her tighter. He couldn't let her leave. Not yet. Not when he was just getting used to the sensation of holding her. Loving her. They'd made love off and on all night and into the morning, taking catnaps in between and short trips to the bathroom or the fridge.

He felt himself growing hard again just thinking about what they'd done to each other, and the only thing stopping him from doing it again was that he'd run out of condoms.

"Naw. You don't have to go." He nibbled her neck. "We'll spend the day together."

"Doing what?" she asked in a teasing tone.

"You decide." He ran a hand along her spine and she arched against him in response.

"Miles…"

"Hmm." He drew a nipple into his mouth.

She moaned. "We can't…keep…this up."

"Oh, I think we can," he groaned, pressing against her, then rolled on top of her. As he moved against the triangular tangle of hair and felt her passive resistance weaken, he remembered. *All out.* He slumped against her.

She twirled one of his short locks around her finger. "Need to make a run to the drugstore, huh?" She grinned, realizing he'd opened a fresh box of six last night, and this would have made time number seven. She pushed him up and away, then leaned on her elbow. She stroked a finger along his thick eyebrows.

"Tell you what. I'll stay, on one condition."

"What's that?" he gave her a sidelong glance.

"You take me home, I get a change of clothes and my notes for my script and we can work together this afternoon."

"I have a condition, too."

"What?"

"We make a pit stop on the way back." He gave her a wicked grin and they both laughed.

They spent the day working, debating ideas, offering suggestions, feeding off each other's creative energy.

As Miles read Tyler's script he saw exactly what Professor Chase saw—a powerful, important story—and now he knew why. She wrote from the depth of her life, what it had been like, and made it come to painful, poignant life on the page. He could see the rolling hill-sides, the lush green of Savannah, the sagging house that held so much love, the countless homes and faceless guardians. And he knew this was a screenplay he had to direct.

"Ty," he said after reading the last page. "This is some heavy stuff."

She lowered her gaze, knowing that now he could see beyond the surface of the words.

"I know I, we, can make this film. And I don't mean some student film. A real film."

She looked into his eyes. "You really think so?"

"I know so. Baby, I can see it. Everything. I mean, it still needs work and you have to finish it. Chase can help you with that. It can still be screened at the university's film festival. That's where it'll get its first bit of recognition. But this is something you want on the big screen."

Her eyes shimmered with hope. "It's all I've ever wanted."

"We can make it happen. I know we can. Let me direct it, Ty. This is the kind of work I've dreamed about doing. Something that has meaning."

She blew out a breath, seeing her dream peeking over the horizon, and making it come true with a man who believed in it, and in her. She'd put her faith, her trust, in him when she cracked open the door, and he hadn't run away.

"Let's do it." She grinned.

The days flew by and winter came roaring in like a lion, dumping several feet of snow on the city for days, which thrilled Tyler to no end. It was the first time she'd ever seen snow and she wanted to be out in it every time Miles turned around. Because it put that smile that he loved to see on her face he put on his boots and winter coat and walked with her for blocks as the flakes sprinkled down around them. And with her, something he'd once considered a nuisance took on a special kind of magic.

They spent all of their free time together, which wasn't as much as either of them wanted, between her job, classes, his students and working out the kinks in both of their projects. Christmas was almost upon them, too.

She talked more and more with Lauren, really talked, telling her about the progress of her relationship with Miles, the fears she'd harbored over the years and how hard she was trying to work them out. Surprisingly, Lauren had understood more than Tyler had given her credit for. And, of course, she talked to Nana Tess almost every day, keeping her up to date on her life and her relationship with Miles.

"I'm sorry I won't be down for Christmas, Nana Tess. But I can't get any time off from my job, and with Christmas being in the middle of the week—"

"You ain't got to explain, chile. It's awright. You spend the holiday with that young man you always giggling 'bout e'ry time you mention his name. Got plenty ta do 'round here." She chuckled. "'Sides, now I won't have to spend all my energy supervisin' you in the kitchen! Lord knows I don't know what man gon' tolerate a woman who cain't cook."

Tyler chuckled. "I'm getting better," she lied, thinking of all the pizza and Chinese food she and Miles consumed. He couldn't cook a lick, either. What a pair they made. "I'll call you."

"I know you will."

"How's Sterling?" She hadn't spoken to him in a while and felt a bit guilty since she'd avoided calling him, not wanting to stir up anything.

"Doin' fine, far as I kin tell. Stops by to see me lack always. Nice boy, that one," she said softly. "Just somethin' 'bout him. He's carryin' something heavy. Cain't seem to set it down, whatever it is."

Tyler frowned. "What do you mean?"

"Jest a sadness 'bout him sometimes. You kin see it in his eyes if'n you look real good."

She thought about that conversation now as she walked along Fourteenth Street looking for unique Christmas gifts, which she knew she could find in the Village. Maybe one day Sterling would be able to lay his burden down, as she'd begun to. But she had Miles to help carry the load. Who did Sterling have?

The knocking on the front door stirred Tess out of the light nap she'd decided to take while rocking in her chair. Slowly she pushed herself up and made her way to the door.

The postman was standing on the other side of the screen door with a big brown box at his feet.

"Hope that blessed girl ain't send me mo' thangs fo' this house." She opened the door.

"Mornin', Ms. Tess. Got somethin' fer ya."

"So I see, Melvin."

"Want me to brang it inside? It's pretty heavy."

"Of course. Didn't thank I was gon' carry it, did ya?" She chuckled and held open the door.

"Where you want me to set it?"

"Right there in the front room."

He put down the box and headed out. "Take care now, Ms. Tess, and have a good Christmas."

"You, too, Melvin." She shut the door and ambled over to the box that came up to the middle of her calf.

"What in the world…" she mumbled, looking at the box. She went into the kitchen and came back with a knife to cut away the brown masking tape. When she finally got it open she was sure she was going to find some fancy bedspread or more kitchen towels, or some frilly nightgown.

With her heart pounding, she pulled out stacks and stacks of papers, all handwritten. And a dark sensation of foreboding settled in her belly.

Some of the pages were yellow with age. She looked at them hard, as if by staring at the neat scrawl she could somehow make out the words, but she couldn't. She was about to call Sterling and have him come take a look when she noticed a single sheet of paper with her name at the top.

She looked over the letter, trying to make out something that made sense. Her eyes stopped on one line that had Tyler's name. She looked at the papers in the box again. She'd been to the doctor enough times to know that even if she couldn't read the words these were notes from a doctor or somebody like a doctor, and they had to do with Tyler. The pages dated back more than twenty years, as if someone had been recording Tyler's life.

A cold sweat broke out all over her body. Whatever was in this box couldn't mean good. What was past was done and best left alone. Whoever sent this box wanted it dredged up. She shook her head. Nobody was going to hurt her baby girl again. Not as long as she had a breath left in her.

She got up from her rocker and went back in the kitchen, searched through the junk drawer and found a roll of masking tape and taped the box back up. She ripped the label that had been addressed to her off the box, balled it up and stuck it in the pocket of her housecoat. Then she called Sterling.

She'd get him to put it in the basement, with all the other stuff. If it hadn't been so dry, she would've told him to burn it, but one flying spark could set the whole area on fire. For the time being she'd keep it in the basement.

On Christmas Eve Sterling drove into Savannah, convincing himself that he needed more film and a small gift for Nana Tess, which he picked up in a small gift shop. But deep inside he knew the real reason for the trip.

He edged up to the building where he'd last seen his father, as far as he could go without being noticed. He wasn't sure why he wanted to see him again. What good would it do? He sat there in his car and waited, anyway.

And then there he was—walking slowly down the path, picking up trash with a pointed stick, greeting the tenants as they came in and out of the building, helping some of the women with their Christmas packages. Everyone who passed either shook his hand, gave him a hug, or a peck on the cheek.

The tightness in his chest began to build. He shouldn't have come. This didn't change anything, only made it worse. All the questions still remained unanswered. How could he have done what he did, and leave him and Nat? Wes was all they'd had and he'd ruined it all—his own life and the lives of his sons. How many Christmases had he spent without his father?

All those years he could never get back. Never. The only good thing that had come out of what his father had done was that he had met Tyler.

But now, even that could never be.

Wes began walking down the lane, heading in his direction. He waited a second longer, then pulled off.

Wes leaned on the stick and watched his son drive away.

"Wake up, sleepyhead," Tyler singsonged, holding a mistletoe branch over Miles's head.

His smile came first, and before she knew what happened he grabbed her and pulled her down on the bed. "Merry Christmas, baby," he crooned, locking her in his arms.

"Merry Christmas." She giggled and rolled away.

Miles sat up and kicked the covers away. "Where's my gift?"

She put her hands on her hips. "You *opened* your gift last night. Remember?" she taunted.

He flopped back on the bed. "Aw, yeah, I remember now. You're a very giving person, from what I recall."

She sat on the bed and twirled one of his locks around her finger. "I have been since I met you."

He looked up at her and her expression was soft, vulnerable, not taunting or teasing, but real.

"You mean that, don't you?"

She nodded.

"Hey." He reached up and took her hand, pulling her down on the bed beside him. "Maybe that's the difference I was looking to make all along."

She pressed her head against his chest, the feeling of safety and security wrapping around her as snugly as a down comforter. Miles had made that happen. She'd taken the risk and he hadn't disappointed her. He hadn't walked away.

She almost believed.

With classes back in session after the holiday break, Tyler and Miles resumed their preholiday routine, with him picking her up from work and taking her to school. It seemed that each day they grew closer, found more things to share, laugh about and talk about, and Tyler was slowly taking down the last layers of resistance, beginning to believe that her future would include Miles.

Sitting in class, she thought about how lucky she was, even after everything she'd been through. She was lucky to have friends like Lauren, Wes and, yes, Sterling, a grandmother like Nana Tess and, of course, Miles. Where would they be now if he had given up on her, let her remain in her shell, keeping everyone locked out?

"Oh, Ms. Ellington, would you wait a moment? I want to speak with you," Professor Chase said. She looked around and the class was emptying out. He finished with his last student and Tyler approached his desk.

"I think your script is ready for submission to the screening committee, Ms. Ellington. You've done a re-markable job with it. It's taken some of my students years to get their scripts into this kind of shape."

"I had a lot of help, Professor, and I really appreciate all of your assistance."

He waved her thanks away. "So, I'd like to submit this next week. The committee usually takes several months to make its final selections. Just wanted to warn you that it's not a quick process. We probably won't have the list of finalists until after the spring break." He laughed. "I think they do it intentionally. Gives them a sense of power."

"Thank you, Professor. Thank you." She smiled, her heart racing. She couldn't wait to tell Miles.

"I knew you'd do it, baby!" Miles shouted, snatch-ing her around the waist and swinging her around.

Tyler giggled in delight. "I still can't believe it. My movie. My movie, Miles."

"I know. I felt the same way when they selected mine last year." He set her down on the floor. "It's the waiting that's the killer."

"That's what the professor said."

"I think you should sit in on a few more of my classes with the students, Ty. Learn everything you can. That theory class you're taking is cool, but nothing beats the real thing."

She plopped down on her couch. "I know, but since my job went from temp to permanent they've been working me senseless. I barely have enough energy to keep up with my classes." She looked up at him from beneath her lashes. "Not to mention keeping up with you."

The corner of his mouth curved up in a grin. "Now we can't have that, can we?" He eased up next to her on the couch and nuzzled her neck.

She popped up and was a half-beat ahead of him when he reached out to grab her and missed. "See what I mean."

"How's the short film coming along with your film students, man?" Greg asked as they sat in their usual hangout. It was just the two of them, everyone else having left for the evening.

"It's looking good. A few more weeks should do it. We did some location stuff. Should be ready to start full casting in about a week or so." He took a swallow of beer.

Greg nodded slowly. "Yo, Miles, man. I know things haven't been too cool with us for a while. A lot of things got said."

Miles pursed his lips and listened.

"And I wanna apologize."

"Forget it, man. It's done."

"We been friends for a long time, Miles. And most of the time I haven't held up my end. I always just took our friendship for granted. I guess what I'm tryin' to say is that…I've always been…jealous of what you had. Everything always came so damn easy for you, man. Everything. Then you found Tyler." Greg lowered his head. "I wanted to be happy for you, but I couldn't, so I kept looking for things to go wrong. You didn't deserve that."

"Look, Greg, it's as you said, we've always been friends. Whether you've been a pain in my ass or not.

We're still friends. Nothing's going to change that." He grinned. "Sorry as I am to say it."

Greg laughed and leaned forward on the table. "So, what's happenin' with you and Ms. Ellington?"

Miles was quiet for a moment, letting the question settle over him, seeing Tyler, trying to sum up all she'd come to mean to him. Finally he spoke. "I think I'm in love with her."

Chapter 24

And Then Comes the Rain

On this marginal date: Patient still harbors feelings of guilt, believing self to be the cause of their situation. Continues to feel responsible for things out of their control.

Tyler was at her desk typing a brief for one of the attorneys at work when her phone rang. She rarely got calls except from Miles calling to say he was running late or Tempest reminding her that they were going out of town and to keep an eye on things.

It was too early for Miles to call, and Tempest and Braxton were in Virginia for the week. Probably a wrong extension, she thought.

"Litigation," she said, pressing the red light and talking into her headset while she continued typing.

"Ty—"

Her heart jumped. "Lauren? Lauren, what is it? You sound—"

"Ty, it's Nana Tess." Her voice broke.

"Oh, God, oh, God, Ren, don't tell me something's happened to my Nana, please."

Her hands were shaking so much she could barely hold the phone.

"Ty, Sterling found her a little while ago. Ty... she's—"

"N-o-o! Not Nana." Hot tears rolled down her cheeks and every head in the secretarial pool was turned in her direction as her heart-rending sobs filled the air.

"Tyler, what's wrong?" Janet Hume stood over her desk.

Tyler looked up and all she could see was the flaming-red hair. Panic seized her and the irrational thought took hold that the woman who'd always come to take her away was going to snatch her from her grandmother again.

"Tyler—"

She dropped the phone. "I have to go...back home, to Georgia. I have to be with my Nana...Tess." Tears streamed down her cheeks.

Janet picked up the phone. "Hello? This is Janet Hume, Tyler's supervisor. She's hysterical." She listened for a moment, keeping a close eye on Tyler, who was trembling in her seat. "Yes, I understand. Is there someone we can call? I'll put her in a cab. Yes. Thank you." She hung up the phone. "Tyler," she said gently.

"I'm going to call a cab for you. Is there someone at home?"

Numbly she shook her head. There was no one there. "Miles. Miles will help me. He'll take me to my grandma," she mumbled over her sobs. "I should've gone home for Christmas. I should've gone."

Janet patted her shoulder. "I'll call a cab."

Janet walked her to the front of the building and waited until the cab arrived. "Take as much time as you need, Tyler. And…I'm very sorry about your grandmother."

Tyler looked at her, reality and fantasy blending, then separating. For an instant she saw herself as she was twenty-four years ago—a frightened little girl being told by the woman with the red hair how sorry she was that she couldn't stay with the Wilcox family, that it was for the best and put her in a car to be taken away. Then it was Janet standing there, and the image faded.

Janet handed the driver a twenty-dollar bill and closed the car door. "Please call if you need anything, Tyler."

What could she need? Now.

It seemed an eternity before the cab finally pulled up in front of Miles's loft. On shaky legs she got out and made her way to the door and took the elevator. Everything seemed to be moving in slow motion. She could barely get her body to respond to her commands. All she wanted to do was wrap herself in the protection of Miles's arms and take him with her to Nana Tess's house. She knew she couldn't do it alone.

She walked down the hall and rang his bell and

waited. She was just about to ring the bell again, thinking that maybe he was in the shower, when he opened the door.

As soon as she saw him she ran into his arms and tried to tell him in disjointed sentences what had happened.

"Tyler, Tyler, you're not making sense. Slow down, what happened to Nana Tess?"

"Miles, honey…who's at the door?"

Tyler froze.

He turned.

Tyler looked past him and right into the smiling face of Mari, who stood boldly in the middle of the room with her blouse open down to her waist.

Something inside of her twisted in excruciating pain. She tore herself out of Miles's grasp and ran—down the hall, down the stairs and out into the street.

For a split second he was paralyzed, until he heard the downstairs door slam and the dog on the second floor launch into a round of barking.

Miles took off after her, shouting for her to stop. When he reached the street he looked up and down to see where she'd gone. Then he spotted her just as she got into a cab and sped away.

He turned, ran back upstairs and found Mari sitting on his couch with a satisfied grin on her face.

He stormed across the room and stood barely a breath away from her. It took all he had not to grab her up and throw her out. "Why did you do that? Huh? You know good and damned well nothing's going on with me and you!"

Slowly she rose and straightened her skirt. "Maybe

I was practicing my acting skills. Finding my motivation, as they say." She laughed. "Don't feel so good when the shoe's on the other foot, does it?"

She snatched up her purse and sauntered out.

He watched her walk away and felt as if the life he'd begun to build had walked out with her.

"Driver, I've changed my mind. Please take me straight to the airport." *No point in going home,* she thought. There was no one there to help. And Miles… Her chest tightened.

"Which airport, miss? We got more than one, ya know."

"Whichever's closer. Kennedy."

"Kennedy it is."

The driver peered at her through his rearview mirror. "Are you all right, Miss? Nobody's chasin' you or nothin'?"

She wiped away her tears and simply stared out the window. How would she ever be "all right" again?

Tyler arrived at Kennedy and made her way to the reservation desk, thankful that her years of being frugal had paid off. She had enough money in her savings account to buy whatever she needed while she was away, and plenty on her one credit card to book her flight. Operating on pure instinct, she got a ticket to Savannah on a flight leaving in an hour, then called Lauren and gave her the information. Lauren promised to meet her at the airport.

She sat in the waiting area, her mind a jumble of thoughts, her insides a mass of pain. Guilt overwhelmed her. She should have known. She should never have come to New York. She knew Nana Tess was sick, but she'd come anyway. The one time she could have done something for someone else and she'd chosen herself, her own wants and needs. A new wave of tears began to build. She didn't go home for Christmas, the first Christmas she'd missed since she was eighteen years old and on her own. And for what—to spend it with Miles—the man who professed to care so much about her, the very same man who as soon as he got the opportunity was with the one woman he said he didn't have anything to do with? How long had it been going on? How many others were there? He was home during the day while she worked. He'd been making a fool of her all along.

She pressed her fist to her mouth. It was just as she'd always known—she couldn't trust anyone with her emotions, because when she did they just threw you away. For twenty-four years she'd lived by that motto, and she'd been protected. She didn't want to think about it, and she wouldn't. Just as she'd banished all the others to the recesses of her mind, she'd do the same thing with Miles. She had to.

When she arrived at Savannah International Airport Lauren and Sterling were waiting. Seeing them both brought home the full force of why she was there. Nana Tess was gone. Gone. She'd never be able to run up the raggedy steps and see her opening the door, listen to her fuss about her eating habits and lack of cooking skills, taste her sweet potato pie, or to call just to hear her voice. Never.

Tyler stood there in the center of bodies jostling back and forth and couldn't move. Deep, wracking sobs shook her body, but still she couldn't move.

Sterling was at her side first, pulling her against his chest. Lauren stroked her hair, uttering soft words of comfort, telling her they were there for her, how much they loved Nana Tess, too, and that somehow it would be all right. They'd pull through it together.

Slowly, wrapped in the comfort of each other's embrace, they went to the car and home.

Miles paced the floor, his cordless phone gripped in his hand. He'd been calling Tyler's apartment every five minutes for the last three hours. He'd driven to her apartment twice. No one was there.

Where was she? And what had happened to her grandmother? He knew it was bad. He'd barely understood what she was saying she'd been so upset. Then…Maribelle.

Every time he envisioned those last few minutes a new wave of rage rushed through him.

He had to find her. Explain. Be there for her through whatever it was she was dealing with. But how could he if he didn't know where she was?

He pressed the Redial button and listened to the phone ring and ring. At a loss as to what else to do, he called Greg. Maybe they could ride around and find her.

"What happened, man?" Greg asked as he stepped up into Miles's Jeep, rubbing sleep from his eyes.

"I don't even know, man. Tyler came to my crib and Maribelle was there—"

"Damn," Greg muttered, shaking his head when Miles had finished.

"The thing that really pisses me off is that nothing was happening. Nothing. One minute we were talking about a role for her in that student film. The next thing I know she's standing in my living room with her clothes half off!"

"Damn, man. You really in it this time."

"No shit."

"You think maybe she went back home?"

"Been by her place. Nobody's there."

"Naw. Naw. I mean home. Georgia. That's where she's from, right? If somethin' happened to her people, maybe she just booked."

Miles turned and looked at Greg for a minute, realizing that was the most intelligent thing he'd remembered Greg saying.

"Yeah, yeah," he said slowly, picturing Tyler taking off like that and knowing that if it had anything to do with her grandmother, she'd be there, no matter what. He could kick himself. He should have thought of that hours ago.

"We're going to the airport," he said suddenly, making a U-turn and heading toward Queens.

"And what you gonna do when you get there? If they do give you any information, then what? You know where she lives?"

Miles stopped at the light, then pulled over to the curb. He crossed his arms over the steering wheel and pressed his head against his arms. He didn't have a clue.

Finally, he put the car in gear and headed home.

"You wanna try her house again, man?" Greg asked from Miles's lounge chair.

"Just did," he said, his voice devoid of emotion. He held his watch up to his face and tried to make out the time through bleary eyes. It was four o'clock in the morning and he still didn't have a clue where she was.

If she was in Savannah as Greg suggested, he still had no way of finding her. His only shot at it was getting in touch with Tempest. But she wasn't around, either.

He threw his legs over the side of the couch and sat up, rubbing his eyes with the heels of his hands. He'd never felt like this before, so empty, helpless. There'd always been a way out of whatever situation he'd found himself in. Either fast talking or…fast talking. There wasn't enough fast talking in the world to fix this.

"As soon as the sun comes up I'm going back over there. Maybe Tempest and her husband were just out on the town for the night or something."

Greg pulled himself up from his reclining position and slowly stood, arching his back to stretch out the kinks. "I'ma run home, get a quick shower and maybe a coupla hours sleep. Call me when you're ready. I'll go with you."

Miles looked up and saw both concern and weariness in his friend's eyes. The flicker of a smile touched his mouth. And for the first time in their almost thirty-year relationship, he saw Greg as the friend he'd always wanted, not the hanger-on, not the Miles wannabe. A friend. He'd actually come through.

"Thanks, man."

Greg patted him on the shoulder. "It'll be cool."

Miles nodded slowly and hoped that it could be.

Chapter 25

If Only I Could

> *On this marginal date: Patient reluctantly discussed the series of nightmares that occur after any traumatic experience. Nightmares are vague upon awakening, but patient stated they feel the terror during dream state. Recurrences may trigger memories from subconscious.*

Tyler tossed and turned all night. Her dreams were assaulted by visions of her grandmother calling for her. Tyler tried to get to her, but her feet were weighted down in the thick marshes that surrounded the island. The more she struggled to get to Nana Tess the deeper she sank, until Nana slowly began to fade. Then her mother Cissy took her place, dressed in the red dress she'd had on that last night. Cissy was yelling at her to get up, but she couldn't, and finally Cissy turned, walked in the same direction as Nana Tess and faded away.

She'd jumped up, only to realize it was a dream. Then she'd drifted back into her nightmarish sleep, to repeat the process.

When the sun finally rose, Tyler was lying in the bed staring up at the ceiling, wishing that the past day was just another nightmare. The sinking sensation in the pit of her stomach reminded her it wasn't. She wanted to pray, to ask God to take the pain away, to make everything all right again. But she didn't even know how anymore. Besides, he'd never listened to her pleas before.

Drawing on her last bit of energy she pulled herself out of bed and forced herself to put one foot in front of the other until she made it to the bathroom.

As she stood under the beating shower water the array of things to be taken care of marched before her. She had to make "arrangements." She shut her eyes. *Arrangements.* She didn't even know what to do. How to do it.

She turned off the shower and heard a light tapping on her bedroom door. Wrapping herself in a towel, she went to her door.

Lauren stood there with a tray containing a plate of toast and tea. "You didn't eat anything last night," she said softly. "You need something." She stepped into the room and placed the tray on the night table, then turned to face her friend. "I know you didn't sleep. I heard you off and on all night."

Slowly Lauren crossed the room to where Tyler still

stood by the door. She caressed her cheek. "I don't want you to worry about taking care of anything. Sterling and I will do it. If you need to call your job and let them know what's happening, I can do it for you. Just tell me what you want."

"I want her back, Ren," she said, her voice breaking. "I just want her back."

"I know, babe." She gathered her in her arms. "But you know that's not possible. And Nana Tess wouldn't want you falling apart. She had a good life, Ty. You know that. She lived it the way she wanted. She was happy and she made everyone who knew her happy. She'd want you to be happy, Ty, and move on with your life."

"But I don't have anybody now, Ren. Nobody."

"You always have me. No matter what."

"I know," she whispered, looking into Lauren's green eyes, and hugged her tighter.

"You want me to call Miles? Does he know what happened?"

She pulled away and straightened. "No." She turned her back to Lauren. "And I don't want you to mention his name to me. Ever."

Lauren frowned. The last thing Tyler needed to add to her woes was Miles screwing up. From her tone, he obviously had. "You want to talk about it?"

She shook her head. "Not now. Maybe some other time. Maybe never."

"Whatever you want." She walked toward the door. "Well, Sterling's downstairs. We're gonna make some calls. I'll get in touch with your job, too. Try to get some rest in the meantime."

Tyler hugged her arms around her waist. "Sure." She

started toward her bed, then stopped. "Sterling was here all night?" she asked, the fact that he was there so early in the morning finally sinking in.

"Yep, all night," she said softly and closed the door behind her.

"Yeah, something happened with her and that guy Miles in New York, on top of everything else," Lauren said, as she thumbed through the phone book. "That's all she needs," she fumed.

Sterling was quiet for a moment, taking in the information. "She tell you what happened?"

"No. Didn't want to talk about it." She began dialing.

"I'm sure it'll work out, whatever it is." Deep inside, he hoped it wouldn't. His thoughts drifted. He heard Lauren talking in the background but wasn't concentrating on what she was saying on the phone.

With Tyler here, even under these circumstances, maybe he'd really have a chance. He'd show her the kind of friend he really was, the man she needed. He'd be there to comfort her. Things would work out this time.

Miles had been parked in front of Tyler's building for hours and he was determined to sit right there until somebody showed up. He decided not to call Greg, figured he'd let him get some sleep, but thinking about it now he wished he had. At least they could have taken turns watching the door. He'd drift to sleep periodically and then jump up, thinking he might have missed someone coming in. He'd lost count of the number of times he'd snapped his neck.

He was a mess, physically, mentally and emotionally, and he couldn't begin to imagine what Tyler was going through, what she was thinking. He leaned back against the headrest and shut his eyes. Maybe if he got just a few minutes sleep, he'd be able to think clearer, figure something out. What, he didn't know.

When he opened his eyes again he was stunned to see it was getting dark. He jerked up and looked at the house. No lights.

Could he have missed them?

He shook his head to clear it. This was crazy. Before long somebody was going to report him as a stalker or something. He opened the glove compartment and found an old envelope. Pulling out a pen he jotted down a short note to Tempest asking her to call him the moment she got in. It was an emergency and it had to do with Tyler, the note read.

On stiff legs he hauled himself out of the Jeep, painfully went up the steps and stuck the note in the door frame. He stood there a moment, not knowing what else to do, then returned to his ride and pulled off.

He sat by the phone, willing it to ring. Every now and then he picked it up just to be sure it was working. He didn't go out, couldn't remember the last time he ate. He'd missed classes and had to reschedule his students. Greg came by after work. They sat and waited. Nothing. For almost two days after Tyler took off, not a word.

He was about to go out of his mind when the phone finally rang in his hand.

He pressed the Talk button. "Hello, Ty?"

"No, this is Tempest. Miles? I just got your message. What's going on?"

As quickly as he could he told her what had happened, leaving out the part about Maribelle. The last thing he needed was for the "sisterhood" philosophy to kick in. Then Tempest, in her attempt to "protect" Tyler from "this man," wouldn't give him the information he needed. If he'd learned nothing else about women, he learned that. They stuck together.

"I have no idea where her grandmother lives, somewhere on the Gullah Islands, the Sea Islands, off the Georgia coast," Tempest said. "But a friend of ours, Sterling Grey, lives there, as well, somewhere close to her grandmother. Tyler said he was looking out for her grandmother while she was in New York. Maybe he could tell you something."

Sterling. "Do you have his number, an address?"

"Hold on a minute."

He heard her put the phone down and his pulse pounded in his temples. He wasn't sure if it was from anxiety or exhaustion. Finally she came back and gave him the phone number and address.

"Thanks, Tempest. I really appreciate this."

"When you do get in touch with her, please tell her if there's anything she needs, just let us know."

"I will."

The instant he hung up he punched the numbers into the phone. His heart was racing. The idea that he'd have to ask Sterling for help in finding his woman would be comical if it weren't so godawful.

The phone rang and rang, then the answering machine came on. He left a message asking that Sterling have Tyler get in touch with him as soon as possible.

The call never came.

* * *

Sterling came back to his house later in the evening to change clothes and shower. He and Lauren had made funeral arrangements for the following day. The home would take care of everything, and Lauren and Tyler were on their way over there to take clothes and the small Bible that Nana Tess always kept with her.

The neighbors on the island had already begun to drop by, bringing food, offering condolences and support. It seemed to help Tyler somewhat, he thought. She'd said it eased the pain to know that so many people loved Nana Tess, that she had made an impact on their lives.

He climbed the stairs and walked into his bedroom and began stripping out of his clothes. When he saw the light on the answering machine flashing he crossed the room and depressed the Play button.

The last voice he expected to hear filled his room.

"This is Miles Bennett. I need to get in touch with Tyler. If she's down there, please have her call me. Thanks."

Sterling replayed the message, wondering how Miles had gotten his number. The only conclusion was from Tempest or Braxton.

So, he was really looking for her. He stared at the phone, debating the right and wrong of what he thought about doing.

He erased the message and unplugged his phone. He wouldn't give Miles Bennett the opportunity to hurt Tyler again.

"Still no word?" Greg asked as he walked through Miles's door.

Miles rubbed his hand across his face. "Naw. I finally

caught up with Tempest and got a number for that guy Sterling who's supposed to live near Tyler's grandmother. Left a message. Haven't heard anything yet. That was this afternoon."

Greg sat down in his favorite lounge hair and stretched out his legs. He stared at Miles and couldn't remember ever seeing him like this. Not when he walked away from his six-figure job, not when he'd borrowed money from him and didn't pay him back, and especially not over a woman. Miles had never cared enough. About anything. It was all on the surface. But that was just the way Miles was. This Tyler was different, though, and Miles had been a different man since the day he met her.

He wondered what it would be like to feel that strongly about someone. So strong that he'd lose sleep, act crazy, drive around for hours. As much as he'd always wanted to be like Miles, now wasn't one of those times.

Suddenly Miles sat up from his spot on the couch. "I'm going to Georgia." He walked across the room and picked up the phone.

"What?"

"Get on a plane and go. Find her. Make it right."

"You don't even know where you're going, man."

"I have an address. Sterling's. I'll figure out the rest when I get there."

Greg stared at him while Miles tried to make flight reservations. He shook his head in wonder. Yeah, his boy had it bad.

Chapter 26

A Long Road Home

The old church that sat in a grove of trees near the edge of the island was filled with island inhabitants, along with an unimaginable amount of beautiful flowers in a riot of colors. Soft piano music played in the background, and whispered voices wafted around her.

Tyler sat stoically in the first aisle, braced on each side by Sterling and Lauren. As she listened to the pastor recite the details of Nana's wonderful life and evoke words of comfort to those who remained behind and reminded them to remain steadfast in their faith, a sense of peace suddenly filled her, as if her soul was being filled after a long drought.

Faith was something she'd never had, but Nana Tess

did. She believed that everything would work out in its own way and time. She believed that God would provide and He always had—maybe not in the way that she would have wanted, but he did.

Even though she'd lived all her life without a real family, a sense of belonging, she'd always wished for something more, and her Nana always encouraged her. In her own way she did have faith. She'd had for an instant faith enough in her abilities to send off her essay. She had faith enough to survive the trauma of her childhood. She'd taken a leap of faith with Miles, and though it hadn't worked out she had gained so much. She'd learned that she was capable of giving, of loving. She looked at Sterling and then at Lauren. They were staring straight ahead.

She bowed her head and whispered her thanks, and knew she had enough faith in herself to move on—just as Nana Tess would have wanted her to do.

Miles had tried every airline under the sun to get a seat on anything flying, but couldn't. The first flight available had been for the next morning, and then it was delayed. By the time he arrived in Savannah and rented a car it was nearly five o'clock in the afternoon.

He got a map from the rental agency and started the ninety-minute drive out to the Sea Islands, hoping that when he found her he'd have the words he needed to say.

The well-wishers were long gone. The house was quiet now. Different. But Nana Tess's presence was still in the rooms, so powerful sometimes Tyler thought that at any moment she would come down the stairs, or call her from the kitchen and tell her to come and eat.

She leaned back against the worn couch and felt the springs poke her in the back. Instead of wanting to insist on getting a new couch, she simply smiled. It was just the way Nana Tess liked it. For a moment she closed her eyes, letting the waning rays of the setting sun that streamed in from the wide front window warm her weary back.

Sterling walked in from the kitchen with a cup of tea, a gentle smile on his face. He'd been a good friend, better than good. He'd looked after her grandmother, stuck by her through this ordeal and never hesitated to ask if there was anything she needed, anything he could do. If she'd learned nothing else in the past few months, she'd finally learned what true friendship was all about, and the joy she'd kept herself from experiencing because she'd been afraid of attachment.

She smiled up at him as he sat down next to her.

"Here. It's chamomile. Supposed to be relaxing." He handed her the cup.

"The way I feel right now, Sterling, if I were any more relaxed I'd be in a coma."

"That's just exhaustion talking."

"Yeah, you're probably right." She took a sip of the steaming tea, then set it down on the scarred cherry wood table.

"Sterling, I can't thank you enough—for everything. You've been—"

"I did it because I wanted to, Tyler. And because I knew it would make things easier on you." His eyes held hers.

"But why would it matter to you? You didn't even know me."

"I...I felt as if I did, from Nana Tess," he added. "And then when I finally met you, well—" He blew out a breath. "Something happened when I met you, Tyler. I wanted to know you better, maybe find a way to make something happen between us. And don't get me wrong, I didn't do what I did for your grandmother, or be here with you through this, because I'm looking for something in return. I know you have someone in New York—"

"That's over," she cut in.

"Oh. I didn't know."

She laughed, but it was a hollow sound. "Neither did I. I guess I thought I had more than I really did."

"I'm sorry."

She swallowed and bit her lip to keep from crying again.

Sterling saw her struggle and pulled her into his arms, stroking her hair. "It'll be all right, whatever it is," he whispered. He felt her shudder in his arms and held her tighter.

Miles eased the rental car down the dirt road and around winding paths, looking for the address Tempest had given him. The houses were few and far between, most of them run-down. Old men sat on porches. Women hung clothes from lines in the front yard. Children ran wild and free. Everywhere he looked, lush green abounded, and tiny creeks ran up and down the landscape. Birds the likes of which he'd never seen cawed and flew overhead.

He felt as if he had been thrown back in time, a simpler time, and he could see how easily one could become drawn into this life and not want to leave its serenity. He understood now why Tyler said coming here always had a way of rejuvenating her, and that her happiest memories had been on these shores.

He drove on past an old yellow house and knew he was close. If there was any sense to these addresses, Sterling's house should be somewhere up the lane.

Moments later he pulled to a stop in front of Sterling's door. He got out of the car and jogged toward the house, which seemed to be in the best shape of any he'd seen so far. Stopping on the porch, he took a moment to pull himself together. He looked for a bell, didn't see one and knocked on the door.

He waited. Knocked again. He went around the side and tried to look in the window. Nothing inside moved.

What to do now? Maybe Sterling wasn't even in town. He thought he remembered Tyler saying something about him being a photographer. Slowly he stepped down off the porch and stood on the road, trying to figure out the best thing to do.

As he looked around his gaze landed on a house he'd passed on his way there. Something struck him. It was from Tyler's script—the faded yellow house, with the sagging porch and the roof that looked as if it carried the burden of the sun for far too long.

His heart pounded. That had to be it. It was close to Sterling's, as Tempest had said.

He started walking, hesitant at first, then with more determination as he drew closer. This was the house. He felt it in his gut. He ran the last few feet, knowing that Tyler was there and that he could make things right between them. She had to listen.

He approached the porch and was just about to step

up when he saw Tyler and Sterling on the couch through the window. She was in his arms, her head resting on his shoulder.

And then Sterling looked up and met his eyes, recognition lighting his gaze. Sterling bent his head and kissed Tyler gently on the brow and she stroked his cheek in return.

Miles felt as if the bottom had just dropped out of his stomach. He wanted to run in there and snatch her away from him, tell her how sorry he was, that they could work it out.

He didn't. He couldn't put himself in that position, be told to leave, that she was with who she wanted to be with and that he deserved feeling the way he did.

And maybe he did. He was finally getting back all that he'd done to all the women in his life, and from the first woman he'd allowed himself to care about.

When Sterling looked up again, Miles was gone. Guilt slapped him. But slowly the sting subsided.

She'd finally gotten some sleep. *Maybe that tea really did help,* she thought, stretching her aching limbs in the creaking bed. She lay there for a moment looking out at the sun hanging over the trees, and wished she could just lie there forever, just stay there wrapped up in memories. She knew she couldn't and Nana Tess wouldn't have wanted her to. Matter of fact, if Nana were there right now she'd be fussing about her still being in the bed.

She had a job to get back to, a semester in school to finish. But she couldn't leave until she knew everything was taken care of—the hard part—going through Nana's things and seeing what she wanted to keep and what could be given away. And then she had to decide what to do about the house. She took a long breath. There was no holding back the inevitable.

When she came downstairs Sterling was in the kitchen fixing breakfast.

He turned when she stepped into the room. "Morning. Thought you might be hungry. There're biscuits on the table and a few slices of ham. I'm just finishing up the eggs."

She smiled. "Sterling, you're too much. I don't even know if I can eat all this."

"Eat what you can." He turned off the stove, brought the frying pan to the table and spooned the eggs into a bowl.

Tyler took a bit of everything, sure she wouldn't be able to eat a thing until she put the first spoonful of eggs in her mouth and realized how hungry she was.

Sterling joined her at the table and filled his plate.

"Where'd you learn how to cook?" she asked, taking a sip of orange juice.

"Been taking care of myself for a long time. It was either that or spend what little money I had on takeout." He grinned and pointed his fork toward her plate. "Thought you weren't hungry," he teased.

"So did I," she said, lifting a second slice of ham and adding it to her plate.

He watched her thoughtfully as he sipped his coffee. How he'd love to wake up every morning with her, see her smile, take care of her.

"What?" she said, catching his stare.

"Nothing. Just thinking. What do you want to do

today? I have some time if you need help with anything.
I know Lauren had to go back to work."

She sighed. "I need to go through Nana Tess's things.
The first place to tackle is the basement. I don't think
I'm ready to go through her clothes yet."

He nodded. "Well, I can help with that. I know she
keeps everything down there." He shook his head. "Just
had me take a big box down there a couple of weeks
ago. When I went down there it looked as if she'd kept
everything her entire life."

"I know. Just thinking about it is tiring."

"Then we'll do it together. No problem."

She smiled. "Yeah. I'd like that."

Tyler hadn't been in the basement in years. She'd
known Nana Tess put everything she didn't use down
there, but she had no idea of the volume of things that
had accumulated over the years. There were boxes
everywhere.

She stood in the center of the floor with her hands
on her hips, not knowing what to do first, and had a
sudden wave of melancholia. Nana's whole history was
down here in these boxes. She wasn't sure if she had
the strength to travel back through her life.

Sterling walked up next to her and put his arm around
her shoulder. She looked up at him and her eyes filled.
He pressed her close.

"Together. Remember?"

She sniffed. "Okay."

"Let's start on that side."

They went to the far side of the room and began
going through the boxes one by one.

After more than two hours they had accumulated a huge pile of everything from forgotten tree ornaments to old clothes, most of which could definitely be thrown away.

"I'm gonna go up and get us something to drink," Sterling said, pulling himself up from his sitting position on the floor.

"Thanks." She went to the next box, which looked even older than some of the others. It had been buried under a pile of old furniture and bags of clothes.

She pulled the box toward her in the empty space she'd carved out for herself and pulled the top open.

At first she thought it was just another box of junk as she began pulling out old papers. Then a small photograph floated to the floor, torn and yellow around the edges with age. She picked it up and her heart lurched in her chest.

It was a picture of her mother—the first one she'd ever seen, but she knew it was Cissy. All she'd ever had all these years was her vague memory. She stared at the photograph in amazement. Cissy was young and beautiful, posing with a man who looked much older. She peered closer, trying to get a better look in the dimly lit room. His face looked familiar, somehow, but she couldn't place it. Maybe he was someone she'd seen when she was a little girl. She stared at her mother. She looked so happy, as if everything in the world were wonderful. Why hadn't Nana Tess shared these things with her? All this time she'd thought everything that was Cissy Ellington was gone. It had been buried right here in Nana's basement.

For a moment she held the picture to her breast, then

went back into the box. She fought back tears as item after item chronicled her mother's life. It was filled with things that were Cissy's: her diploma from high school, a grade school yearbook, old report cards, childhood crayon drawings, stuffed animals.

She pulled out the red dress, and her heart almost stood still. A pounding began in her head as that night came rushing back. The sights, the smells, the yelling...

She had been terrified as she curled up in her bed. She could still feel the terror now, remember how her mother was screaming at a man.

She couldn't hear what he was saying. He was talking too softly. Then she heard glass crashing against the wall, and her mother came storming into her room, in that red dress. Her mother was coming at her, and she was so scared and then a big shadow was in the doorway....

"Sorry I took so long," Sterling said, then stopped when he spotted her curled in the corner. "Tyler, what's wrong?" He put the glasses down on the top of a box and sat down beside her.

She was rocking back and forth, holding on to the red dress, tears streaming down her eyes.

"Tyler, please. Tell me what's wrong." He put his arm around her shoulder.

"I...she was going to hurt me, Sterling. She was going to hurt me again."

"Who?"

"My mother. Oh, God. My mother." She covered her face with her hands. "She always hurt me when she got drunk. Always. But I never told. Never. I though if I was good, cleaned the house, didn't make a mess and stayed really quiet, she wouldn't hurt me." Sobs shook her body as she rocked back and forth. "She was drunk that night, too."

"What night? Tyler, you're not making sense."

"The night she died!"

"Come on, let me take you upstairs." He tried to pull her to her feet.

"He didn't do it, Sterling." Her eyes raced around the room as if searching for something. "It was an accident. He…he was trying to keep her from hurting me."

"Who?"

Frantically she began tossing aside objects from the box that she'd dumped on the floor until she found the picture. "It's him. He didn't do it." She held the picture out to him with shaky hands.

Sterling stared down at the photograph and felt the air rush from his lungs.

"No," he said in a hoarse whisper. "Can't be. It can't." He shook his head. "Can't." He sat back on his legs and stared at the picture.

Tyler swiped her hand across her face and tried to make sense of what Sterling was saying. "It is him. I know it," she said, gulping in air.

He turned to her, his face contorted in pain. "That man in the picture—he's my father. Wesley Grey."

"What?" Nothing was making sense. How could this man be Sterling's father? He'd gone to jail because the law believed he'd killed her mother, and so had she. Had Sterling always known? Then the name filtered through her jumbled thoughts. Wesley Grey? Wes?

She snatched the picture from his fingers and stared down at the keen features, the wide eyes and engaging smile, the smooth, chocolate-brown complexion. It *was*—Wes—almost thirty years younger, but it was Wes—the caretaker of her building, the one who'd treated her like a daughter. The man she'd helped send to jail because of her silence.

Suddenly a wave of nausea overtook her. She jumped up and ran up the stairs.

When she came back from the bathroom even more shaken than when she'd gone in, Sterling was seated at the kitchen table, the box at his feet. He was holding a small leather-bound book in his hands, tears were rolling down his face.

"I didn't know," he choked. "I blamed him all these years. Hated him all these years. He was in love with her."

"With my mother?" she asked, desperation in her voice. She came and sat across from him, putting her hand on his. "Tell me what you know, Sterling, please."

He hesitated, trying to find a place to start. "My father was a business manager for nightclub singers," he began. "My brother Nat and I lived with him after our mother died...."

Sterling talked in slow, halting tones, sometimes racing forward, then retracing his thoughts. Wes had been Cissy's business manager according to what Cissy had written in the diary that Sterling held in his hand. She knew he was in love with her, but felt he was too old. He treated her well, put up with her drinking and her rages, and looked out for her daughter when he could.

"When my father was convicted of killing your mother, Nat and I got split up and sent to foster homes. Nobody wanted to take on two young black boys." He waited, looking at her.

The stirring began in her stomach when she looked back into his eyes. Slowly she shook her head. "It can't be you."

"Yes, it's me, Tyler, the little boy who lived in the Wilcox house. Who walked you to school, helped you with your homework, sat up with you at night when you cried for your mama."

"But...you...your name—"

"Sterling's my middle name. As soon as I was old enough I made it my legal first name. I wanted to put that whole life behind me. Wanted to forget. And I did. At least most of the time."

She covered her face, trying to put the pieces together. The two of them had spent almost all their lives in denial of the truth, denial of who they were. She hadn't wanted to remember the abuse from her mother, the drinking. So she'd erased it, and turned her mother into a fairy princess who could do no wrong. And for that an innocent man had gone to jail. How could she ever forgive herself?

And Sterling, too, had created his own world—a world where his past didn't exist, where who he was and who his father was didn't exist because it was easier that way to deal with the pain. Both of them did.

"We have to go and see your father. You need to. I have to," she said, pushing up from the table. "I know where we can find him."

Slowly Sterling stood. "So do I."

Chapter 27

More Than You'll Ever Know

By the time Tyler and Sterling arrived in Savannah and drove to her old building, the sun was beginning to set. They'd talked during the long drive, really talked— about their childhoods, their losses and the ways each of them had handled their pain.

She listened to Sterling talk about his father, the man he'd believed he hated all those years. He had just been a young boy who felt abandoned and needed the love of his father. He had to find someone to blame. So he blamed Wes.

And she, so afraid of rejection because of who she was, had built a world of fantasy where all the ugliness of her past didn't exist.

They'd all suffered.

Sterling pulled to a stop at the end of the drive. Tyler looked at him and took his hand. "We can do this," she said, drawing on a strength she didn't know she had.

They got out of the car and walked into the lobby, Sterling entering a step behind Tyler.

And there he was, wiping down the chrome finish of the glass doors with an old white rag, humming an offbeat song.

He turned at the sound of footsteps, and the first person he saw was Tyler. His weatherbeaten face broke into a sunshine smile. "Ms. E. Welcome home!" He started to approach, then stopped when Sterling came into view.

He looked from one to the other, not sure of what to say, what to do. He breathed in short, stilted breaths, "Matt? Matthew?"

Sterling answered to the name he hadn't responded to in nearly two decades. "Yeah, Dad, it's me."

Wes's body began to shudder as he fought to control the sobs that overtook him.

Hesitantly, Sterling approached, his heart aching as he looked at the stooped body of his father. Then all at once he took him in his arms, holding him, trying to push back all the years they'd missed, all the time they'd lost as father and son.

"Dad…please forgive me."

The three of them sat around the small circular table in the room that Wes used as his apartment, and talked late into the night.

What had happened to Cissy was an accident, he'd

said. "I was tryin' to get her away from ya, Tyler. Didn't wanna see her hurt you no more. I...grabbed her, too hard, and pushed her away. But she was so drunk she lost her balance and slammed her head against the edge of the dresser." He shook his head as the old sadness settled over him. "I wouldn'ta hurt Cissy for nothin' in this world. I loved her. Tried to get her to do right. You got ta believe that."

"I do. I do, Wes. I know it wasn't your fault."

"When you came here that afternoon, lookin' for a place to stay, I knew I was being given another chance. A way to make it up to Cissy, through you."

"And you always looked out for me, just like...you tried to do that night."

He nodded, then turned to his son. "I can't blame you, son, for givin' up on me. Not wantin' ta have nothin' ta do with me. But I kep the faith. Knew one day I'd have a chance to make it up ta ya." He pushed himself up from the rickety stool, walked over to the small dresser and opened the drawer. He fumbled through a stack of papers until he found what he was looking for.

He sat back down. "Here." He handed Sterling the papers. "This is for you and your brother."

Sterling unfolded the documents and read that he would inherit Midwood Manor.

He looked at Wes. "I—don't understand."

"I invested in some small-time stocks when you boys were toddlers. Forgot all about 'em. When I got out, they'd amounted to a lotta money. I used it to restore this building." He smiled. "I own it."

* * *

Sterling drove Tyler back to her grandmother's house after promising his father he'd come back the next day and spend some time with him.

They stood in front of Nana Tess's door.

"When Nana Tess died, I tried to understand why," Tyler said as she looked up to the cloudless sky. She turned to Sterling. "Now I know. Though it's still hard, I know it wasn't for nothing. If she hadn't, who knows when, or if, we would have ever found out the truth. It might have been too late to make amends to Wes…to your father. We might have never found a way to share the truth about ourselves with each other."

"There's something I need to tell you," Sterling said. "All these years, I believed that I was in love with you. I was really in love with the *memory* of you, the memory of how good you used to make me feel when we lived in the Wilcox house. I carried that with me all these years. And when I saw you again, I wanted to make what I'd been dreaming of a reality. But that can never happen. I tried." He swallowed and looked away. "Miles called for you. He tracked you down and called my house. I erased the message. He came the afternoon after the funeral. I saw him outside your grandmother's window when we were sitting on the couch."

She took a step back. "Miles was here—?"

He nodded. "I'm sorry, Tyler."

He came for me. He came. She looked at Sterling and wondered how he could do such a thing. But right then it didn't matter. If she'd seen Miles at the time or spoken to him when he'd called, she wouldn't have been ready to hear what he had to say. She knew that now.

Her thoughts rushed to the last time she'd seen him and Mari. And she looked at her life, Sterling's, Wes's, and knew without a doubt that nothing was as it seemed.

Miles went through his days more by habit than anything else. He could barely focus on his work. He wouldn't talk to anyone. The only thing that saved him from making a fool of himself in front of his students was that school was on spring break. He'd even broken down and gone to Tyler's job, thinking that maybe she had come back. She hadn't.

It had been more than a week and he still hadn't heard anything from her. Not that he expected to. She was probably too wrapped up with Sterling.

Every time he thought about it he wanted to hit something, someone. But he didn't have anyone to blame but himself for Tyler finding her way to Sterling. He was so used to things just going his way that he'd never thought for a minute that it wouldn't. He should have known better than to have Mari up in his apartment. He'd been stupid, too sure of himself, and now he was paying for it.

He pushed away from his computer, unable to concentrate, and turned it off just as the phone rang. Reluctantly he crossed the room and picked it up.

"Yeah."

"Miles. It's Tyler. I'm coming home in a few days and I was hoping you could meet me at the airport."

His heart started to race. "Ty, baby. Are you all right?"

"I am now. It's been really hard, but I'm all right."

Her voice broke. "My Nana's gone, Miles. But I'm going to be all right."

"Ty, I'm sorry. I—just say the word, baby, and I'll fly down there."

"No. I need to do the rest of this by myself. Try to understand."

"Whatever you want, as long as you're coming home."

"I'll call you to give you the flight information. I have to check with a Realtor and put...Nana's house up for sale, tie up some loose ends and I'll be back."

"I'll be waiting for you. And Ty—it wasn't what you thought."

She was silent for a moment. "I believe you."

A wave of relief swept through him like a tide. "And Ty—"

"Yes?"

"I love you."

"I know."

Tyler stood in front of her grandmother's house, the For Sale sign stuck in the red earth, seeing all her days there—the nights spent in the creaky old bed, Nana Tess rocking in her chair, gathering eggs for breakfast, on her hands and knees scrubbing her floors until they gleamed, passing on a wise word of advice, and most of all hanging up the phone and shutting the door without saying goodbye—until that last day. She smiled, letting the memories settle over her, burrowing their way down, ready to bloom when she needed them.

Lauren walked up behind her and put a hand on her shoulder. "Ready, hon?"

Tyler turned, her eyes shimmering. She pressed her lips together and nodded.

Arm in arm they walked toward the car where Sterling was waiting.

Tyler walked up to him and wrapped her arms around his waist, pressing her head against his chest. He held her close, inhaling the clean scent of her hair, feeling it tickle his nose just like it had when they were kids. "Don't forget our deal," he whispered.

She arched her neck and looked up at him, frowning. "What deal?"

He grinned. "You know the one when you cast me as the dashing leading man in your major motion picture."

Tyler laughed. "Oh, that deal."

They hugged one last time before she got in the car. "You take care of Wes."

"I will. He'll be sick of seeing me soon."

"Make sure you come and see me when you come to New York."

He looked at Lauren, who grinned as if she had a big secret. "Maybe Lauren and I will make the trip together."

Tyler eyed her friend, who gave her a wide-eyed innocent stare. Tyler shook her head. *Sterling and Lauren. Don't that beat all?*

"I'll keep on top of the real estate agent and let you know what's going on. You sure you don't want to hold on to the house?"

She sighed. "I've thought about nothing else for the

past few days. I wish I could. But I can't afford to keep up with the taxes and all the repairs that need to be done."

"You're probably right. I still can't believe everything that happened with Sterling, and his father, your mom."

"I know. I'm still trying to digest it all. But it helps knowing that my mother had someone to love her."

"Yeah," she said, thoughtful. "So, you want me to send those boxes to your address in New York?"

"Yeah. I didn't get a chance to go through that last box. And I want the one with my mother's things."

"You should get them next week."

"Thanks again. Seems like that's all I've been saying lately."

"Hey, we Good Samaritans love the applause," she said, patting her chest. She laughed. "They're calling your flight."

She hugged Lauren. "Take care of Sterling," she whispered in her ear.

"Oh, I intend to."

Miles paced the waiting area of the airport, checking his watch every few minutes as if the act could somehow speed up her flight. He checked the board again and her flight number lit up.

She'd arrived.

He peered over heads, trying to see if he could spot her. The departing passengers poured through the gate and she wasn't among them. He checked the board again. That was the flight number she'd given him. Where was she? What if she'd changed he mind?

"Miles."

He turned toward the sound of her voice and something inside of him shifted, then settled. He brushed past the bodies that blocked his way and captured her in his arms, spinning her around.

She pressed her face against his neck, savoring his familiar scent, feeling his heart pound against her chest. She arched her neck and looked into his eyes. "I have so much to share with you."

"I've been waiting a long time to hear you say that."

Lying next to Miles on his bed, Tyler told him everything that had happened since her grandmother's death, from finding the box with her mother's belongings and having to sell Nana Tess's house to finally making her peace with Wes, and he with his son.

"I spent so many years feeling like a victim, being afraid," she said, as she twirled one of his locks around her finger and he stroked her back. "I wasted so much time, Miles."

"I don't think there's anyone who can go through life and not want to do things differently, Ty. These past few weeks we both came to some heavy realizations about who we are and the people around us. It wasn't easy. But necessary."

"I know." She sighed.

"You've been saying that a lot lately," he teased, pulling her beneath him.

"Maybe I'm finally getting wiser."

He kissed her long and slow. "We can only hope."

She pinched his behind.

Chapter 28

Pieces of Dreams

After two days of doing nothing but making love and talking long into the night, Tyler insisted that Miles drive her home.

"I do have a life outside of this bedroom, you know," she said, slipping into a pair of jeans.

"But it can't be half as much fun." He gave her a wicked leer.

"Says you," she tossed back.

He fell across the bed and clasped his hand to his heart. "You wound me," he moaned.

She laughed. "Don't give up your day job."

"I don't have a day job, remember?" He laughed and wasn't quick enough to dodge the pillow that came his way.

They both finally got dressed and headed out.

"You want me to pick you up in the morning and take you to work?" he asked as he pulled to a stop in front of her building.

"That would be great. I don't think I'm up to the trains just yet."

"I'll be here at seven. You be ready."

She leaned over and kissed him. "I will." She opened the door and got out.

"See you tomorrow."

She waved and ran up the steps and inside. No sooner had she closed the door behind her than Tempest poked her head out.

"Tyler. Are you all right? We were so worried."

"Yes. I'm fine. Well, almost fine. But I'll be okay."

"Two boxes were delivered this morning. From Savannah. Braxton took them upstairs and put them in front of your door."

"Thanks."

"Need anything?" she asked gently.

"No. Just some sleep."

Tempest leaned against her door frame. "Miles was really worried about you." Her eyebrow arched.

"I know." She smiled. "Good night."

"'Night."

She ran up the stairs, opened her door and pulled the boxes inside, thankful that Braxton had brought them upstairs. The box she hadn't opened felt as if it weighed a ton. She picked up the box with her mother's things in it and put it in her bedroom closet, then came back out into the foyer and pushed the bigger box into the living room. She'd get to it later, she decided. What she wanted to do right then was take a long soak in a steamy hot tub.

Fluffed dry and oiled down, she slipped into a cotton gown and searched her closet for something to wear to work, then got her notes together for class, which resumed the next evening.

She padded across the cool wood floors and into the kitchen. After fixing a cup of tea she was determined to get some sleep, but when she walked back through the living room, she glimpsed the box. She knew if she started going through it, she'd be up for hours, but...

Taking a seat on the couch, she pulled the box toward her and began ripping off the masking tape that held it shut.

She opened the flaps and was greeted with nothing more than stacks of papers. She blew out a breath of annoyance, but then something caught her eye.

On this marginal date worker was assigned to place four-year-old black female who has become displaced due to death of mother. According to police reports, said female was present at the time of mother's death but appears not to remember what happened. Search for nearest relative will begin immediately.

"What...is this?" She began rifling through the papers and page after page chronicled the life of a young girl who traveled through the foster care system, analyses of her behavior and the medical reasons for it, backgrounds on the families she was sent to. And the reason why she was removed from the Wilcox family even though—she now discovered—they'd wanted to adopt her.

On this marginal date it has come to this worker's attention that client has been inadvertently placed in the same foster home with the son of the man accused of killing her mother. Should client become aware of this, additional trauma may ensue. Recommendations for immediate removal has been made.

Her heart was pounding. Everything, every word written for more than ten years, was about her. How had her grandmother gotten these?

She read on, and all the memories kept rushing back with vivid clarity; the schools, the doctors, the families, all with explanations attached. She read the evaluations from the doctors who clinically described her symptoms of withdrawal as normal for the type of trauma she'd experienced. Every step was documented, as if she were a case study. As awful as that realization was it helped her to understand that what she'd felt, what she'd harbored in her heart for so many years, was truly a result of what she'd been through—not because people weren't trustworthy, caring, worthy of her affection. They were all part of a system without a heart, and they had to find a way to function within it as best they could.

Hours later she finished the last page, which merely stated that she was now at the age of majority and free to live on her own without state supervision. *Without supervision.*

Slowly she began to return the papers to the box. Then she saw a folded piece of paper stuck on the side of the box. She unfolded it.

Dear Ms. Ellington,

I was the social worker for your granddaughter Tyler for fourteen years. During that time I tried to do what I could to get her into the best homes once you were no longer able to take care of her. But even the best efforts are often not enough, and the children suffer. Unfortunately we are bound by a system that functions by rules, not emotion, and "in the best interests of the child" gets lost in the bureaucracy of it all.

I am sending this package in the hope that you will give it to Tyler. I don't know what has become of her, as I lost track of her years ago. I hope that if she does read my notes it will help her to understand herself, come to grips with her life, and help her to realize that I did the best I could. I know I'm not much longer in this world, and I know I have to do this one thing before I go.

Sometimes at night I still see her face staring up at me, begging me not to take her to another home. And my heart aches for her, and the countless children like her. Maybe she can take what I have given you and find a way to make a difference. So that what happened to her won't happen to other children.

For me, it was more than just a job. Please give my regards to Tyler and tell her I think of her often.

Regards,

Lydia Sinclair, CSW

Tyler held the letter to her chest. "Thank you, Ms Lydia. Thank you."

On the ride to work Tyler told Miles about the notes and showed him the letter.

"Wow," he said after reading the letter. "How are you with all this?"

"I'm okay. It explains so much."

"Are you going to do anything with them, as she asked?"

She turned to him and smiled. "Yes. I'm going to find a way to use them in *our* movie."

That was when the idea hit him. As soon as he dropped her off at work he went straight home and made a call—a call he thought he'd never make in his life.

"Hello, Dad. I need your help."

When Tyler walked into the secretarial pool each of the women came up to her to give condolences, invitations to lunch, or just to talk. Their thoughtfulness touched her, and she realized she had a whole office full of people who cared and she hadn't even known it.

Halfway through her morning Janet stopped by her desk to welcome her back and ask if there was anything she could do.

"I'm fine, really. But thanks. You've been great."

"Well, it's good to have you back." She started to walk away.

"Janet."

She stopped and turned around.

Tyler smiled. "Maybe we can have lunch one day."

* * *

When Miles dropped her off at the university the first person she saw was Professor Chase, who seemed happier than usual to see her.

"Ms. Ellington, I have wonderful news. Your script was selected by the committee to be screened."

"What!" She beamed. "Are you sure?"

"Absolutely. Here's the list of names to prove it." He pulled out a sheet of paper from the breast pocket of his sports jacket and showed it to her. And there it was, her name right at the top of the list of five.

"You're going to have to get busy. You need to get together with the film department people and pick a camera crew, think about locations shots and a cast. Don't let the other candidates get the jump on you. Then the best directors and cameramen will be all booked up."

She grinned. "Oh, I think I have a lock on a director."

Epilogue

Somewhere over the Rainbow

"Miles, you still haven't explained to me how in the world you got the university to agree to let us shoot in Georgia," Tyler said, wiping perspiration from her forehead with a very used Kleenex. July was about the hottest month of the year in Georgia, not a great time to be location hunting. It must have been close to one hundred degrees and it seemed as if the air-conditioning on their rented car had taken a break.

"Why don't you just relax? You're just the lowly screenwriter. I'm the brains behind this operation." He turned the car onto the narrow two-lane road.

"Right."

He chuckled.

"And what makes you think the new owners are going to let us shoot on their property, anyway?"

"Listen, baby, I have it all worked out. You'll see. Just sit back and enjoy the scenery."

She huffed and folded her arms beneath her breasts and gave him a sidelong glance. He was up to something. She just knew it. She could tell from the sneaky smirk on his face.

Up ahead, just over the ridge was the area where her grandmother's house was. Her heart thumped. She hadn't been back there since the funeral. Suddenly she didn't think she could deal with it.

He slowed the car. "Come here."

He slid his hand behind her head and pulled her to him, kissing her long and deep. He moved away and she signed, the thrill of his kiss still coursing through her.

"Now, I want you to do me one favor."

"What's that?"

He pulled a handkerchief out of his pocket. "Put this on."

She frowned. "Why?"

"Just do it, Ty. Please. Indulge me."

She twisted her lips and snatched the scarf from his hands. "I don't know what you're up to," she said, tying the scarf around her eyes.

"That's the whole point. Now sit right there. I'll help you out." He hopped out of the car and came around to her side. "Just hold my arm. And don't peek."

"Miles—"

"No talking, either."

She felt herself walking down a short incline, and she

could visualize herself running up and down that path when she visited her grandmother as a little girl.

"Just a little farther," he said.

Her heart started thumping.

They came to a stop. "Okay. Don't move." He walked around her and untied the scarf.

She opened her eyes and couldn't believe what she saw. The yellow was no longer faded, the steps were fixed, there were new windows and a brand-new roof. It was the house of her girlhood memories. Exactly. Her eyes filled and she spun around.

"Miles...I don't understand. It's—"

"It's yours."

"What?"

"Yours, free and clear."

"But how—"

He put his arm around her shoulder. "Remember when we talked about making a difference, making changes?"

She nodded, trying to push back the knot in her throat.

"I called my father. First time I'd done that in more years than I can count. Told him that for once I needed him to do something for me that *I* actually *wanted*. That it was important to someone very important to me. He pulled some strings with the Realtors down here and I bought the property in your name."

"You—bought it?"

"Yeah." He stepped up to her and looked down into her eyes. "I thought it would make you happy."

"Oh, Miles." She threw her arms around his neck. "It does. It does."

He pressed her close. "And...I thought it'd be the

perfect place to shoot our film—and spend our honeymoon. What do you think?"

She jerked back and stared at him. "Are you—are you asking me to marry you?"

"Trying."

For the first time since they met she saw the charismatic, totally in control Miles Bennett actually look scared.

"I think we'll make beautiful movies together," she murmured. She cupped his face in her hands. "I love you, Miles Bennett."

He lowered his head. "I think that's a wrap, folks," he said an instant before his lips touched hers.

Now she could play the role she'd been destined to portray herself, and an appendix could be added to her file: *Client finally finds true happiness.*

CASE CLOSED

USA TODAY BESTSELLING AUTHOR

BRENDA JACKSON

IRRESISTIBLE FORCES

Taylor Steele wants a baby, not a relationship. So she
proposes a week of mind-blowing sex in the Caribbean
to tycoon Dominic Saxon, whose genes seem perfect.
No strings—just mutual enjoyment. But when it's over,
will either of them be able to say goodbye?

"Brenda Jackson has written another sensational novel...
stormy, sensual and sexy—all the things a romance reader
could want in a love story."
—*Romantic Times BOOKreviews* on *Whispered Promises*

*Coming the first week of May
wherever books are sold.*

KIMANI™
ROMANCE

www.kimanipress.com

KPBJ06405080

Book #1 in

THE THREE MRS. FOSTERS

THIS
TIME FOR
GOOD

FAVORITE AUTHOR

CARMEN
GREEN

About to lose her family business because of her late
husband's polygamy, Alexandria accepts Hunter's help.
But she's not letting any man run her life—
not even one who sets her senses aflame.

"Ms. Green sweeps the reader away on the lush carpet
of reality-grounded romantic fantasy."
—*Romantic Times BOOKreviews* on *Commitments*

Coming the first week of May
wherever books are sold.

KIMANI™
ROMANCE

www.kimanipress.com

Down and out...but not really

Indiscriminate
Attraction

ESSENCE BESTSELLING AUTHOR
Linda Hudson-Smith

Searching the streets and homeless shelters for his missing
twin, shabbily disguised Chad Kingston accepts volunteer
Laylah Versailles's help. Luscious Laylah's determination
to turn "down-and-out" Chad's life around has a heated
effect on him. But Chad's never trusted women—
and Laylah has secrets.

"Hudson-Smith does an outstanding job...
A truly inspiring novel!"
—*Romantic Times BOOKreviews* on *Secrets & Silence*

*Coming the first week of May
wherever books are sold.*

KIMANI™
ROMANCE

www.kimanipress.com

KPLHS0660508

her kind of

Man

Favorite author

PAMELA YAYE

As a gawky teen, Makayla Stevens yearned for
Kenyon Blake. Now he's the uncle of one of her students,
and wants to get better acquainted with Makayla.
The reality is even hotter than her teenage fantasies.
But their involvement could damage her career…
and her peace of mind.

"Other People's Business…is a fun and lighthearted story…
an entertaining novel."
—*Romantic Times BOOKreviews* on
Pamela Yaye's debut novel

*Coming the first week of May
wherever books are sold.*

KIMANI™
ROMANCE

www.kimanipress.com

KPPY0670508

"Byrd proves once again that she's a wonderful storyteller."
—*Romantic Times BOOKreviews*
on *The Beautiful Ones*

ACCLAIMED AUTHOR

ADRIANNE byrd

controversy

Michael Adams is no murderer—even if she did joke about killing her ex-husband after their nasty divorce. Now she has to prove to investigating detective Kyson Dekker that she's innocent. Of course, it doesn't help that he's so distractingly gorgeous that Michael can't think straight....

**Coming the first week of May
wherever books are sold.**

ARABESQUE®

www.kimanipress.com

KPAB1000